THE FLAGLER LEGACY

A Novel
by
David Forster Parker

Routes of Florida East Coast Railway

The Flagler Legacy is a work of fiction in which the story, as well as most of the characters and their activities, have no relation to real persons or events. However, a few political leaders and primary characters of the era are identified, but their actions and statements are mostly fiction created by the author. Many political and bureaucratic events related to the Florida East Coast Railway are factual, interspersed with fiction by the author. The bulk of the story is the author's creation, as are any errors in relating historical data.

PTC Communications, as publishing advisor for this novel and all information contained herein, declare this as copyright property of David Forster Parker and it may not be reproduced in whole or in part in any form or by any means without express written consent by David Forster Parker.

P.O. BOX 51604
JACKSONVILLE BEACH, FL 32240
904.992.9888
INFO@PTCCOMMUNICATIONS.COM
WWW.PTCCOMMUNICATIONS.COM
ISBN: 978-0-9832094-3-0

DEDICATION

This book is dedicated to the memory of
Henry Morrison Flagler
1830-1913

Net Worth: USD $60 million at the time of his death (about 1/651 of the US GNP)

Children:
Jennie L. (1855-1889)
Carrie (1858-1861)
Harry Harkness (1870-1952)

ACKNOWLEDGEMENTS

Although this novel is a work of fiction, many of the historic figures, communities and events identified in the text are factual. But the novel's fictional characters and events attributed to them and their possessions are my creation.

The story contains a compendium of my knowledge, information and observations based upon several years of research on Henry Morrison Flagler and the Florida East Coast Railway which he founded in 1895 and owned up until his death in 1913. Research also was conducted on Edward G. Ball, the railway's chairman from 1961 until his death in 1983. This research included interviews with some of his former employees who prefer to remain anonymous. Place names and locations are known to me from my three decades of residency and consultancy in Florida and other locations.

As with past publications, I have relied upon my older and wiser sister, Margaret G. Vincent, for guidance as well as criticism of the storyline and other components. I am indebted to Janine Murray for the final edit of this manuscript. My third son, David W. B. Parker, once again served as editor and publishing advisor as well as final book designer through his company, PTC Computer Solutions and subsidiary PTC Communications. Of course, the research results and observations are my responsibility as author. I also give thanks to family friend Stevan Jones for his advice on legal issues, although I am solely responsible for the translation of his advice into the text.

I am indebted to my wife, Marilynn, and my four sons—Chris, Stephen, David and Dan—for their support and memories contributing to experiences in this story.

List of Main Characters

(Alphabetic by last name, * Denotes real person, <u>underline</u> denotes twelve primary characters)

<u>Abdullah, Mohammed</u>	Criminal enforcer and assassin for hire, aka Big Moe
Atkins, George	Senior Legal Counsel, Florida East Coast Railway
<u>Ball, Edward*</u>	Chair, Florida East Coast Railway, Trustee, DuPont Trust, 1902-83
Brzezinski, Zbigniew*	US National Security Advisor
Carter, James Earl*	Thirty-ninth President of the United States of America, 1977-81; b. 1924-
<u>Chekov, Dimitri</u>	Illicit Arms Dealer and Assassin (aka Daniel Chester, David Cochrane)
Coburn, Samuel	Florida Circuit Court Judge
Cosgrove, Edward	Reporter, Florida State Assemblyman
<u>Dempsey, Joshua "JD"</u>	Agent, U.S. Central Intelligence Agency; Explosion Task Force Staff
<u>El Saud, Hassad</u>	Wealthy member of Saud family, & terrorism financier (aka Henry Stanton, Henri St. Pierre)
<u>Flagler, Henry M.*</u>	Founder/Partner, Standard Oil Company; Florida Developer, 1830-1913
<u>Hale, Jordan</u>	Senior Agent, Federal Bureau of Investigation (FBI)
<u>Harris, Nigel</u>	Senior Agent, British Intelligence Service (MI6)
Hennessy, Sean	New York night club owner, 1890s
<u>Jones, Chandra</u>	Television News Reporter, Jacksonville Station WJTR
Kenan, Jack*	Brother-in-law of Henry Flagler, Chairman of FECR, 1913-1945
Malone, Charles	Director, United States Central Intelligence Agency (CIA)
Mason, John	Judge Florida Circuit Court, Justice Florida Supreme Court
<u>McBride, Margaret</u>	Deputy National Security Advisor; Explosion Task Force Chair
McCloud, Ebeneezer	Florida State Senator
O'Shea, Patrick M.	Renowned Irish tenor vocalist, 1859-1935
O'Shea, Patrick M. Jr	Grandson of above, Trustee, Patrick Michael O'Shea Trust (PMO Trust), 1897-
<u>O'Shea, Patrick M. III</u>	Son of above and Jacksonville attorney 1927-
<u>O'Shea, Patrick M. IV</u>	Son of above, and Harvard Law Graduate, Florida Bar, 1950-
O'Shea, Molly	Daughter of Patrick M. O'Shea Sr.; mother of P. M. O'Shea Jr., 1873-
Paissant, Georges	Deputy Director, French Security Service, Sûreté
Solomon, Bessie	Historian, Florida Times Union daily newspaper
Tindale, Aubrey	Director, US Federal Bureau of Investigation (FBI)

PROLOGUE

The history of the world's civilizations is marked by class distinctions and autocratic rule over the majority of populations. Strong people grew stronger and the remainder grew weaker in terms of both personal well-being and public influence. Eventually, leaders of the weak emerged to react with physical violence against assumed unjust policies of the strong. Through hundreds of years of internal conflict, the reactionaries became known as "terrorists" and they continue to this day to disrupt both dictatorial and democratic governments.

Terrorism generally is described as individuals or groups causing violent conflict in opposition to government organizations. Examples are recorded under a wide range of names in historical writings. Scholars often cite the roots and practice of terrorism as traced to the first century, AD, when the Jewish "Sicarii Zealots" assassinated collaborators with Roman rule in the mid-eastern province of Judea. Every century thereafter contained examples of violent uprisings, with some rating worldwide publicity such as the French Revolution's "Reign of Terror" in the eighteenth century. It was here that Jacobins employed mass executions by guillotine of some 40,000 victims to enforce obedience to the emergent state. They referred to themselves as terrorists.

The invention of dynamite in the nineteenth century escalated the death rate by such uprisings. Bombing became the violence of choice for emergent terrorist groups. According to historic scholars, such acts of violent anarchism, often associated with rising nationalism and anti-monarchism, was the most prominent ideology linked with the term terrorism. In the late nineteenth century, for example, anarchists committed assassinations of the Russian Tsar Alexander I and the U.S. President William McKinley.

During the twentieth century, acts of terrorism were related to a diverse array of anarchist, socialist, fascist and nationalist groups. On June 28, 1914 the assassination of Archduke Franz Ferdinand of Austria and his wife Sophia on the main street of Sarajevo sparked uprisings that resulted in World War I. A worldwide trend of anti-colonial uprisings continued through following decades.. Some historians include the violence and intimidation of Stalinist Russia and Nazi Germany as extreme acts of terrorism.

Some of these terrorist organizations, including the Fenian Brotherhood opposing British rule in Ireland, the Haganah and Irgun and PFLP opposing the British Mandate of Palestine in Israel, and the Muslim Brotherhood opposing British rule in Egypt, carried on their terrorist activities through several decades. The practice became worldwide with the Viet Minh rebels against colonial France in Vietnam, Mao's great march across China, Castro's success against Batista in Cuba, the PLO and Fatah in Palestine, the Basque ETA in Spain, the Red Army and Red Brigades in Germany, the FLQ in Quebec, Canada, the Japanese Red Army in Japan, the Tamil Tigers in Sri Lanka (longest continuing terrorist group, 1976-2009), the Mau Mau in Kenya, the MK in South Africa, and the Ku Klux Klan, Weathermen, SDS and Black Panthers in the United States.

By the 1970s, terrorist organizations had spread fear amongst peaceful people across the world, and, for populations in many countries, the fear was expanding with secret threats from well-financed international groups acting independently. Leaders of these groups appeared convinced that the growth of acts of terrorism could achieve revised political and religious policies to benefit their own beliefs. Terrorism could be effective in reaching political goals.

Rick O'Shea returns home to Jacksonville, Florida in 1977, with his new Harvard law degree, eager to assist his family to correct the recent elimination of the trust fund bestowed on his great grandfather and subsequent heirs by the wealthy Henry Morrison Flagler in 1897. With assistance from an ambitious and attractive female news reporter, Chandra Jones, the two begin research on recent legal cases defending the trust fund deletion. But, unidentified opposition to their research leads them into the middle of a massive terrorist plot designed to simultaneously blow up the centers of five major American cities.

The history of the world's civilizations is marked by class distinctions and autocratic rule over the majority of populations. Strong people grew stronger and the remainder grew weaker in terms of both personal well-being and public influence. Eventually, leaders of the weak emerged to react with physical violence against unjust policies of the strong. Over hundreds of years of internal conflict, the reactionaries became known as "terrorists" and

they continue to this day to disrupt both dictatorial and democratic governments.

Map of France illustrating Marseille, Nice and Monaco as well as Paris.

ONE

"Holy Mackerel! . . . Martha, come out and see this. The whole sky is . . ."

But Martha never made it to the front porch. She and her husband of fifty-five years were killed instantly from the explosive shock wave that obliterated every house on their street just west of the Broward Yard railway junction in central Jacksonville.

The massive explosion was ignited just after five o'clock on Sunday morning, when most residents of the city were asleep, and only a dozen security employees were at work in the northern freight terminus of the Florida East Coast Railway. They all died instantly along with many residents of adjoining neighborhoods.

The deafening noise of the blast woke all but the hearing-impaired within a thirty-mile radius. Its brilliant orange, yellow, red and purple flames turned a black night into brilliant colors, magnified by clouds of grey smoke rising above the inferno for several hours.

Residents throughout the city ran out of their homes in nightclothes to ascertain the origin of the inferno that continued to expel a series of explosions and shock waves for thirty minutes after the initial blast. Opinions ranged from a senseless accident to a major act of terrorism, with countless creative ideas in between.

Some residents feared that it might be a tanker barge of fuel oil in the St. Johns River just north of the Broward Yard. Others assumed the source was railway tanker cars waiting to be shipped south to Florida cities on the east coast. Still others imagined a renewal of the vitriolic union strike that recently was reported to be settled after a dozen years of physical violence extending throughout the railroad to Miami, some 350 miles south of Jacksonville. But most residents seemed more concerned about spraying their homes with garden hoses to prevent flying ashes setting new fires.

Night workers at the new headquarters of the Times-Union newspaper on the north bank of the St. Johns River had the best view of the explosion, as well as the best sensation of the flames. Newspaper reporters summoned from their homes were surprised to learn that they were to interview fellow employees as the primary witnesses to the explosion.

Media reports called it Jacksonville's worst disaster since the great fire of 1901 demolished the downtown center north of the river.

Although streets surrounding the Broward Yard were immediately closed by police, reporters televised the scene by helicopter in response to demand for national network reports on the disaster. No Broward Yard night shift workers had survived for interviews, and Florida East Coast Railway executives did not become available for comment until later that morning.

The President of the United States—Jimmy Carter— held a special televised briefing at noon that day condemning anyone responsible for this disaster. He announced that emergency funds would be available immediately to the local government and the Florida East Coast Railway to initiate repairs. The President also announced the formation of an emergency task force to report directly to him on the cause of the explosion.

Like most Jacksonville residents, Rick O'Shea was awakened by the devastating early morning explosion in Broward Yard. His apartment in the old Saint Nicholas district of Jacksonville, south of the St. Johns River, was only a few blocks from the blast site. His windows weren't blown out like several of his neighbors. But he did lose some of his new dishes which fell from kitchen cupboards when their doors swung open from the impact of the blast.

Rick's dishes were new because he had moved into the second-floor walk-up apartment only a month before. It was furnished with hand-me-downs from his many relatives in Jacksonville, particularly his ninety-eight-year-old grandmother who still resided on her own in a large and over-furnished house on the banks of the St. Johns River in Jacksonville's South Arlington district. His six sisters also had contributed possessions to his new home.

The tall and handsome twenty-six-year-old, Patrick Michael O'Shea IV, always known as Rick by his friends and family, had returned to his hometown after receiving his law degree summa cum laude from Harvard University earlier that year. His father, Patrick Michael O'Shea III, known by clients and friends as Mike, was a successful attorney in Jacksonville. He had proudly offered his son a clerical position in his office during his studies to sit for the Florida Bar examination. There was little question that, as the only son and only law school graduate in Mike's family of seven children, he would be offered a partnership with his father after he passed the Florida Bar Exam scheduled for the coming week.

However, this early morning blast, apparently in the main terminus of the Florida East Coast Railway, could interrupt his plans if the blame was directed toward his family. This possibility instantly entered his mind because of the lengthy feud between the O'Shea family and the current chairman of the railway. In fact, his major objective in returning to Jacksonville was to restore his family's legal position as the holder of an historic family trust, established by the railway's founder, Henry M. Flagler.

The 1897 O'Shea Trust Fund stipulated that it was to be financed by the Florida East Coast Railway in perpetuity. And so it had been funded by the railroad at the beginning of each year, from 1900 through 1974. But the funding stopped abruptly after a 1974 judgment of the Florida Supreme Court ruled the trust invalid upon petition by the powerful current chairman of the railway, Edward G. Ball.

As Rick stared out the window at the orange flames rising high into the early morning sky, he pondered the potential legal actions that could be launched by Chairman Ball if there were any possible suggestion that the O'Shea family might be involved. He felt certain that no family members were involved. But, he made a mental note to discuss this issue with his father and grandfather on Monday morning.

TWO

Miami Beach, Florida
August 28, 1977

"Gentlemen, I salute you with a victory toast," said the stocky, white-haired man of apparent senior years at the head of the luncheon table. He raised his glass of champagne toward his five companions in the top-floor executive suite of the elegant Fontainebleau Hotel in Miami Beach.

The "Don," as he was known to the others, was dressed in a casual sports coat and open-neck shirt. The tall, muscular African-American at the other end of the table also was dressed in sports coat and open-neck shirt, the sports coat not quite hiding the holstered gun underneath. He was the arson team captain, known as "Big Moe," derived from his adopted name of Mohammed Abdullah. The other four men at the table were white Americans of average age, size and appearance with sport shirts overhanging denim jeans. Each raised his champagne glass in salute.

The older man continued: "The Broward Yard explosion appears to have been perfectly timed and executed, just as we planned—an excellent piece of work for which I commend each of

4

you. Big Mo advised me by phone this morning that you set the Semtex ignition bombs on the liquid natural gas tankers and planted the two bodies outside the administration building as I directed. You then met him at the I-95 Rest Stop with the stolen van twenty minutes prior to the explosions. He told me that you cleaned the van thoroughly before leaving it unlocked with the keys in plain sight. He then delivered you here in his minivan to join me. Do you have any questions or comments? No? Then let's have lunch."

Big Mo opened the door to the suite, ushering in three waiters who efficiently served the group with hot soup and sandwiches, prior to re-filling their champagne and water glasses, and then quietly departing.

After a brief dining pause, the Don continued. "Each of you has an envelope of cash in front of you, as we promised, in addition to the retainer fees you received at our first meeting three months ago. As we agreed, the second envelopes at each place contain airline tickets to four different Caribbean Islands with flights leaving at different times this afternoon. You are not to share your destination with anyone else, including your colleagues at this table. In addition to the airline tickets, the second envelope contains reservations at an all-inclusive resort where you have agreed to remain for seven days incognito. An expertly forged passport also is in the envelope for your new identity.

"In exactly seven days, you will use the second airline ticket to fly to our final meeting at the named hotel on the island of Providenciales, known as 'Provo' by the residents, in the surrounding British protectorate of Turks and Caicos. It is there that you will receive your final fee for this assignment. Any questions? No? Good! A new assignment may be defined for you at that time, providing that you have carefully complied with all of the rules that we agreed upon with each of you, most particularly the rule concerning the prohibition against alcohol and friends or acquaintances of either gender during your resort vacation. Do each of you understand and re-confirm your adherence to these rules?"

Each of the four men responded in agreement.

"Good, because the penalty for non-compliance is immediate termination—no excuses will be tolerated. Your resort stays will be monitored. I am certain that each of you remember your understanding of these terms, including the rewards and penalty for non-compliance. I will leave you now. Please enjoy your lunch and then Mohammed will accompany you to the airport in his van. I look forward to seeing each of you within ten days."

The Don then rose and exited the suite.

The Don, also known by security forces in several countries as Dimitri Chekov, an international broker of drugs and guns, closed the door behind him. On his way to the elevator, he ripped off the fake beard, moustache and hairpiece to reveal a man at least twenty years younger than his prior appearance, and with a shaved head containing not a single hair. He discarded his disguise and washed the dye from his eyebrows in a lobby washroom before taking a taxi to the Miami airport for the return flight to his apartment home in Atlanta.

THREE

St. Augustine, Florida
August 30, 1977

The first session of the Broward Yard Explosion Emergency Task Force was held in a meeting room at Flagler College, a majestic building renovated from the original Ponce De Leon Hotel completed in 1896. It still retained the architectural grandeur stipulated by the Florida development pioneer, Henry M. Flagler, for the first of the several resort hotels he founded along the eastern coast of Florida at the turn of the 20th Century.

A mature, grey-haired woman of average height and dressed in a tailored blue business suit rose at the end of the conference table to address the six men and two women appointed to the task force.

"Ladies and gentlemen, I am delighted that every expert invited to participate in this Broward Yard Explosion Emergency Task Force is here today. Not one person turned me down. As you know, my name is Margaret McBride. President Carter asked me to set aside my duties as deputy to our National Security Advisor in order to chair this task force. I will report your findings and recommendations directly to him.

"The National Security Advisor, Zbigniew Brzezinski, provided his personal guidance to me in identifying you eight as the most capable security and law enforcement officials. The objective is to identify the person or persons responsible for this explosion and ensure that they are brought to justice. Now, are there any questions before we proceed?"

"Yes, Madam Chair . . ."

"Please stop right there, Richard," interjected McBride to the Senior Secret Service Agent who she had known for many years. "I really must insist that we avoid formalities in addressing each other. My name, as you know well, is Margaret, and each of you has a first name sign in front of you. So please adhere to this rule in order to expedite communications. Now, your question?"

"Well, in the true spirit of informality, I believe that several of us are curious as to how long it took you to memorize the spelling of the National Security Advisor's name?" Laughter broke out around the table, and even McBride joined in before admitting, with a twinkle in her eye, that she was unable to answer on the grounds of national security.

"Before we get underway, I would like to introduce our two staff members. Janet Sproule, sitting at the small table to the left, is a senior court stenographer with our office who I requisitioned to keep the team's records. Records will be available in printed form to any of you for reference. Sitting to my right is Agent Joshua "JD" Dempsey who is on loan from the Central Intelligence Agency for the duration of this task force. He will follow up any leads that we can generate. However, it is important to note here that we have received formal letters of cooperation from all federal and Florida security and law enforcement agencies, as well as from the Duval County Sheriff's office covering the city of Jacksonville."

McBride summarized the usual rules and guidelines for the task force, which will be passed out to each member by Ms. Sproule. She then called upon the Florida East Coast Railway senior counsel, George Atkins, to brief the group on the history of the Florida East Coast Railway, from its founding in 1895 by Henry Flagler, up to the current management by Edward Ball, chief executive of the Alfred du Pont Testamentary Trust that controls a majority ownership position in the railway.

Atkins, a distinguished-appearing man with a full head of white hair and facial age wrinkles to match, first advised that the company was known in Florida and throughout the railway industry by the acronym FECR. He will refer to it by these letters in future. Then he handed out a single page summarizing the company history in the following series of bullet points:

Florida East Coat Railway (FECR) Historic Summary

- Henry M. Flagler, a founding partner in Standard Oil with John Rockefeller, resigned from that position in 1895 when he became committed to developing the east coast of Florida with new resort hotels and railroad access. Flagler had previously purchased three small local railroads adjacent to St. Augustine, which he amalgamated into the new Florida East Coast Railway (FECR) in 1895.

- Between 1904 and 1912, FECR was responsible for one of the greatest railroad engineering and construction feats in the history of the United States: the fabled Key West Extension, which opened with Mr. Flagler's triumphant entry into the island city on January 22, 1912. He remained the sole owner of FECR until his death in 1913.

- FECR consisted of over 525 miles of railway track down the east coast of Florida from Jacksonville to Key West between 1985 and 1912— subsequently reduced to the current 351 miles when a 1936 hurricane demolished key portions of the Key West link.

- He also built resort hotels at several station stops, as well as in the Bahamas. He initiated communities at Palm Beach, Fort Lauderdale and Miami, and operated ferry service from Miami and Key West to Cuba and The Bahamas.

- Flagler died in 1913 at the age of 83, leaving an estate of over $60 million dollars to his third wife, Lily Kenan Flagler, and his only remaining child, Harry Harkness Flagler (born to Flagler's first wife, Mary Harkness in 1870).

- FECR was managed successfully for many years by Lily's brother, Jack Kenan, up until the national real estate collapse of 1926, and the subsequent stock market crash of 1929, events which caused the company to declare bankruptcy and become a ward of the court in 1931.

- FECR, in collaboration with other railways, continued to operate high quality passenger service from northern cities to Florida resort destinations through 1943. At that time, during the height of World War II, it terminated passenger service in lieu of military priorities and expanded freight service from Florida to northern and western destinations through connections with other railroads.

- FECR was declared bankrupt again in 1961, with a court-ordered re-organization under control of the majority ownership entity of the Alfred DuPont Testamentary Trust, which was managed by DuPont's brother-in-law, Edward Ball. Ball used Trust funds to purchase de-valued FECR mortgage bonds and gain control of FECR ownership during the 1930s, and he was named chairman of the FECR in 1961. He loaned money from the St. Joe Pulp and Paper Company, another entity owned by the DuPont Trust, to pay FECR debts and remove it from bankruptcy.

- Over the next dozen years, a turbulent labor dispute was initiated by a union strike in January, 1963. Ball resolved it by firing all the union employees and replacing them with non-union workers. Many bombings and violent demonstrations against FECR occurred during this period. Over 200 crimes were committed by the former union members. After they blew up two trains in February, 1964, the FBI became involved and several union leaders were sent to jail.

- The largest minority shareholder, a trust established by Flagler in 1897 for his close friend, Patrick Michael O'Shea, brought litigation against Ball's management, but it was denied by the Federal court. Ball also achieved annulment of the O'Shea Family Trust (PMO Trust) by the Florida courts, thus saving the FECR an annual payment of close to one million dollars for funding the family trust. This decision was upheld by the Florida courts despite appeals of these decisions by the O'Shea family attorney, Patrick Michael O'Shea III.

As of this date, Chairman Ball appears fully in control of FECR and its two associated firms—Florida East Coast Industries and Florida East Coast Land Company—despite this latest bombing now under our investigation.

After pausing for lunch across the street at the historic Casa Monica Hotel, also formerly owned by Henry Flagler, the task force members interacted with each other in order to introduce

10

themselves and reveal initial reactions to the explosion and the historical summary. They agreed to meet again in one week's time.

In closing, McBride handed out copies of the following news article distributed by the American Press wire service on August 28, 1977 for printing in newspapers across the country and beyond.

Explosion like an 'Atomic Bomb'
Forty-two killed in Florida rail yard explosion

By Carl Schmidt & Maria Maxwell

American Press

JACKSONVILLE, FL. Fires were still burning many hours after the devastating explosion shot huge fireballs into the early morning sky from the Florida East Coast Railway's Broward Yard freight terminal in the center of this east coast city of one-half million residents.

According to initial estimates by the Mayor's office, a dozen railroad employees and thirty occupants of nearby homes were killed instantly in the blast that some observers likened to an atomic bomb. City hospitals were jammed with over one hundred injured victims. The huge explosion before dawn awakened residents over thirty miles distant from the blast site.

Although investigations were just beginning about the cause of the explosion, railroad officials did confirm that some twenty tank cars loaded with fuel oil and liquid petroleum gas were in the yard, ready for trans-shipment to other destinations.

Each tank car carries 30,000 gallons of liquid. The question is not their flammable content, but rather the cause of ignition—those tanker cars are all sealed tight.

According to James Nesbitt, a witness about one-quarter mile from the blast site, "it was really scary, the shock waves from the multiple blasts and the flames shooting up to heights literally covering the sky. Some fireballs must have extended over 300 feet into the air."

Local officials confirmed that fire marshal inspections, after the fires are extinguished, could take months to determine the cause of ignition. The more important questions of who did it and why may never be resolved.

The President of the United States appeared on television a few hours after the explosion to announce that federal aid was in process for the city and the railway. Furthermore, he had already appointed the Deputy National Security Advisor, Margaret McBride, to chair a task force of disaster and terrorism experts to identify the cause of the blast and person or persons responsible.

FOUR

New York City
Circa January, 1895

Henry Flagler, former founder and partner in the Standard Oil Company with his friend John D. Rockefeller, and more recently the developer of a new coastal railroad and hotels in Florida, was enjoying an evening with his good friend, Sean Hennessy, at one of the latter's three supper clubs in Manhattan. Flagler, now age fifty-four and retired from Standard Oil, was spending the winter in New York in support of his second wife, Alice, who was undergoing treatment at a New York clinic for a deteriorating mental disorder. Now living alone in his New York home, he gladly accepted the frequent offers from Hennessy to join him for dinner and entertainment.

"Henry, me boy," smiled the rather overweight and genial host, "I can promise you a real treat tonight. I have persuaded the renowned Irish tenor, Patrick Michael O'Shea, to come to New York for the winter and sing at my clubs. Patrick's wife recently died and left him with a teen-age daughter who is an exceptional musician on the pipe organ. So, as you will see when we open the curtain, I have installed a first-rate pipe organ just for her. Hopefully, the two of them can recover from their loss by performing for my guests."

"Ah, my friend," smiled Flagler. "Your generosity is only exceeded by your canny instinct to make a profit. Congratulations are in order." He immediately called for another bottle of champagne for the two of them.

No sooner had the two men finished their dinner than the tall, handsome Patrick Michael O'Shea emerged with his magnetic smile from the side curtain onto the stage and launched into an historic Irish Sea chantey, without accompaniment, to the delight of the club's customers. He then paused to instruct the opening of the stage curtain and proceeded to introduce himself and welcome his daughter Molly to accompany him on the impressive pipe organ installed on one side of the stage.

Molly was an attractive, fully developed young woman of considerable beauty who curtsied to the audience prior to playing a rousing Irish jig, while her father stood to one side clapping along with the audience. The smiling tenor then stepped forward and captivated the audience with a series of Irish ballads and folk tunes accompanied by Molly. He closed this segment of their performance by reciting the story of the grieving Irish father burying his youngest son, killed in revolutionary fighting against the English. His exceptional mastery of vocal technique brought tears to many in the audience with his rendition of "Danny Boy," and he and Molly left the stage to standing applause and cries for more.

Flagler joined the rest of the audience in standing applause. Finally resuming his front row seat, the distinguished-looking Flagler turned to his host with a broad grin, "Sean, this is indeed a magic experience for me. I have never heard such a fine voice. And the addition of his lovely young daughter on the pipe organ is an added treat. Once again, I offer sincere congratulations, my friend."

Over the next few weeks, Flagler was a regular diner at the Hennessy club. O'Shea and his daughter would join him at his front-row table after performances, and trade stories about life in each of their countries. One night, toward the end of the New York theater season, Flagler begged Hennessey's indulgence to allow the O'Shea couple to be his guests at his Palm Beach residence and entertain his guests for several weeks the following winter. Of course, he would pay their regular fee plus travel expenses. Hennessy readily agreed to relinquish his star performers the following winter, knowing full well that most of Flagler's "friends" were wealthy New Yorkers who would bring more patrons to his clubs when they returned to the city.

Entertainment by the O'Sheas at the Flagler Palm Beach mansion and at Flagler's new Florida east coast hotels in the winter of 1896 proved to be a spectacular success. Patrick Michael O'Shea, and his equally talented daughter Molly, became the toast of the wealthy "snow-birds" from New York and environs. Flagler had purchased the finest pipe organs from European craftsmen for his hotels and mansions in St. Augustine and Palm Beach to ensure that Molly was fully-equipped to perform in concert with her father.

Flagler wired Hennessy in New York after the first month of performances that he must renew their agreement for the following year. He even promised the club owner a share of the two Florida performance hotels' dinner revenue. He also welcomed him as a guest in his Florida homes. Hennessy wired back his acceptance within a few hours.

FIVE

Palm Beach, Florida
Circa February, 1897

The second winter season in Florida for Patrick Michael and Molly O'Shea had been even more successful than the first, with sold-out performances in both hotels as well as eager guests at the Flagler mansions in St. Augustine and Palm Beach.

But, in February, Molly became stricken with illness which caused her terrible headaches and stomach upset. In order to provide her the best of care, her father returned her to New York, accompanied by two nurses, in Flagler's private rail carriage. Flagler contacted his personal physician to attend her upon arrival.

She had been in New York only one day when the physician announced her illness to O'Shea by wire. Molly was pregnant and due to give birth in September. The physician provided drugs for her sickness and assured her and her father that she was in excellent physical health. So, Molly returned to Florida and finished the season accompanying her father.

Molly gave birth in New York on August 31, 1897 to a boy that she named after her famous father, Patrick Michael O'Shea, Junior. Despite whispered conversations among Flagler's household staff, there was never any public mention of the baby's father. Rumors abounded throughout the Palm Beach social set that Flagler may have sired the child, but no confirmation was ever forthcoming.

When the O'Sheas returned to Florida in December of that year, Flagler retained an experienced nursemaid for the additional member of the O'Shea family. The baby soon became the feature attraction of the Flagler household.

On the last day of December, 1897, Henry Flagler called his attorneys to his home and directed them to establish a trust fund for his dear friend, Patrick Michael O'Shea and his descendants. The trust was to be financed in perpetuity by Flagler's Florida East Coast Railrway. The annual fee would be $500,000 to be paid to the trust on January 2nd of each year beginning in 1900 and increasing by 2 percent annually. At that time, and up until his death, in 1913, he was the sole owner of the Florida East Coast Railway.

The Flagler attorneys advised him that, in accordance with English Common Law, as continued in American law, any trust established "in perpetuity" was defined as to be terminated twenty-one years after the death of the last remaining original party to the trust. Therefore, in stipulating that the trust should be passed to the oldest heir named Patrick Michael O'Shea, Molly's baby born in 1897 would be acknowledged as a party to the trust. Assuming that he lived a long life, the 21-year termination would be effective from the date of his death.

The trust stipulated that the current heir would manage the trust and receive one-half of the annual fee, with one-quarter being paid in equal shares to all living direct descendants on January second and the remaining one-quarter be placed in a PMO Investment Fund to be administered by the living heir as a "permanent family resource for such needs as he deems relevant to the O'Shea family's well-being."

SIX

Jacksonville, Florida
August 29, 1977

The law office of Michael O'Shea was located on the tenth floor of the Jacksonville Bank Building in downtown Jacksonville, north of the St. Johns River. On this afternoon, the day following the massive explosion south of the river, three men were seated at the attorney's conference table: Patrick Michael O'Shea Junior, the only child of Molly O'Shea and now in his eightieth year; Patrick Michael O'Shea III, the attorney listed on the office entrance and known by his many friends as Mike, age fifty-eight; and Patrick Michael O'Shea IV, a graduate of Harvard Law School and just announced new member of the Florida Bar, whose family and friends know as Rick, age twenty-six. Earlier that day, after Rick's successful acceptance to the Florida Bar, his father had invited him to become a partner in his law firm.

The son and grandson retained the handsome family features of the senior O'Shea, except for the elder man sporting a full head of white air in contrast to the dark brown hair of his offspring. They each were served cold drinks by Mike's silver-haired longtime secretary, Maryanne Magee.

"Dad, I'm glad that you could join Rick and me this morning. The explosion Sunday morning is bound to reverberate on our family and I, or I should now say, we, need your counsel on a family position other than passive silence when the authorities come calling."

"I am always available, Mike," smiled the white-haired family patriarch, still looking fit despite his age. "Although, I should add that my counsel is cheap, compared to what you charge your clients."

"Yes, but my income, and now Rick's income, are the result of expensive educations that you paid for out of the PMO Investment Fund, so your continuing support is most welcome. By the way, how is Grandma Molly doing?"

"I saw her yesterday, and she looks fabulous at almost one hundred years. As you know, she attributes her good health to never having been married, but I believe that still playing the church organ all her life is a more likely cause. Anyway, let's turn to the family business at hand."

"Right," responded Mike. "I have spoken to all male members of our next generation during the past two days, other than your grandsons, the two Stephens brothers, who were reported killed in the explosion."

"What on earth were they doing at Broward Yard?" asked his father.

"Well, sir, I asked the same question, and I was surprised to learn that they have been employed by the railroad since last March as apprentice dispatchers. They earned extra wages by volunteering to work nights."

"Hmm," muttered the senior O'Shea. "You can rest assured that Ed Ball will use their presence there to try and pin this explosion on our family for past incidents attributed to us in defiance of his armed strike-breakers."

"Excuse me, Grandfather," interrupted Rick. "You are leaving me behind. I remember the initial strike back in 1963 when I was attending Bishop Kenny School, but I don't recall any violence. And I know little about this man, Ed Ball, other than he is the chairman of the railway and responsible for having our family trust annulled."

His father chose to answer before the oldest O'Shea. "Hold on a minute, Rick. You've got some catching up to do. We sent you off to Branford Academy in Virginia for high school, and you missed the years of greatest violence between the railroad employees and company management. Also, prior to this period, back in the 1930s and '40s, the manager of the Alfred du Pont Testamentary Trust, Ed Ball, bought up a majority of cut-rate mortgage bonds on Florida East Coast Railway property, resulting in that trust being awarded management of the bankrupt Florida East Coast Railway by the Fourth Federal Circuit Court. Ball proceeded to lock out all union employees, causing a battle that lasted from 1963 until it was settled by further court action in favor of Ball in 1976, just one year ago. At that time Ball also owned the local newspaper, the Florida Times-Union, and he suppressed all news of the violence."

At this point, Rick's grandfather cut in, "By extraordinary good fortune, Rick, when the Florida East Coast Railway, usually called FECR, was declared bankrupt in 1931 and thereafter supervised by the court, the chairman was Henry Flagler's brother-in-law, Jack Kenan. Jack's sister Lily married Henry in 1902 and remained his wife until his death in 1913. Jack considered us family, and he kept me informed of the cheap mortgage bonds being purchased by Ball. So, being responsible for our family investment fund, I jumped on that bandwagon and began buying similar FECR mortgage paper, with the result that our PMO Investment Fund became the largest minority shareholder of FECR behind the DuPont Trust.

"During Kenan's chairmanship, the company hired many members of our family. Our family members supported the railroad unions against Ball when he took an adversary position in 1963. And Ball despised us along with the leaders of the unions. However, to the best of my knowledge, no member of our family was ever involved in the sabotage bombings and related violence carried out on FECR by unhappy union members."

Just three blocks from the O'Shea law office, on the sixteenth floor of another bank building, the short, bald figure of Edward Ball sat behind a very large desk in a very large corner office with windows overlooking the blue expanse of the St. Johns River flowing from the south. On the other side of his desk sat the two top executives of the Florida East Coast Railway, reporting to their chairman.

When granted management of the newly organized company in 1961, Ball paid its debts from funds borrowed from the St. Joe Paper Company, another DuPont Trust holding. This new funding enabled FECR to emerge from bankruptcy.

But two years later, in 1963, the union employees of the company went on strike for higher wages, resulting in years of violence extending from Jacksonville to Miami, during which time Ball dismissed all of the union employees—many of them O'Shea relatives—and replaced them with a non-union work force. He also won court cases in 1974 and affirmed in 1976 upholding his actions. And, in that same year, he received a decision from the Florida courts terminating the O'Shea Trust, thereby saving FECR an annual expense approaching one million dollars.

During this time he became known as the most powerful man in Florida because of the vast holdings of the DuPont Trust. Ball's influence was exerted through his control over a vast DuPont business empire that included a statewide network of banks, newspapers in major cities, the state's largest property owner—St. Joe Paper Company—and the Florida East Coast Railway along with its ownership of several resort hotels and ferry boats. At one time, he controlled over one million acres of land. He married once in 1933 and was divorced in 1943, but rumors of occasional secret mistresses persisted throughout his later life.

Ball had no interest in running for political office, but his management of many investments throughout the state allowed him to acquire enormous political power. He was the key figure in a group of twenty north Florida politicians called the "Pork Chop Gang" that controlled the state government from the 1930s to the 1960s. This coalition supported racial segregation and set conservative policies for many statewide issues. His ownership of the local Florida Times-Union allowed him to suppress news of the 'strike' violence. He became known for his favorite before-dinner toast: "Confusion to the Enemy."

Ball succeeded in improving the railroad's efficiency by cutting costs at all levels, including funding for the Patrick Michael O'Shea Trust. Ball's elimination of funding for the O'Shea Trust was never reported in newspapers or by public notice, but rather carried out quietly by FECR attorneys collaborating with the Florida courts.

Outsiders later estimated that his sister Jessie Ball DuPont would not have approved this cessation of funding to possible heirs of Flagler, but she had died in 1970.

"Of course, as the O'Shea family attorney, your father immediately brought legal suit against the FEC companies and Edward Ball for illegal action based upon the original trust language that it would exist in perpetuity. The company defense claimed that the railway's 1931 bankruptcy negated all claims against the newly organized company.

"Wow," exclaimed the youngest O'Shea. "This issue is far more complicated than I imagined. It is difficult to plan where to start."

"Yes it is," replied his grandfather. "But this family has been waiting for you to complete your education and return home to resolve it for us under your father's guidance. We all have great confidence in you, Rick. But now, I must return home for my noonday nap. Call me if you need me." And the senior O'Shea rose from his chair and walked out, leaving his two descendants to tackle their family's difficult issues.

"Make no mistake about it, this explosion was created by expert arsonists, probably former military veterans," began Ball. "But, I am not so concerned about finding them as I am about identifying the people who paid them. Who gains from this act of terrorism? The union fight is over. The O'Shea family lost in court. The railroad doesn't have any enemies. Can you gentlemen suggest who might be behind this senseless act of mayhem?"

The two executives both stared back at their chairman raising their shoulders in negative response. They had nothing to add.

SEVEN

Washington, DC
August 31, 1977

Not many people are invited to the Oval Office of the President of the United States. But the four people invited to this office today were familiar faces: Federal Bureau of Investigation Director, Aubrey Tindale; CIA Director, Charles Malone; National Security Advisor, Zbigniew Brzezinski; and his deputy, Margaret McBride. After refreshments were served, President Carter turned to Ms. McBride.

"Margaret, we are all here to listen to your progress report on the origin of the Jacksonville Broward Yard explosion. Please proceed."

"Yes sir! First of all, the Jacksonville Fire Marshall and the Florida State Fire Marshal both concur that this explosion was a very professional piece of arson, with each of at least ten tank cars filled with explosive petroleum products armed with remote-controlled 'Semtex' bombs that were ignited by radio signal from several miles distant. All employees on-site were killed instantly. The two bodies of O'Shea cousins found on-site were employees who had been killed prior to the explosion and placed within the blast zone. We presume they were added to shed blame on that family, who had been quarrelling with FECR management for many years.

"Our task force of carefully selected experts believes that these bodies were placed as false leads. They are convinced, from evidence of the source of the explosion, that the perpetrators were professionally trained bomb experts—probably trained by our own military—who were hired by foreign terrorists to undertake this explosion and leave clues of local involvement. Our investigator, Agent Joshua Dempsey on loan from the CIA, has turned up a number of presumably illegal activities funded by FECR management over the past decade that terminated the O'Shea family trust with consequent savings to the FECR. However, these findings are tangential to our investigation and will not be pursued. I have authorized Dempsey to pass on this information to Patrick Michael O'Shea IV, his friend and former classmate at Harvard Law School.

"We also have instructed Agent Dempsey to continue collaboration with his MI6 contact to uncover foreign funding sources—no results to report thus far, except that I would like to express our gratitude to Director Malone for assigning such an astute agent to our task force."

"Many thanks, Ms. McBride," replied Malone. "We share your opinion of Dempsey and look forward to further results from him."

"I am already impressed by the rapid results of your task force, Margaret," stated the President," but we must press on. I am uncomfortable that this unexpected mass killing could be a test run for future attacks of even greater impact. So, all of your agencies must increase your mutual efforts to identify these people, whoever they may be. Can any of you offer any ideas for further investigation?"

"Hearing no further response, I thank you all for attending. Oh, Margaret, please wait for another minute or two."

After the others had left, President Carter asked Ms. McBride to return to her seat, and he moved to a chair directly in front of her.

"Margaret, you have done an excellent job thus far, and I am truly grateful. But, I remain deeply concerned that the Jacksonville explosion may be a harbinger of even stronger attacks to come. I want to assure you that my staff is instructed to forward any call from you at any time that you need assistance. My private number is on this card that I am offering you. Please don't hesitate to request reinforcements if you feel they are needed."

"You have my word, sir. I will contact you when I learn more."

EIGHT

Jacksonville, Florida
August 31, 1977

Chandra Jones' appearance at the entrance to the private Shamrock Club on Jacksonville's Southside was greeted with genuine pleasure by Patrick Michael O'Shea III, the welcoming chairman of the eightieth birthday celebration for his father, the patriarch of the O'Shea family.

Chandra Jones was a remarkably beautiful woman who inherited the finest physical characteristics of her five ethnic ancestries. She stood almost six feet in height with her conservative three inch brown pumps; her tailored two-piece, fawn-colored suit complemented her light brown skin of flawless complexion. The tasteful necklace contained small precious stones that highlighted her prominent brown eyes in a lovely face framed by the cascading waves of her auburn hair. Her shade of lip gloss complemented the natural skin color, framing a dazzling smile of perfect white teeth. At the age of twenty-six, she had achieved the enviable position of weekend anchor for Jacksonville's most popular television station. For this assignment, she was accompanied by her equally tall but rather bland-looking cameraman.

"Ms. Jones, I am delighted to see you again," exclaimed the athletic-looking Mike O' Shea with a broad smile on his sixty-year-old face. "Please join our celebration and feel at liberty to stay as long as you like and enjoy our party. But, to start off, I would like to introduce you to my wife, Jennifer, prior to escorting you to meet my father and my son, also named Patrick Michael O'Shea."

Jennifer, an immaculately groomed woman of about the same age as her husband, stepped forward with a welcoming smile to shake hands with the television news reporter.

"Why thank you, Mr. and Mrs. O'Shea," responded Chandra with a genuine smile." I am truly pleased to be here in the midst of one of Jacksonville's most distinguished families. Thank you so much for the invitation. Please meet my cameraman, Jimmy Brozovitch."

The cameraman shook hands with the O'Sheas quietly, and then Mike gently took Chandra's arm and led her toward the front of the large hall to where a dozen people were standing in line to greet Patrick O'Shea, Jr. on his 80th birthday. He was sitting in a large chair next to a table filled with gifts and greeting cards. Chandra's escort paused briefly to speak with the folks in line, and then politely requested that Ms. Jones be given priority opportunity to meet their patriarch. The people in line smiled graciously at the local television celebrity before quietly melting in with the growing group of spectators gathered to watch their patriarch greet Ms. Jones, carefully recorded by the silent cameraman.

"Ahh, Ms. Chandra Jones," exclaimed the elder O'Shea in a strong voice. "I watch you every weekend — the highlight of my week." He raised both hands up to her and continued, "My birthday is fully complete, now that you have graced me with your beautiful presence."

She took both his hands in hers and replied, "What a nice thing to say, Mr. O'Shea. Thank you! And happy birthday! I would very much like to conduct a brief interview with you if you could spare some time from your guests."

"Absolutely! Mike, would you please ask the guests to give us a few minutes alone?"

"Certainly, Dad," replied his son, but with a slight frown on his face. "Would you mind if your grandson joins the two of you?"

"No, not at all. I believe that he has drifted over to the bar, surrounded by those lovely young girls. Tell him that he can find us in the directors' room." He then rose without assistance and took

25

the reporter's arm to guide her toward the smaller meeting room adjoining the main hall while his son went to the microphone to explain the recess to the over one hundred guests in the hall.

A few minutes later, after the elder Patrick O'Shea and his guest were seated according to cameraman Jimmy's direction, the tall and very fit-looking youngest Patrick O'Shea joined them. Luckily for Ms. Jones, her partial African-American heritage provided a skin color that camouflaged her embarrassing blush as she looked up into his deep blue eyes with fascination. But her reporter discipline captured the moment, and she extended her hand politely to greet the newcomer: "Mr. O'Shea, please join us, while I interview your grandfather."

Chandra Jones had prepared very carefully for this interview and she had consulted books and news articles about the history of the O'Shea family, and why all of the first-born males were given the same name to qualify as inheritor of the trust established by Henry Flagler at the turn of the century. But, she had not anticipated the wily behavior of Patrick O'Shea, Jr. No sooner had she fixed the old gentleman with her most disarming smile than he leaned over and gently grasped her arm as he commandeered the interview.

"First of all, Ms. Jones, I should explain that I have been subjected to clever reporters throughout my entire life—none as pretty as you, I might add—and they all ask me the same questions about our family history and whether we have any proof that we are descended from Henry Flagler. The answer, of course, is no, we do not."

"But, Mr. O'Shea, I . . ."

"Just let me give you my answers first," O'Shea carried on in his strong voice, "and you can then ask about any missing pieces. We do have a legal trust fund that Henry Flagler personally established for our family that paid us an annual stipend, allowing us to educate our children and our children's children, while being able to afford a better-than-average lifestyle, including this annual party.

That is, the fund did pay us all annually until the Florida East Coast Railway was commandeered by Mr. Edward Ball after his DuPont Testamentary Trust Fund achieved majority ownership upon the unfortunate FECR bankruptcy . . ."

"Exactly, Mr. O'Shea, so . . ."

"Please wait a bit, Ms. Jones, I have not finished providing answers. Ball then managed to have the fund legally annulled and terminate our rightful inheritance. We believe this annulment to be illegal and we brought litigation against Mr. Ball and the Florida East Coast Railway and its affiliates. That litigation also was quashed by Ball's attorneys and his-hand-selected judges."

"But, what about . . ."

"Have patience, Ms. Jones. There have been rumors that we organized the bombing and other acts of violence against the railroad during the lengthy workers' strike from 1963 to 1976. We did not. Furthermore, there never has been one shred of evidence that an O'Shea or any member of our family was involved in violent action of any kind. We always have worked within the law to regain our inheritance."

"Yes, I know, but . . ."

"The ultimate climax of Mr. Ball's legal shenanigans occurred in 1975, after the strike action was all but over. We then proved by exception that every member of our family employed by the railroad prior to, and even during, the strike was unfairly fired on the basis of unsubstantiated rumors. And we continue to maintain that our trust was illegally struck down."

"Yes, indeed, sir, but . . ."

"Ms. Jones, your energetic persistence is paying off, and my aged body is having difficulty in answering all of the questions that you would like to ask. However, I personally have spent a good part of my life fighting to prove these facts. The reason that my grandson is here with us in this interview is because my final days are numbered and he must inherit this fight from me in accordance with his Harvard law degree, that was made possible by this fund. "

"Now," he paused to take a breath, "the last question that you want to ask me is whether our family played any role in the nasty explosion that destroyed the Broward Yard rail junction last Sunday. The answer is absolutely not. Members of our family have never engaged in illegal tactics of any kind toward the railroad or any other corporation or individual."

"Absolutely, sir, but . . ."

"In conclusion, Ms. Jones, I am delighted that you could come to my birthday party, and I am pleased to have joined in this interview with you. If you have any questions about my response, please ask them of my grandson who is completely briefed on the history and current status of this family. Thank you so much for being here."

Then, without another word, Patrick Michael O'Shea, Jr. rose from his chair and returned to the party, leaving Chandra Jones staring at his departure with her mouth open.

"Ms. Jones," said the youngest Patrick O'Shea, "please let me apologize for my grandfather's rather abrupt behavior. He has been questioned on these issues for most of his life and he is frustrated by the court actions against our rightful cause. All of us know that we were wrongfully dealt with by forces that we believe went beyond the law, and their extra-legal actions still go on. There is little doubt, that, within the next few days, we will be accused of this latest bombing. But, as my grandfather has stated here tonight, and many times in the past, we do not act outside the law."

"But, Mr. O'Shea," she replied. "I am interested in the O'Shea saga, and I would like to learn more about it. Can I ask you more questions?"

"Sure, I will be happy to respond. But not tonight! This is an evening of celebration and we intend to keep it that way. Thank you for being here, and thank you for listening to our plight. Please stay and partake of our food and drink. But, on behalf of our entire family, I must request that you do not ask any further questions of anyone tonight. Thank you. My friends call me Rick. I wish that you would too. Now, please join me in the main hall for a drink. "And Patrick O'Shea IV rose and offered her his arm to escort her to the bar.

As Rick placed drink orders at the bar for the three of them, the usually silent Jimmy Brozovitch leaned toward Chandra to whisper: "Holy Moses, Chandra, you have been ambushed. I don't believe that I have ever seen you so muzzled."

"Well, you're probably right, Jimmy, but, in the immortal words of good ol' Yogi Berra, 'It ain't over till it's over'. "

The two of them then joined Rick to meet more members of the O'Shea family, who also were fans of the charismatic television star. Finally, she had to beg forgiveness for departing to meet her evening news deadline.

At eleven o'clock that evening, Mike O'Shea, as most family and friends referred to Patrick Michael O'Shea III, arranged to have a large television screen rolled into the hall, so that everyone could catch a glimpse of the evening news and a few phrases from Chandra's "interview" with Patrick Michael O'Shea, Jr. After the brief television showing, Mike O'Shea grasped his son by the arm and whispered, "It would not be a bad idea for you to follow up with the lovely Miss Jones. She could provide us some good publicity."

The younger O'Shea smiled at his father's suggestion, and replied, "You know, Dad, that sounds like one of the best ideas I have heard tonight."

NINE

North of Provo Island
September 2, 1977

The Watson brothers had their three sport fisherman boats in pristine condition for each of their charter group reservations that morning. All three parties arrived on time at Blue Haven Marina on the eastern end of Providenciales Island, better known by residents as Provo. The three brothers quickly welcomed them aboard and were soon headed out to the Atlantic Ocean.

The oldest brother led the way in his 32-foot Bartram setting a due north course as the shortest route to the Atlantic bottom drop-off where the best game fish are found. He had four American men aboard, ready for some serious game fishing. His brothers followed with their fishing clients, each in turn heading his boat to the east and west flanking positions safely distant from each others' trolling lines.

The three boats were about ten miles offshore when they paused for the men to bait their hooks and then begin a slow troll northward. Suddenly, both younger brothers were shocked to witness a gigantic explosion where the oldest brother's boat had been. Orange, yellow and red flames shot skyward, followed by ugly grey and black smoke. The younger brothers, aided by their single crew members, rapidly pulled their lines back into their boats and headed for the blast site. They circled the site but were unable to get close because of the intense heat. Neither boat was able to spot any sign of human remains, in fact they could not identify any debris beyond small pieces of fiberglass from their brother's hull.

Both remaining brothers had simultaneously contacted coastal patrol headquarters in Cockburn Town by radio, and confirmed that a British frigate patrolling the north shore would rendezvous with them within twenty minutes. By the time the larger craft arrived, the fire had all but disappeared and few identifiable remains could be seen. Two surface craft were launched from the frigate and searched diligently without significant success. Officers of the navy ship interviewed everyone on the two remaining boats before recording the details for an official report.

The two brothers refunded their passengers and headed for home. Their priority was to gather the Watson family together and lend support to their brother's wife and children. Local police interviewed them on shore and collected the four passports of the American passengers filed with the charter contract. Although the news article on the sport fishing boat explosion, killing four Americans and the captain and deckhand off the northern coast of the island of Providenciales, was major news in the Turks and Caicos Islands, it barely made the inside page of the Miami Herald.

However, in attempting to notify the Americans' next-of-kin, the local police were amazed to find that all four American passports were forgeries. Their report to the chief of police in Cockburn Town resulted in an immediate contact with the British Foreign Intelligence Service (better known as MI6) in London, England requesting the assignment of a senior agent to the case.

Within hours, Senior Agent Nigel Harris was on a flight from Nassau in The Bahamas to the neighboring British protectorate of Turks and Caicos. His director in London had advised him to defer his Bahamas assignment and concentrate on the Provo explosion, which, at first blush, had the appearance of a homicide. Agent Harris already had determined to contact his old friend in the American FBI once he reached Provo.

TEN

Jacksonville, Florida
September 2, 1977

It was a gorgeous late summer day in central Jacksonville when Chandra Jones entered the popular Wine Cellar restaurant. She found Rick O'Shea waiting at a table in the garden shaded by historic oak trees. After polite greetings, they decided to select menu items before Chandra broached the topic of her interest.

The Wine Cellar, with its pastoral garden as well as its elegant indoor dining, is a popular luncheon location for attorneys and business professionals with offices in central Jacksonville. Thus, it was no surprise to find attorney Patrick Michael O'Shea IV seated at a garden table with television reporter Chandra Jones two days after their introduction at the senior O'Shea birthday party. However, it was somewhat surprising that Chandra had invited the young O'Shea on the pretext of learning more about the history of his family for her follow-up half-hour special, scheduled for a Sunday time slot the following month. But, as requested by O'Shea, no cameraman was present at this strictly "off-the-record" luncheon meeting.

"Let me get this straight," Chandra requested, after they had submitted their lunch orders to the waiter, "your great-great grandfather, Patrick Michael O'Shea the First, was the beneficiary of a trust created by Henry Flagler in 1897 that received annual funding from his wholly owned railway company and continued in perpetuity to fund descendants of the same name. Is that right?"

"Well, almost," replied O'Shea "First of all, if we are going to discuss my family at length, let's use their common names to save time. My grandfather is the only one called Patrick by family and friends. My dad goes by Michael or Mike, and I have been called Rick since birth."

"Wow, that is a lot easier. I was resorting to numbers in my personal notes, but I assume that you prefer Rick rather than IV?"

"Correct! Now, the trust annual funding was actually split with one-half to the current senior heir, my grandfather, one-quarter to be divided equally among each living blood relative and one-quarter to an investment fund that heirs can borrow from to pay for education, health care or similar needs approved by the senior heir. I doubt if I could have attended Harvard without Mr. Flagler's gift."

"And, if I've got it right, the fund was declared illegal in 1974 by court order, subsequently confirmed by the Florida Supreme Court to the petition by the three FECR funding entities, all under the direct control of Edward Ball, who still serves as chairman of all three entities. "

"Yes, after sixty years of annual payments!" replied Rick. "However, it should be noted that the FECR bankruptcy of 1931 was also key to this action, insofar as it reduced the value of company shares and enabled Ball, through his chairmanship of the Alfred I DuPont Testamentary Trust, to purchase cheap FECR mortgage bonds which eventually totaled fifty-five percent ownership and allowed him to be awarded management control of FECR by the federal court and to re-organize FECR, and subsequently take control of the other two original Flagler companies—Florida East Coast Industries and the land affiliate, Flagler Development Company. Florida East Coast Industries was made a holding company of the other two companies and became owned by the DuPont Testamentary Trust and controlled by its chairman Ed Ball."

Chandra said, "Your grandfather believes that your family was wronged by Ed Ball's actions. Is that correct?"

"Correct!"

At that moment, the waiter returned with their orders, and both of them concentrated on eating their food. But, after a few mouthfuls, Chandra returned to her interview.

"Rick, you are employed in a law firm with your father. Is that right?"

"Correct again," smiled Rick in response. "Michael O'Shea Law specializes primarily in civil litigation and real estate transactions."

"Do you have any outstanding litigation on the O'Shea family inheritance?"

"No, we do not. My father was frustrated by the 1974 decisions against us and attempted to petition the court for new hearings, but he was refused on three occasions with somewhat different requests. He and I both believe that we were improperly treated by the court in 1974 and we have been trying to find a friendly legislator to investigate our case, but no luck so far. He wants me to run for the Florida Legislature so that we can investigate our own case—that is definitely not for publication—and I have been reluctant to enter the world of politics."

"Okay," Chandra replied with a magnificent smile. "I have an idea that we might explore, if you are willing to confide in me?"

"Well now, that is appealing, but what is your definition of 'confide'?"

The reporter's face turned serious and she looked the attorney right in the eye before responding. "Sean, my editor at the television station, reviewed my clip of the O'Shea party and invited me into his office yesterday. He told me that he was familiar with the O'Shea family story because of informal chats with his aunt, Bessie Solomon, who is about to retire as historian for the Florida Times-Union newspaper. He phoned her on my behalf and she agreed to meet with the two of us and share some of the press articles and background files from the so-called 'Ball era' of the paper, when he monitored news articles.

"According to my editor, Bessie is probably the best source of information about issues affecting your trust, but she is understandably concerned about leaving the paper with an unblemished record. So, you must promise me to keep her information off the record. I already have spoken to her and agreed that our conversations would be confidential and I took the liberty of pledging your confidence as well as mine. Can I have your pledge on her behalf?"

"Wow!" exclaimed Rick as he returned her direct eye contact. "I am overwhelmed that you have taken this interest in our family. The answer to your question is absolutely yes. You and Bessie have my agreement to keep her identity confidential. Furthermore, I am humbled that you included me in your investigation."

"Well," responded Chandra as she lowered her eyes, "I must confess that I have an ulterior motive. You are a source of O'Shea family information that is essential to my investigation. In short, I need your input to validate and expand Bessie's information."

"Curses," said Sean. "I was assuming that you just wanted my services as a bodyguard."

"Well, let's hope that won't be necessary," she smiled.

ELEVEN

Nice, France
September 3, 1977

The large white yacht of Prince Hassad El Saud was anchored among other impressive yachts in the sun-bathed Mediterranean Sea. The lone visitor had just arrived from the airport by taxi and water taxi. He was welcomed aboard by a steward dressed in white, and shown to a below-deck cabin where he found a light lunch awaiting him. The lunch tray also contained a note advising him to enjoy a short rest prior to his four o'clock meeting with the Prince.

At five minutes before the meeting time, Dimitri Chekov greeted his employer on the yacht's afterdeck, where the Prince was seated at a table beneath a large green umbrella. The handsome Arab was dressed in white pants and a colorful shirt. His clean-shaven and well-tanned face gave no indication of his royal status in Saudi Arabia. In fact, he resided most of the year with his wife and three children in Monte Carlo just a short drive east along the Riviera. A steward served them soft drinks and they began reviewing their priority action plans.

After two hours, the Prince told Chekov that he had an evening engagement but that Chekov would be served dinner on-board and he would see him in the morning.

During the night, while Dimitri Chekov enjoyed a peaceful sleep, the Yacht Cleopatra pulled up anchor at Nice and slowly cruised a few kilometers east to a fresh anchorage in the placid waters of Monte-Carlo Bay. Prince Hassad El Saud was scheduled to speak at a local business reception that morning in the America Room of the Monte-Carlo Bay Hotel and Resort. The new anchorage permitted him to be taken quickly to the hotel in the yacht's motor launch. He left word for Dimitri to meet him for lunch on the yacht's afterdeck upon his return.

The enigmatic Russian was already seated beneath the afterdeck umbrella sipping a fruit drink when the Prince joined him in the early afternoon. He sat down at a place setting already including his favorite mango fruit drink. The deck steward immediately served a lobster salad to each of the men and then quickly disappeared into the interior of the yacht to ensure privacy for the Prince and his guest.

"Well, Dimitri, did you have a good rest?"

"Yes, indeed, Your Highness. I never even noticed the yacht moving to this new location. I gather that the famous Monte Carlo Casino is just down the street from our anchorage?"

"It is indeed; would you like to try your luck?"

"Thank you, but no, I have never believed in luck."

"An excellent rule," replied the Prince. "But, perhaps what I am about to propose to you will change your mind. Can I assume that you have some flexibility in this regard?"

"Absolutely, Your Highness. I am at your service, whatever, it may be."

"Very well, then, please listen carefully. As you know, I am one of the male members of the Saud family. My grandfather founded the Kingdom of Saudi Arabia and later founded the Aramco Petroleum Company which is the primary source of our wealth. However, as direct descendants of the Wahaibi tribe, we practice the strictest form of Islam. The holy Koran, containing the words of our great prophet, Mohammed, guides all of our actions.

"But, our current King, my uncle, has chosen to bend our religious teachings by cultivating friendship with the United States of America, a country that uses an enormous amount of oil and it buys most of it from Aramco. We can tolerate the Christian beliefs of its people and even the influence of its wealthy Jews. But we cannot abide them adopting the land of Israel against all historic rights of settlement in the Middle East. Therefore, some of my trusted cousins and I have embarked upon a secret Jihad to devastate the United States economy. Does this fact frighten you."

"Not in the slightest, Your Highness," replied the wily Russian without hesitation. "I have pursued a career of selling my services to the highest bidder. You are that man. I am prepared to carry out all of your orders regardless of the impact on my current land of residence. You will recall that my birthplace is Russia. I was raised in a country that was no friend of the United States. I have no problem at all inflicting harm upon the Americans. In fact, I look forward to such an opportunity."

"Thank you, Dimitri. Your answer is as I expected. I can assure you that the rewards will compensate you for any danger that you might encounter. Now, I will brief you on an extraordinary plan already underway. But please remember that any breach of confidentiality about this plan will result in your instant death. Before I proceed, please confirm that you agree to complete secrecy about this plan. You are the only non-Muslim to be informed and my cousins are concerned about your reliability. I have vouched for you, so my own life is at risk if you fail me."

"I will not fail you, Your Highness. You can rest assured of my dedication to you."

"Very well, my friend, I am comfortable with your promise. Before telling you of our plan, I should also inform you that, in addition to the quite considerable salary that I pay you from my own pocket, my cousins and I are today depositing one million Eurodollars in a Swiss bank account in your name. You will be given the account number on the day that our plan is executed in America. We expect that day to occur within the next few weeks. Your efficiency will hasten that day." Chekov remained discretely quiet, despite his urge to jump up and down for joy.

The Prince then proceeded to describe an extraordinary plan requiring the ownership of the Florida East Coast Railway and its management to carry out what appeared to be the biggest act of terrorism in history. And he, Dimitri Chekov, would be the coordinator.

TWELVE

Poti, Georgia
September 4, 1977

A gorgeous pink and purple dawn was breaking across the eastern Black Sea as the commuter plane from Istanbul began its descent into Poti Airport on the coast of Georgia. Dimitri Chekov glanced out the port window to see several freighter ships docked in the Poti Seaport basin. The port was alive with machines unloading metal pods from train cars and transferring them to the ships. He smiled contentedly with the thought that managing to secure employment with Prince Hassad El Saud was the best break of his life.

The pilot executed a perfect landing and Chekov joined the other passengers descending the portable stairway and forming a line to present their passports to the Georgia immigration officials. Upon gaining entry to this former Russian satellite, he carried his small overnight bag quickly past the silent customs official and out to a waiting taxi at the curbside. He directed the driver in perfect Russian to take him to the freighter Polar Star at the Poti Seaport. Although tired from his double flight from Nice to Istanbul and then the commuter flight to Poti, he was eager to inspect the Castle Investment Group cargo prior to its departure from Poti on its long journey to Port Everglades outside Fort Lauderdale—the most expensive cargo shipment that he was ever likely to oversee.

He paid the driver his "outrageous" fare, totaling two dollars in American currency, and advised him to return in two hours for a return fare. Then the expatriate Russian ascended the gangway to his scheduled meeting with the ship's captain and the cargo agent from Turkmenistan. The sailor at the gangway welcomed him in Russian and beckoned him to follow as he continued up to the bridge of the ten-thousand-ton freighter designed for container transport.

Two men stood waiting for Chekov on the bridge. One was the captain who introduced himself to the newcomer and then presented the cargo agent from Turkmenistan, who had accompanied the shipment by train to the Poti dockside. He pointed out the five containers on flatbed rail cars awaiting Chekov's inspection prior to loading onto the freighter. Chekov smiled politely at the captain before informing him that he would not be needed for the actual inspection, and he and the cargo agent then proceeded down to the dock.

Prior to approaching the cargo containers, the cargo agent and Chekov paused to exchange identification and predetermined passwords. Once they both were satisfied that the other was a legitimate representative of the original contract signers, they proceeded to unlock and open the end door of the first container. The interior was packed from top to bottom with large wooden boxes labeled in both Russian and English as machine tools for shipment to a company located in Baltimore, Maryland for trans-shipment through Port Everglades via the Florida East Coast Railway. The cargo agent explained that there were two rows of these boxes filled with tools at the rear door of each container to satisfy the curiosity of a customs official. The real cargo was imbedded behind the boxes. Chekov informed him that he must inspect the primary cargo in each container. The cargo agent carefully masked his annoyance and called upon four dock workers with a front-end loader that he had hired earlier for this likelihood.

The dock workers proceeded to unload a double row of wooden boxes in the first container labeled in English as metal tools. As they were removed, a larger metal box was revealed about two meters square, leaving a narrow passageway on one side for access beyond it to a metal tank occupying the remainder of the container. The metal box was accessible by a sliding panel, but Chekov moved past it to the large tank. Chekov borrowed a small hammer from the dock workers and tapped on the large tank. The sound clearly indicated that it was full of something, as specified in the contract. He apparently was satisfied with his findings and instructed the agent to restore the interior while he proceeded to undertake the same examination on the other four containers.

Although each container was identified with a different company and address in another American city, Chekov discovered that one of the boxes labeled tools in the third container contained a unique notation in the address naming a specific person named Harry Jackson as the recipient. He pulled out his knife again and slit the wrapper on this box to find, as expected, a metal container with a hinged lid. Upon opening the lid, he found five metal divisions with identical pieces of equipment. The top of each contained a timer as well as the specific city that it was to match. These were the expected wireless ignition switches for each of the six massive bombs manufactured on contract for a fictitious company located in Malta.

Chekov then instructed the patient cargo agent to re-assemble the interior of each container in its original state ready for trans-Atlantic shipment. He then re-boarded the freighter and climbed to the bridge. The captain was waiting for him with a clipboard containing the cargo release for a signature. But Chekov had one more piece of business to conduct prior to signing the release. First, he requested the captain to step inside where they could speak out of sight of any interested bystanders.

In his native Russian language, he told the Georgian captain that he needed these containers to be spread about the other cargo. As the captain's expression began to appear unhappy, Chekov explained that he was aware that this request would require more time and expense. As he spoke, the wily Russian extracted a large roll of Eurodollars from his pocket, and proceeded to count five thousand onto the navigation table—a very large bonus for the captain of an aging freighter. When he finished counting, confident that the captain had counted simultaneously, Chekov asked if the captain felt that this cash would cover the extra time and work involved, knowing full well that the captain would pocket the entire amount. "Well," the Russian concluded, "I am adding another thousand just to be certain. We may require your assistance in future."

He then returned to the dockside where the cargo agent and his workers were still putting the container interiors back in order. He rewarded the agent and his four workers another handful of Eurodollars for their extra effort. By the time he boarded his taxi, he was smiling quietly to himself that his job in Poti was well concluded.

Dimitri Chekov was feeling very tired from his extended trip to Europe and Asia as he exited security in the Atlanta airport. The large figure of Big Moe was waiting at the curb with their usual limousine driver. The small driver quickly stored Chekov's carry-on luggage in the trunk and opened the rear door for him. Big Moe was already inside raising the security window between the seats as Chekov joined him.

After summarizing his trip for Big Moe, Chekov instructed him to purchase round-trip tickets to Jacksonville for the next afternoon, and to be sure to bring his illegal entry tools. Hopefully, they can return in the late evening if all goes as planned. In the meantime, he was eager to get to his apartment and to an early bedtime.

THIRTEEN

Jacksonville, Florida
September 6, 1977

Margaret McBride welcomed her investigator to a private meeting room in the Crown Plaza Hotel overlooking the St. John River. Joshua Dempsey, better known to his friends as "JD," had been loaned to her by the CIA two weeks prior and spent most of his time in Florida with state and local law officials sorting out the details of the Broward Yard explosion.

JD's report to McBride essentially cleared any complicity by the O'Shea family despite two of their members found dead at the scene. However, in searching legal files, he discovered possible bribery to a circuit court judge who then was promoted to the Florida Supreme Court and subsequently motivated a colleague to reject the same case as an Appellate Court judge—an infraction apparently picked up by the appeal attorney but rejected to be heard by the Supreme Court after both judges died from natural causes. The plaintiff was the Patrick Michael O'Shea Trust represented by attorney Michael O'Shea.

McBride found this illegality of interest, but her primary attention was focused on JD's phone conversation with FBI Senior Agent Jordan Hale who had briefed Dempsey on a boat explosion north of the Turks and Caicos Islands (a British protectorate). Four Americans were killed in the blast, each one carrying a forged passport with false addresses.

Furthermore, a known criminal using the name Mohammed Abdullah flew out of the island of Providenciales that same morning, landing in Miami and boarding a flight to Atlanta—his last-known address, but since vacated. He is a person of interest in the boat explosion. The British MI6 Senior Agent, Nigel Harris, had asked Senior Agent Hale about his knowledge of Mohammed Abdullah, but he only had outdated FBI file information. So, he phoned Dempsey.

JD was knowledgeable about Abdullah, also known as "Big Mo," from a prior drug smuggling assignment and was able to direct his British counterpart to a street address in Atlanta which, unfortunately, also proved unoccupied. However, of greater interest was the fact that his CIA file indicated that this man currently had been employed as an enforcer by the international criminal middleman, Dimitri Chekov, who also lived in Atlanta.

Furthermore, the boat explosion tests by MI6 indicate that the explosive was 'Semtex', the same explosive used in the Broward Yard explosion. Suspicions abound of a connection tying the dead men to the Jacksonville disaster—possibly a clean-up of the arsonists. McBride asked him not to leave Jacksonville for a few days while she reported to President Carter. In the interim, she gave him freedom to report the legal irregularities to his former college friend, Rick O'Shea.

Rick O'Shea had just put his specialty lasagna dish in his apartment oven for dinner when his guest arrived. He answered the doorbell and absorbed a crushing hug from his former college room-mate at Harvard, JD Dempsey. O'Shea had been delighted to receive JD's phone call two hours previously to report that he was in town for a couple of days and looked forward to an evening together, assuming that his old roomie was well provisioned with food and drink as well as a guest room.

Actually, JD was carrying a 12-pack of beer as well as his suitcase and computer bag. He set them all down in the entry and unpacked two beers before sitting in the nearest chair. After several more beers and the delicious lasagna, JD confessed that, despite his allegiance to CIA policies, he had a confidential story that he felt obliged to reveal to his old friend. He had cleared permission to do so with his supervisor just two hours ago, before phoning Rick.

He then proceeded to reveal the information that he had related to Deputy McBride earlier in the day to a wide-eyed O'Shea, who professed his absolute confidentiality to his college buddy regardless of his clearance. It was just the kind of knowledge that he had hoped to find in order to re-open the FECR case terminating the Patrick O'Shea Trust Fund.

"Since you are in my home, I will avoid hugging you for fear that the neighbors may be watching, but, my friend, you could not have brought better news to me."

"Well then, I guess we better add a little icing to the cake," replied JD with a smile. And he immediately opened his briefcase to extract written details of the court proceedings that he had just revealed. "My boss doesn't want these notes, so I am giving them to you in partial re-payment for the test you helped me with when I inadvertently stayed out all night with an un-named co-ed in Cambridge."

"Naturally," laughed Rick, "my memory is completely blank on that incident. But, regardless, I accept your notes with many thanks."

"Great! That certainly calls for another cold one." And the two men returned to celebrating their reunion.

FOURTEEN

Jacksonville, Florida
September 6, 1977

Rick O'Shea arrived at the riverside Florida Times-Union newspaper office exactly on time and found Chandra Jones already in reception waiting for him. He greeted her with a handshake and asked if she had notified Bessie Solomon.

"She has indeed," boomed a strong voice from a smiling white-haired woman emerging from the hallway next to reception. Although her face and mature body indicated a woman in her sixties, she displayed the energy of a much younger woman. She shook hands with each of them and motioned them to follow her to an elevator that lowered them two floors to a huge file room organized much like a library. Bessie explained that they had only been in this

45

building for a year and had yet to transfer most of their historic library to microfilm.

They followed her to a small room equipped with a metal table and four metal chairs. Bessie poured coffee for each of them and sat down with her palms upturned on the table. "Now," she said, "what secrets of Jacksonville would you like to know?"

Actually, she already had been briefed by her nephew, Chandra's TV editor, and she was able to relate a series of surprising stories beginning with the celebrations and defeats of the FECR followed by the exploits of Alfred DuPont and Edward Ball, prior to DuPont's untimely death in 1935. She described the DuPont purchase of several hundred acres on the southeast bank of the St. Johns River four miles south of the city center and their plan for a new community with their own riverfront estate as the centerpiece. The estate was named Epping Forest in honor of Jessie DuPont's family home in England. Their new home was a masterpiece by a talented local architect. After his death in 1935, she opened the mansion to world leaders for meetings on several occasions. After her death in 1970, the home was placed on the National Historic Register along with its grounds and boat docks.

Bessie also mentioned the dark days of the Florida Times-Union newspaper when it was managed by Ball and his political cronies. They chose to print nothing about Jacksonville's most shameful day in 1967 when bloody race riots left dozens of both black and white residents dead and hospitalized as well as many more blacks arrested for false charges. Prior to that terrible day, she related how the paper successfully buried the story of Ball's vacation misadventures in France during 1958.

According to Bessie, Edward Ball acquired substantial gambling debts (over five million dollars) dating from an infamous, but secret, 1958 weeklong vacation in Monte Carlo with a French 'showgirl'. Although his companion was well paid for her time, she subsequently told the story to another client who was a confidant of a wealthy member of the Saudi Arabian royal family who purchased the debt from the Casino and hired an international criminal named Dimitri Chekov to threaten Ball with disclosure subject to immediate payment. But, despite his small stature, Ball was a very tough character, and he had many friends in high places. He told Chekov to go ahead and do his best to ruin Ball's reputation. He could handle it.

Upon receiving no satisfaction, the wealthy Arab apparently created a plan to use Ball to create a takeover of the FECR and use it to smuggle drugs from Miami to northern cities with rail links to FECR. Chandra could not take notes fast enough, but O'Shea was comfortable with his pocket recorder.

"Now, where do you want to start?" Bessie questioned with a twinkle in her eye. She clearly was enjoying this foray into her vast knowledge mine.

"Bessie, you undoubtedly have a huge warehouse of confidential information," O'Shea postulated, "and a great deal of it seems to be in your memory as well. But my purpose is not to cause personal embarrassment or blackmail. I only want the facts pertaining to FECR legal action against the O'Shea family from 1972 to 1976, and the judges involved in these cases."

Although Bessie may have been disappointed by this relatively narrow topic, she retained her good humor and stood up with open arms. "We've got it," she exclaimed with a smile, "but it may take me an hour or so to dig it up. Why don't you young people go have some brunch and return in an hour? Just come down past reception and I'll be here waiting for you."

"But," Chandra exclaimed, "can't we be of help to you in the search?"

"No, I work alone. I've always worked alone. You run along and I'll get set up for you."

Rick and Chandra took the opportunity to explore Worman's Bakery a few blocks from the newspaper building. It was a famous center city breakfast and lunch cafe featuring fresh pastries that neither one of them had experienced.

They sampled several pastries and talked about their quite different childhoods in Jacksonville: he in a prominent catholic school and she in an old public elementary school in a largely African-American neighborhood on the north side of the city. He had been sent to an expensive private school in Virginia for the last three years of high school, whereas she worked hard to excel at an all-black high school with minimum standards.

Neither she nor her family had sufficient funds to send her to college, but she was determined to advance herself without credentials. Somewhat to her embarrassment, her good looks prevailed to land her a junior position at the WGTR television station.

The continuing publicity over city leaders' efforts to institute peaceful solutions to racial issues moved the station manager to bridge the color barrier and allow her to report on events in the largely African-American northern part of the city. She proved her worth as a street reporter and last year was promoted to weekend anchor, the only such "black" news person in Jacksonville. Once again, however, she felt that she had to rely upon her good looks to achieve popularity. Now she was determined to report more important stories, and she had chosen the O'Shea family history as her first.

They arrived back at Bessie's "dungeon" headquarters a little later than planned, but their new friend was waiting patiently with several file folders piled on her table.

48

Bessie gave them a big smile to welcome them back. "I have some good news and some bad news," she announced. "The bad news is that some of the files have been pilfered and reports on the legal proceedings affecting the O'Shea family are incomplete. But the good news is that my filing system was in disarray at that time because of moving from our old building, so whoever did the pilfering missed most of the really important background information that was not printed. So, we have lots of stuff for you to review, but it is in loosely written format. I'm afraid that it will take you a good deal of time."

Rick immediately jumped up and took off his jacket. "Let's get started, then. I'm ready to roll." And he immediately pulled files to his side of the table and began putting them in order.

Chandra proved equally enthusiastic as she, too, pulled files her way and suggested that they order everything by year first, prior to making notes.

"Good idea, Chandra. We can pile the earliest years at your end of the table and the latest at my end. Bessie, we promise to put everything back in order when we finish."

Rick and Chandra had spent all afternoon in the basement of the Florida Times-Union building carefully reading every piece of documentation on the legal cases between FECR and the Patrick Michael O'Shea Trust. Although the 1974 trial records were not verbatim, the actual references to trial testimony were sufficiently clear to understand the arguments of both parties. The unsigned reporter who had authored the notes had a clear writing style and there appeared to be no question, at least in Rick's mind, that the FECR attorney, George Atkins, had not proven a sufficient case to support the 1931 bankruptcy of FECR as a basis for terminating the annual payment to the Patrick Michael O'Shea Trust. He reasoned that the bankruptcy might well have been grounds for negotiating a lower annual payment, but not the complete termination that the judge ruled.

At the same time, Chandra was reviewing notes from two years later (1976) when the Appellate court ruled against the appeal by Mike O'Shea that the earlier Circuit Court ruling was not substantiated by Florida case law on bankruptcies. A bankruptcy under federal Chapter 11 required a negotiated settlement with all creditors in agreement, rather than the Chapter 7 ruling for dissolution of the company and proportionate share agreement of assets certified by the court. Clearly, in this case, two essential factors were missing: (1) the debts were not negotiated for proportionate sharing, and (2) the target company had been declared bankrupt under the Chapter 11 provision of re-organization under court supervision rather than the Chapter 7 provision of dissolution. It appeared to be a flagrant mixing of the two different solutions.

She also came across the fact that Judge Samuel Coburn, within three months after ruling on this case then received a promotion to the Florida Supreme Court in Tallahassee, the state capital. At that time, judges for the Appellate Court were filled with Supreme Court Justices on a rotational basis to conserve funds. The new appointment of Samuel Coburn drew the bench for the O'Shea appeal. Of course, Mike O'Shea objected to the same judge (now Justice) hearing an appeal on his own ruling. So Coburn was self-recused in lieu of another new appointment to the Supreme Court, Justice John Mason. It seems that both Coburn and Mason were nominated by a single man, Senator Ebeneezer McCloud, representing St. Johns County where the FECR headquarters was located. Senator McCloud had served many years in the State Senate and was considered an institution in government. By coincidence, his daughter had risen through the ranks of Florida East Coast Industries and, in 1975, she was promoted by Chairman Ball to the position of Senior Vice President of Human Resources at a considerable increase in salary.

The reporter who had drafted these notes made circles around each of these names and linked them with a red pen. He or she clearly suspected collusion among these officials, but, of course, the news editor rejected the story for lack of solid facts to support the allegations.

In the interim, Samuel Coburn died of a sudden heart attack in the spring of 1976, and, when Mike O'Shea appealed to the Supreme Court, Justice John Mason was selected to write the Court Rejection to hear the case.

Just reading about this patently clear series of miscarriages of justice caused Chandra to become infuriated to the point that she slammed her clipboard down on the table causing Rick to look up in alarm, and Bessie came running in from another room to calm her young friend. So, Chandra felt obliged to explain her anger over the notes that she had just reviewed.

"Well now," rejoined Bessie with a smile. "I may have just the right tonic for your anger."

"I doubt if anything could help me sleep after reading these notes," replied Chandra.

"Really? What if I informed you that the young reporter who made those notes quit in anger after the refusal of the editor to run his story? His name is Edward Cosgrove and you interviewed him a few months ago when he got elected by a substantial margin to become a Florida State Assemblyman for a portion of St. Johns County, including suburban St. Augustine."

"Wow! Is that really true?" asked Chandra.

"My dear, I don't do lies. Check your own appointment book."

Chandra blushed at her mistake. "Oh dear, I don't mean to suggest . . . that is, I just didn't think before putting my foot in my mouth. Please forgive me."

"Of course, my dear, don't give it another thought. I can promise you that I won't. But, please follow up with Mr. Cosgrove. Just don't reveal where you learned of his notes."

"Absolutely! Rick and I already pledged our confidence to you. But, Rick, if this guy still has the passion showing through these notes, I won't need any support material. Yah-hoo!"

FIFTEEN

Jacksonville, Florida
September 6, 1977

The only entrance to Ed Ball's condominium penthouse overlooking the St. Johns River was by his private elevator It required two keys to operate from the lobby, one held by the building doorman and one by Ball. Thus, the five-foot-five-inch tall Ed Ball felt very secure as he emerged from the elevator foyer into his spacious living room at the end of his working day.

His shock was overwhelming when he confronted the frightening vision of Dimitri Chekov and his huge black accomplice sitting on his sofa staring at him. He sputtered with a mixture of anger and fear in attempting to address them in an authoritative voice, which emerged in a rather squeaky whisper as he demanded to know how they got into his apartment.

Chekov replied that their secrets of access were irrelevant. They were here to discuss the sale of the FECR. He suggested that Ball take a chair and listen carefully. Ball appeared frozen in position until Big Moe slowly unwound his long body from the couch. Ball quickly seated himself in the closest chair.

After Ball was seated, the big black man cleared off the coffee table in front of him and spread out a color draft of a magazine article entitled "The Secret Life of Edward Ball," and featuring lurid pictures of his former Monte Carlo companion on the first page. Big Moe turned the page to show pictures of Ball with this woman in shocking bedroom scenes on the inside pages. The elderly executive sat back in his chair, clearly exasperated by these scenes of one careless week of his life.

Chekov then explained that he represented the man that owned Ball's note for over five million dollars before interest. It would be returned to Bond without question within one hour after the sale of FECR to a perfectly respectable American company called Castle Investment Group Inc. of Wilmington, Delaware.

"Attorneys for that company will present themselves at your office the morning after tomorrow—September 8—with a certified check for ten percent of the total sales price of fifty-two million dollars, an amount which is estimated to be five million dollars above the company's market value. No compensation will be demanded for the devastated Broward Yard. It is included in its present condition.

"Also, existing mortgage debt will be included at its present value and paid off by the new owners. In the unlikely case that you are not prepared to sign the sales agreement by noon of that day, the details of your 1958 French adventure will be front page news by the end of the week. We may throw in another explosion just to emphasize the point to any critics you may encounter.

"Do I make myself perfectly clear, Mr. Ball?" Ball just sat and stared straight ahead. "Mohammed, perhaps Mr. Ball is ill. You might take him to the terrace for fresh air and a clarifying view of the city from the rail."

As Big Moe began to move, Ball replied in a quiet voice, "Physical violence will not be necessary. I will sign the documents as you have proposed."

Chekov smiled quietly at him, "A very wise decision that you will not regret, Mr. Ball." He and Big Moe rose from the sofa and proceeded directly to the entry hall. After dropping the apartment keys on the hall table, the two men entered the elevator and were gone.

Chekov and Big Moe caught the evening flight from Jacksonville back to Atlanta, comfortable with their evening's persuasion of the formerly powerful Edward Ball.

After Big Moe and his limousine driver delivered Dimitri Chekov to the front door of his Atlanta condominium from the airport terminal, he walked quickly to the front entrance and on to the elevator with a quick wave to the doorman. He unlocked the door to his apartment and turned on the lights. The Russian was as surprised as had been Ball to see and intruder this time – Prince Hassad El Saud sitting in Chekov's favorite chair sipping his best malt whisky. Two large men stood behind him without movement.

The Prince smiled up at him, "Have no fear, Dimitri, your time has not yet come. I just dropped by to receive your assurance that Mr. Ball is prepared to sign our agreement tomorrow. Is that correct?" Chekov quickly revived his senses.

"Absolutely, Your Highness. You can count on it." The Prince rose from his chair and replied, "I certainly hope so . . . for your sake. Sleep well, my friend." And the three men left.

SIXTEEN

St. Augustine, Florida
September 8, 1977

The FECR headquarters office buildings were just north of King Street, several blocks west of the historic city center of St. Augustine. News media reporters had gathered in advance of the eleven o'clock presentation, even though they were well aware that Ed Ball prided himself on starting meetings precisely on time. Chandra Jones and her cameraman were set up directly in front of the speaker platform to ensure optimum coverage, although she was well aware that this announcement would be a blow to her new friend Rick O'Shea.

As expected, sharply at eleven o'clock, the diminutive Mr. Ball strode up to the microphone on the platform in the lobby of the FECR headquarters just as Chandra completed her taped introduction. Ball immediately began to read his prepared statement; namely, that FECR management had determined that the shareholders would gain from selling the company for the premium price of $52 million in cash. The buyer, Castle Investment Group of Wilmington, Delaware, a well-financed and experienced company, had promised to keep management personnel in place as well as the operating personnel. Train schedules would be maintained for all freight shipments.

Ball went on to state that the contract had been signed with the contingency of a sixty-day due diligence provision during which financial details would be negotiated to confirm the final price. No work stoppage was anticipated. Any questions could be addressed to Mr. Theodore Thompson, FECR Vice President of Public Relations.

Ball then introduced the Senior Attorney of the Castle Investments Group who read from a written statement that his company was delighted to be acquiring this eighty-year-old railway company with its rich history of service to communities and industries on the east coast of Florida. He assured current employees of the company that Castle Investments Group planned no organization or personnel changes, and they looked forward to becoming a responsible corporate citizen of St. Augustine and Northeast Florida.

The speakers then departed the platform and entered limousines for transportation back to their chartered plane at the St. Augustine airport. The entire program lasted a total of twenty minutes and Chandra added some additional background to close the story over an additional five minutes. She was not particularly happy with the broadcast insofar as the news would be unlikely to rate headlines on the evening news, or even deserve a weekend special unless she could add a human interest tag from some interested source. She immediately thought of her new friend, Rick O'Shea, and vowed to give him a call as soon as she returned to the office.

Mike O'Shea, accompanied by his son and his father, had watched the FECR announcement on television in Mike's conference room. Although they had been advised of the sale on the preceding day's evening news, they were still in a state of shock over the announcement. The task of recovering their payment agreement from FECR just got much more difficult with the apparent sale of the company.

Thirty minutes later, Rick finished reporting the good news of legal irregularities in the court protocol as revealed by his friend JD Dempsey. However, petitioning the court to re-open these cases would be much more difficult under a new owner. But, surely even their trust payment of a million dollars would not, in itself, be sufficient reason to suddenly sell the company. The sales negotiations must have been in process for several weeks, if not months. There must be another reason.

Rick suddenly sat upright in his chair and turned to his father: "Dad, what do we know about Castle Investment Group?"

"Frankly, Rick, I don't know anything about them. Why do you ask?"

"What if they are a front for a foreign purchaser who wants a railway for planned criminal activities."

"That seems a little far-fetched to me, but where are you going with this?"

"It may be far-fetched, but if we could prove the presence of a foreign buyer of questionable reputation, we could petition the federal court to deny or at least defer the sale, thereby allowing us time to petition the Florida courts to re-open the FECR litigation against our trust."

"By George, Mike, the boy may have something here," interjected the elder Patrick. "The federal law on foreign ownership could be applicable if Rick is right. But, what gave you the idea, Rick?"

"Three different government agencies—MI6, CIA, and FBI—are pursuing the involvement of unknown foreign interests in the Broward Yard explosion and its connection to a fishing boat explosion in the Turks and Caicos Islands which killed four Americans with forged passports. It seems to me that we may have stumbled onto something bigger than restitution of our trust fund. Furthermore, if we could identify the foreign interest, we could use it to halt this sale and focus on recovering our trust funding. Grandfather and Dad, I believe that this may be worth investigating. What is your view?"

"Well, I can give you my view," voiced a female voice from the open conference room door where the three men turned their attention to find Chandra Jones listening to Rick's monologue.

"How long have you been listening?" demanded Rick in a sharp voice.

"Only a few minutes. I came by to ask you some questions and the door was open. Furthermore, you were talking about the same things I wanted to ask about, and . . ."

"One minute, please, Miss Jones," interjected Patrick O'Shea. "We just saw you on the television broadcasting from St. Augustine, and suddenly you show up here claiming to be exploring the same stuff that Rick is talking about. Doesn't that strike you as rather strange?"

"Yes it does," she replied, as she entered the room and sat in a chair. "So, either Rick and I are exchanging ESP or, more believably, we both have hit upon the same idea for different reasons. Regardless, I will tell you that I finished the St. Augustine broadcast and realized that it did not have sufficient news value to headline the evening news or even make a good weekend feature. So, I started to think of how we could make it more newsworthy, and I remembered that the explosion was in the Broward Yard and federal agencies are currently searching for a foreign source. So, why does a relatively unknown company from Delaware want to pay a premium price for a railroad that has been bankrupt twice? The answer to that question might solve a number of issues in one fell swoop. I imagined that you gentlemen might be working. So, I rushed over here to get your opinion, and I heard Rick singing the same song."

"So, here we are," responded Mike. "Some hypothetical ideas that will require serious research to examine, but with no clear strategy as to how to proceed—assuming, of course, that it is worthwhile to proceed."

"Ms. Jones," began Patrick senior, "first, let me apologize to you for my bullying tactics at the party. I'd had a couple of drinks and lost control. We older people do that once in a while."

"Thank you."

"Second, I understand that you and Rick have been doing some quiet research on our legal issues in the newspaper files. Clearly, you seem to work together quite well. I suggest that the two of you apply the same teamwork to coordinate with the federal agencies to see if we can get a line on this hypothetical overseas

58

terrorist. I agree with both of you that we could kill two birds with one stone. Now, Mike, if this is too big a drain on your office budget, The PMO Trust will reimburse you. I would like to go full speed ahead and see if we can either identify this person, or at least petition the federal court to block this sale. Is everybody okay with this plan?"

All three of the others nodded in agreement.

"Great, then I can go home for the afternoon cocktail hour." And, off he went.

"I must add," said Rick, "that turning our attention on the Castle Investment Group means that we must defer our successful research of the legal irregularities involved with the FECR versus the PMO Trust, The issue is which topic deserves priority attention?"

"Frankly," responded Mike, "there is no question in my mind. Once the FECR sale is complete, our potential for a hearing with the Florida courts diminishes rapidly. The new owners will present strong arguments against arguing a completed case in favor of their new company. I believe that the two of you must resolve the Castle ownership issue before we return to our appeal. I suggest that you jump on the Castle ownership without delay, assuming that Chandra's editor is agreeable."

Rick and Chandra looked at each other and nodded their agreement. They decided to meet at the main branch of the Jacksonville Library first thing in the morning to begin research.

SEVENTEEN

Jacksonville, Florida
September 9, 1977

Rick and Chandra mutually decided that they would try an early morning session at the Jacksonville Library, using library references, prior to contacting Agents Jordan Hale and JD Dempsey. They met at the main branch when it opened at nine, and proceeded immediately to the reference desk to enlist the professional librarian's assistance in efficient research on the Castle Investment Group.

The reference librarian was a pleasant grey-haired lady in her sixties with time to spend on their needs without delay. They explained that they were about to do business with this company in Wilmington, and they needed to track its credentials and ownership. First, she reminded them that the Better Business Bureau is a second source, but that she would search her files first for them.

They quickly learned that Castle Investment Group, Inc. was incorporated in 1973 by three American senior officers who jointly deposited ten million dollars in initial capitalization. Prior to formation of the new company, each of the three officers had reputable careers as officers of similar investment firms and each had masters degrees in finance from reputable universities. All three had homes of substantial value with families in the Delaware and New Jersey area. They checked each of these background statements for authenticity before proceeding. No flaws of any kind were discovered.

In terms of investment, the company primarily had invested its capital in conservative market funds. The only capital assets were a large vacation home in the gated Amelia Island Plantation resort community just north of Jacksonville and a small farm with a two-story house and outbuildings outside Darien, Georgia, a small tourist town on I-95 highway between Brunswick and Savannah. These investments totaled less than one million dollars so the major company expense was composed of salaries to the three officers, salaries for support staff, company vehicles, and office rent for their headquarters in Wilmington, Delaware. They did not appear to have any current revenue sources.

Rick and Chandra returned to the O'Shea law office after lunch and contacted the Better Business Bureau with no results, either positive or negative. They then placed calls to JD Dempsey at the CIA and Jordan Hale at the FBI. Both agents responded within an hour to report that they, too, had been investigating Castle Investment Group and both agencies had discovered substantial phone and fax traffic between Castle and a French law firm located in the city of Marseille. Of equal interest, Dempsey's MI6 contact, Nigel Harris, reported that the French firm was founded just three months prior to the founding date of the Castle firm—a coincidence? Maybe! French records are not as accessible as American records, but it appears that there is a relationship between the two firms.

Chandra and Rick presented all of this information to his father to request his opinion on whether there was sufficient evidence to support potential foreign ownership. Mike responded that their findings were not conclusive, but, given the tight timetable, it might be useful to tip their hand by petitioning the federal court for a stop or at least a deferral on the sale. He directed Rick to draw up a petition while Chandra returned to the newspaper files.

EIGHTEEN

Wilmington, Delaware
September 12, 1977

The office of Castle Investment Group Inc. was on the fourth floor of a relatively new building in downtown Wilmington. The entrance lobby featured a walnut reception desk and dark green walls with brown leather waiting chairs and exhibited the aura of a successful investment firm.

Upon his arrival at ten o'clock on the Monday morning after the FECR purchase announcement, Dimitri Chekov was asked to take a seat for a few minutes while the receptionist went in search of the president. But instead of taking a seat, Chekov followed the receptionist through the door leading into the private offices to the president's large office.

The receptionist began to announce the arrival of Mr. Chekov when the Russian strode right by her and announced himself: "Dimitri Chekov. Where would you like to do our business?"

"Well I . . . how do you do, Mr. Chekov. I believe that we can move to the conference room. May I offer you some coffee?"

"No coffee; let's get to work."

The Castle president, an immaculately dressed man of about fifty years, maintained his composure and ushered Chekov into a large conference room with seating at a walnut table for twelve persons. Two other men entered the room having overheard the rough announcements of Chekov, and each announced his name without handshakes as the other two principal partners of the firm. The four men sat down at one end of the conference table and an aide entered with what appeared to be account ledgers, and set then down in front of Chekov. He ignored her and addressed the president.

"I do not anticipate that this meeting will take very long. As you have been informed from Marseille, I represent the owner of the Marseille attorneys and this firm. The owner originally sent you ten million U.S. dollars for capitalization and instructed you to purchase three items. Did you complete these purchases?"

"Yes, we have," responded the president. He opened the ledger book and pointed out the three entries at the end of a long list of furnishings, monthly rent, office supplies and equipment and salaries. "The current balance, as you can see, is just shy of four million. We will be happy to explain details, if you prefer."

"Not at all. You will be visited by two accountants for that purpose within the next few days. My purpose is to ensure that you are prepared for the big picture, beginning with the purchase of the Florida East Coast Railway, for which you paid a deposit of over five million dollars last week."

"That is correct, sir, and we have a team of two lawyers, two accountants and one engineer en route to St. Augustine right now to begin due diligence. As you know, we have sixty days to complete this investigation."

"Please contact them this afternoon and tell them plans have changed. The owner now needs to close within thirty days, so inform your team that they will receive double pay to cut their time in half. This new timetable is not negotiable. They will agree to complete it in thirty days or be replaced immediately. I need an answer from you today, and the clock starts ticking now.

"Further, you must prepare the purchase documents within the next two weeks and submit them to the seller's attorneys at that time, allowing them two weeks to prepare for closing. Is that clear?"

"Yes indeed, Mr. Chekov, but that is a very tight timetable."

"Yes it is, but you can do it. The alternative is to resign today, and I will find another team. Any comments? I need each of you to respond in the affirmative right now, or leave the premises,"

The four men glanced at each other for a few seconds after which the president uttered a "Yes" followed immediately by two other echoes of "Yes."

"Fine. Now that we have that matter resolved, let's turn to the sale closing. Over the next two weeks, you will receive five special delivery packages of ten million American dollars in cash in each package. These packages will be addressed to and co-signed by the president—nobody else is to open these packages. The president will be solely responsible for the contents being safely deposited in a local bank. The balance is more than enough to support a cashier's check for the exact closing agreed by the due diligence team. The president will sign that check. The remainder may be used for expenses only related to this transaction—no mingling of funds. A separate account ledger must be used. Is that clear?"

Each of the three replied "Yes."

"Very well! There being no questions, I need not detain you further except to caution you that this transaction must be kept confidential among the men in this room and your due diligence team. Under no circumstances can the French connection be revealed. Any leak of this information will result in the harshest of penalties. By the way, information about the two properties you purchased in Georgia and Florida are also confidential by the same penalty. I will need keys to both of these houses right now, before I leave. Thank you for your attention."

Chekov then rose and proceeded toward the entrance, pausing only briefly to pick up the two sets of keys.

NINETEEN

Jacksonville, Florida
September 12, 1977

It was ten o'clock when the three O'Sheas and Chandra Jones assembled in the Michael O'Shea conference room. Armed with coffee and water, the four faces were very grim. The petition drafted by Rick requested termination of the FECR sale to Castle Investment Group, Inc, on the grounds that the firm was under ownership of the European law firm of Renand, Baham and Cabut, located in Marseille, France. The petition claimed that this law firm was under suspicion of maintaining a relationship with a terrorism organization pledged to harm the United States of America.

"You did a good job, Rick, but I am pessimistic about the outcome," stated his father. "We simply are not able to produce a solid fact supporting our claim."

"On the other hand," responded Patrick, "we have nothing to lose except the cost of their trip to Richmond . . . and possibly a tongue-lashing from the Fourth Circuit Court Judge. But, Rick has been tongue-lashed before. Right, Grandson?"

"Absolutely, sir! No problem!"

"Frankly, that is why I suggested that you be accompanied by Miss Jones. There are not many male judges who verbally assault pretty women," stated Patrick with a grin.

"With equal frankness, sir," replied Chandra, "I wouldn't touch this trip with a ten-foot pole, if I didn't need the verbatim for my story."

"We know that, Chandra," chimed in Mike, "and we are all grateful to have you on our team. Please excuse any of our remarks that may sound sexist."

"So excused," she replied with a bright smile, and then paused to add, "at least for this morning's conversation."

The three men all chuckled over her response, after which Rick rose with Chandra and they took their departure to catch the flight to Richmond.

At precisely two o'clock Rick and Chandra entered the Federal Fourth Circuit Court to present Rick's petition to the presiding judge. They both were surprised to see a woman on the bench rather than the previously scheduled Judge Charles H. Bancroft.

"So, that shoots Grandfather's strategy," Rick whispered to his companion. Chandra smiled in response.

"First of all," began Judge Mary B. Simpson, " before we get started, I should like to make it quite clear that I am not Judge Charley Bancroft. I regret to report that he is in hospital suffering from a kidney stone. I am sure you join me in wishing him a quick recovery. As the sign states, I am Judge Mary Simpson, duly accredited to hear your pleas."

"Now the first item is a petition from Attorney Patrick Michael O'Shea IV from Florida under privilege of reciprocity. Are you present, Mr. O'Shea?"

"I am, your honor."

"Are opposition attorneys representing Castle Investment Group present?"

"We are, your honor: Richard Maclean and Dennis Neilson, both stated members of the Virginia Bar."

Rick was then invited to present his petition orally—he had previously submitted it to both the judge and the opposition attorneys.

Attorney Maclean then argued for Castle that the petition was frivolous and that his client intended to launch a counter-suit for defamation of character.

Rather than defer judgement, Judge Simpson ruled that the petition was insufficient in support of its claim, but the issue was of sufficient concern that she would grant the petitioner thirty days to strengthen the petition. "Adjourned!"

"Interesting," whispered Chandra, "that's exactly what your father said would happen."

Rick and Chandra slowly walked down the long flight of steps from the courthouse, and paused at the bottom gathering area for a short rest before heading down the street to find a taxi. A loud shout caused them both to look up: "WATCH OUT!"

Rick reacted just in time to see a large delivery van jump the curb directly in front of them. Without a word, he grabbed Chandra and literally threw her into a landscape island full of evergreen bushes. The momentum caused him to follow her flight and land on top of her, barely missing being struck by the truck's front corner by inches.

"Wow! That was a close call," uttered Rick, just as a policeman rushed up asking if they were injured. "No, I don't believe so. How about you Chandra?"

"I am fine except for this large body on top of me," she replied.

"Sorry about that. Give me your hand and I will help you up."

Chandra allowed herself to be assisted by Rick and the policeman to her feet. The policeman immediately contacted his station to report the runaway truck, which had already disappeared around the nearest corner. Other than the driver being white, no witnesses volunteered any distinguishing identification. The policeman took their names and phone numbers and Rick hailed a taxi to take them to the airport.

TWENTY

Washington, D.C.
September 12, 1977

Once again, the top security advisors to President Jimmy Carter assembled in the Oval Office to hear Margaret McBride's latest report from the Broward Yard Explosion Task Force. In addition to the National Security Advisor, and the Directors of the CIA and the FBI, Margaret had received permission to include Agent Joshua Dempsey who had carried out all of the investigative work for McBride's task force. The President welcomed each of his visitors, and then turned to McBride.

"Margaret, I believe that everyone has arrived. Please go ahead with your report."

"Thank you, Mr. President. In addition to my own notes from the meetings of the task force, I have brought with me today CIA Agent Joshua Dempsey, who has been the workhorse behind the task force. He can respond to any questions that you may have." Dempsey held up his hand for identity, but being the youngest person in the room was sufficient to single him out. McBride then continued.

"When I last reported to you two weeks ago, our task force had been able to identify the Broward Yard explosion as the work of trained explosion people This finding ruled out any involvement by members of the O'Shea family, who had been embroiled in controversy with the Florida East Coast Railway over an inheritance left by the founder, Henry Flagler. The two bodies of O'Shea family members found at the scene were employees of the railway, but did not bear any evidence of involvement in the explosion. On the contrary, they appear to have been killed in advance of the explosion and planted at the scene to purposely mislead investigators into concluding O'Shea involvement.

"Of far greater importance is another connection we have discovered with the help of a British Senior MI6 agent named Nigel Harris. It seems that four Americans killed in a fishing boat explosion near the Caribbean Island of North Caicos held forged passports and were seen in the company of a known American criminal named Mohammed Abdullah. Abdullah flew from the nearest island— Providenciales— back to this country on the same day as the explosion, Furthermore, the explosive 'Semtex' was used in the boat explosion as well as in the train yard explosion. Of course, these are not conclusive evidence of connection, but they have caused us to involve both FBI and CIA agents in efforts to identify these four men and trace their suspected employers.

"In summation, let me state that it is our firm belief that the two explosions are related and we believe that they are sponsored by well-funded foreign terrorists. Although we do not have the identity, or identities, of these foreign terrorists, we have turned over all of our findings to both FBI and CIA agencies for investigation. It is our conclusion that the Broward Yard explosion was a first example of plans for other explosions yet to occur in vulnerable locations in the continental United States. We urge further investigations by our security forces to research this issue with greater diligence than our task force can muster. Therefore, we respectfully submit, Mr. President, that the task force be terminated and further efforts be conducted jointly by the FBI and CIA. Thank you."

President Carter thanked Ms. McBride for her diligent coordination and accepted her report. "Any questions, gentlemen?"

"Yes," stated CIA Director Malone. "First of all, Margaret, a job well done! My congratulations! But I am curious about these two known criminals, Mohammed Abdullah and his apparent superior, the Russian, Dimitri Chekov. They both were reported living in Atlanta. Are we close to apprehending these men. As you have suggested, they appear to be the link with these foreign terrorists."

"Hold on just a minute, Charley," interjected FBI Director Tindale. "Margaret correctly passed on that search to our team. I am informed that they traced Abdullah to two different Atlanta addresses, one supplied by Agent Dempsey, I believe. But the tenant had cleared out ahead of our team. However, I understand that they are hot on his trail. Is that correct, Agent Dempsey?"

Before responding, JD glanced at McBride for approval. "Yes sir, your description is accurate, but I might add that we also identified Chekov's apartment, but he was apparently out of the country. I believe that your people have his address under surveillance."

"Good," added President Carter. "It seems that Dempsey has handed over his role to the FBI and they have it in hand. But, the real task will be to capture Chekov and bring in our CIA resources on his foreign travels. I assume that your people are monitoring the FBI in-country work, Charley?"

"Absolutely. Agent Dempsey continues to be fulltime on this case, even though he no longer reports to Margaret. I am not suggesting that you shouldn't worry, Mr. President, but we have other resources at the ready just as soon as we get some solid leads."

"Right, but I do worry. At this point, we have no idea of their attack timetable. So, as the real estate people say, 'time is of the essence' and the stakes could be very high. Thank you all for joining me and I look forward to some better news."

Everyone rose and quietly exited the office.

TWENTY-ONE

FBI Senior Agent Jordan Hale had just opened the door leading into his house from the garage when his eight-year old daughter rushed out of the kitchen to hug and kiss him, the best part about coming home. His ten-year-old son then sauntered in casually to report that there was a lady on the phone from his office. Jordan put an arm around his rapidly aging young adult, thanking him for bringing in the new wireless phone.

"Hello, this is Jordan Hale, sorry to keep you waiting, but I was just this minute walking into the house."

"No problem, Agent Hale. This is Suzan Pringle, the evening operator at the office. I have received a call for you from our station Agent Abe Greenberg in Jackson, Mississippi, requesting an urgent return call from you. I still have him on another line if you would like me to transfer you?"

"Yes, absolutely! Thank you, Suzan," he agreed. His wife, Marta, embraced him and kissed him on the cheek careful not to disturb his call. Being married to an FBI agent had its own protocol for greeting formalities. She would welcome him later after the kids retired.

"Hello, Jordan, Abe Greenberg here. I'm sorry to interrupt you at home, but I have an incident here that may be just what you may be looking for. Do you have a couple of minutes?"

"You bet, Abe. Good to hear from you, by the way. It's been a long time."

"It sure has— my last training program in Washington where you were lecturing on kidnapping. I really enjoyed that course."

"Well, thank you, Abe; that's good to hear. Now, what have you got going on down there?"

"Right, sir. About an hour ago, central time, a middle-age woman came into the office to report that her husband had been missing for over two weeks, and she was concerned about him. It turned out that his skill was in demolishing buildings and he had taken a small contract assignment in Macon, Georgia. He thought that he would be gone for a few days, but, in any event, he would phone to update her after the timing became more precise. Two evenings later, he phoned to tell her that the job was bigger than he expected and he would be gone at least a week, but she never heard from him again.

"Of course, I consoled her about men losing track of time, and so on, but after I took her name and some particulars on her husband, she pulled out a picture of him. I can assure you that I recognized him immediately as one of the four passport pictures that you distributed ten days after the Jacksonville explosion. The fact that he was a demolitions expert sealed my confirmation, and I put in the call to you right after I sent her back home with assurances that we would locate him."

"Well, Abe, I'm afraid that, if you're right on the identification, she will never see any part of him again. But, if your recognition is right, we do know what happened to him and I need to interview that lady right away. Please confirm that she will be at home tomorrow afternoon, and I will find a flight into your city to meet at her house. Many thanks, Abe. You may have given us a critical lead into a major murder case. I'll see you tomorrow."

Hale immediately phoned the office and asked Suzan to book him on the quickest flight to Jackson, Mississippi, the next morning. Then, he took his seat at the dinner table to convene the nightly (or at least on those nights when he was home) family meeting hour.

TWENTY-TWO

Jackson, Mississippi
September 14, 1977

It turned out to be a beautiful day for flying and Hale connected with flights in Atlanta and on to Memphis without delay, thereby managing to catch the commuter flight to Jackson and arrive right on schedule. He had given his arrival time to Abe Greenberg, but he was still surprised to see him waiting outside security.

"Hi Abe, it was very optimistic of you to rely upon my scheduled arrival after three flight changes. Anyway, thank you for being here. Do we have time for lunch before our appointment?"

"You bet," replied Abe. "She doesn't expect us until two. That's my car at the curb. Hop in and we'll head to my favorite lunch spot. It's good to see you, Jordan. You are looking fit and healthy. But, I thought that you had been here long enough to adopt a southern accent."

"Nah, that's why the Bureau sends us Jewish guys down here. We are already accent prone from going through the Academy. It's a type of job security."

"I see," replied Hale with a chuckle. "I don't suppose there's a long line-up waiting for your job?"

"On the contrary, Jordan. This has turned out to be a pretty good posting. Jackson is a fine old city, despite its name for one of our worst presidents. Not that racial issues don't crop up occasionally, but, for the most part, the citizens are law-abiding and well-behaved. I like it here."

Upon arrival at the restaurant, the two agents continued their small talk, purposely avoiding any premature discussion of the woman they were about to visit and her suspected criminal husband.

They took their time enjoying southern barbeque with local vegetables that lived up to Abe's advance billing.

They arrived at the modest house in a pleasant neighborhood a few minutes before two, and found the owner waiting for them at the front door. She was a somewhat overweight woman in her late forties with a friendly face that contained a worried frown exhibiting her worst fears concerning her missing husband. The two men gave her friendly smiles and introduced themselves with identification, then followed her into a clean and tidy living room with chairs for each of them. They refused any refreshments after their heavy lunch, and Hale took the lead in the ensuing discussion.

"First of all, Ma'am, please tell me your husband's full name and age? Also, do you have any identification for him?"

"Yes, his name is Walter Joseph Mason. He is 51 years old and I managed to find his honorable discharge papers from the Army. As you can see, he was much younger then, about ten years ago. We both grew up in this city and so we returned here after his army duty, but he was not able to find a permanent job. So, one of his army friends from Atlanta contacted him and found contract demolition work which paid quite well, even though it required quite a bit of travel and it was sporadic. However, along with my part-time job at my brother's dry cleaning store, we managed to get by and even purchase this house."

"Were there other army friends who worked with him on these contracts?"

"Oh yes, five or six trained demolitions experts from his army days often worked together, depending on the size of the building or other structure that had to be demolished. In this latest contract, they only needed four men. I have already phoned their homes, but only two were married and their wives expressed the same concerns as mine that their husbands have not returned or called. But, the team leader is not married and I only talked to a message recorder at his house in Atlanta. I have written down all four names, with addresses and phone numbers for you to follow up on. I also added two other men that he frequently works with, assuming that you might also like to speak with them."

"Thank you, Mrs. Mason, for an excellent package of information. I can promise you that a team of experienced agents from the Federal Bureau of Investigation will pursue each one of these leads and that I personally will stay on this case until we find your husband. Please feel free to phone Agent Greenberg here if you come across anything else that might seem useful. Abe, do you have anything to add?"

"No, I believe that you have covered all of the questions that come to my mind. But, as Agent Hale has stated, do not hesitate to phone me if you come across any other information that might be useful. Thank you, Mrs. Mason; you have been most helpful."

The two men shook hands with their hostess and left.

Within an hour of interviewing Mrs. Mason, Agents Hale and Greenberg were contacting FBI offices in each of the cities included in the address list: two in metropolitan Atlanta (including the assumed "team leader"); one in Huntsville, Alabama; and two in Birmingham, Alabama. The two who they assumed were not in the fishing boat explosion deserved priority interviews, but all five households were on the "urgent attention" list and due for action immediately. Hale also made courtesy calls to CIA Agent Dempsey in Washington and MI6 Senior Agent Harris in London to notify both of them of this break in the case and that he would keep him abreast of results of ongoing interviews.

The entire process went so smoothly that Hale was able to phone his wife to tell her that he planned to return home that evening. Agent Greenberg then drove him back to the airport to catch the first of three flights back to Washington.

TWENTY-THREE

Amelia Island Plantation, Florida
September 14, 1977

Amelia Island Plantation is an 800-acre gated resort community on the southern part of Amelia Island, the northernmost Atlantic Ocean barrier island in the state of Florida. Most of the detached homes, attached homes and condominium homes have seasonal owners with primary homes in other locations, mainly Atlanta and northeast Florida. The growth of nearby Jacksonville has generated an increasing number of permanent residents who commute into the city for employment.

One such new owner recently purchased a large home of six thousand square feet with six bedrooms, including two bedrooms over the three-car garage. The new owner, Castle Investment Group, Inc. of Wilmington, Delaware, rented the property to Mr. and Mrs. Henry Stanton with their three young children, formerly of Montreal, Canada where the children attended French immersion schools. Mr. and Mrs. Stanton also speak French as well as English.

On this first morning in June, a Mr. Daniel Chester applied at the community's main security gate to visit Mr. Stanton. The resident gave his approval by phone in English. Thus did Chekov initiate a new meeting place with Prince El Saud, now known as Henry Stanton. His wife was re-named Claudette Stanton. The visitor drove his inconspicuous grey Chevrolet sedan into an open garage and was welcomed by one of the two security men, who immediately closed the door behind him and ushered Chekov, now addressed as Mr. Chester, through the garage entry into the house and showed him to Mr. Stanton's spacious study facing the rear of the house, well separated from the children's play areas. The two men shook hands and took facing seats.

"Welcome to Florida, my friend," said the new Stanton. "Did you have any problem closing your Atlanta apartment and traveling here under your new name?"

"No trouble whatsoever, Your Highness."

"Please forget that title," admonished his employer. "Refer to me as Stanton from now on. Our old names are terminated and we have excellent new identities for all of your needs."

"Yessir, I won't forget again."

"Good! The second thing is that I don't want you spending much time at this house. We already have three men here. That's enough. I have taken a twelve month lease on a two-bedroom waterfront condominium under your new name. It has basement parking with an electronic key. Therefore, there is no need for you to show your face very often. Do not eat, drink or swim inside the Plantation. I want you to be as invisible as possible. Understood?"

"Yessir!"

"Excellent! Now tell our Castle people to move ahead with the FECR purchase immediately. Forget the fine print of due diligence. We need to own that company within the next two weeks. Next, have you checked the progress of the cargo?"

"I have, and the Polar Star is proceeding through the Mediterranean Sea. It should reach Gibraltar in three or four days."

"Good. I will have a complete new crew ready to take over. The existing crew must disappear completely. I mean without a trace. You better plan on monitoring that operation personally. We cannot leave any tracks. Have you employed a competent team?"

"The very best Corsican hit team available! They will be in Gibraltar before the Polar Star arrives. And I will fly over to confirm that their expensive fee is money well spent."

"That sounds perfect. I plan to stay here with my family until further notice. You have your untraceable phone number to contact me, but only when absolutely necessary. And be careful of your language even then. This is my hiding place in open sight. Do not do anything to jeopardize it. Is that clear?"

"Perfectly clear, Mr. Stanton!"

TWENTY-FOUR

Jacksonville, Florida
September 14, 1977

The conference table at the Michael O'Shea Law Office was surrounded by the three O'Shea generations in addition to Chandra Jones.

"Lady and gentlemen," began Mike O'Shea. "We have very good and very bad news. The bad news is, not only did the judge defer the petition for lack of sufficient evidence, but a truck took a swipe at Rick and Chandra on the sidewalk outside the courthouse. In short, these people, whoever they may be, are playing hardball. I don't plan to lose my son and heir regardless of the issues at stake."

"But Dad," broke in Rick, "perhaps they were just trying to scare us."

"If so, they succeeded. I'm scared."

"So," spoke up Patrick, the elder, "what's the good news?"

"Well, actually, the good news is quite good. Chandra reports that the newspaper files are full of ammunition to get our trust financing back, and she even has a prime prospect for a political supporter. The problem is that we cannot bring our full efforts to bear until we stop this unbelievable sale of FECR—only thirty days to go. In addition, although Rick struck out with the Castle ownership revelation, the FBI has just stumbled on a break that could lead to revealing the sponsor of the Broward Yard explosion."

"How so?" questioned Patrick.

"A woman in Jackson, Mississippi reported a missing husband to the local FBI. Her picture of him matched one of the forged passport pictures, and furthermore, the husband is an army-trained demolitions expert. In addition, she gave up the names and addresses of five other army buddies who usually worked together, but only four were needed for the current job. So, we are waiting on some good interview results from our FBI friends."

"That is good news," added Chandra. "But, I'm afraid that it is too little, too late. The FBI must uncover two or more layers of superiors before revealing the kind of ammunition we need to stop the FECR sale—thirty days may be too long."

"You may be right," interjected Rick. "I think that we cannot stand still. We must get some inside dope from France. And I nominate myself to go after it. Nigel Harris claims that the French Government will not disclose ownership records. So, I think that we must use subterfuge by infiltrating the French legal firm supplying the money.

"And just how would you do that?" questioned Chandra. "You are not exactly trained for infiltration work."

"No, he is not," concurred Patrick, "But I can't help noticing that my grandson does manage to impress a lot of young women, like, for example, legal secretaries and receptionists. In fact, although I cannot fathom his intentions, Rick has introduced us to a rather beautiful woman who probably has the same effect on young lawyers. In short, we have at this very table a potential two-person team of potential infiltrators. I would be willing to wager that these two attractive persons, disguised as front scouts for a hypothetical American firm needing legal assistance in southern France, could wrangle our ownership information within a couple of days."

"But we don't know anything about these attorneys, Dad."

"So, hire a human resource firm in England or France — I'll bet your friend Nigel Harris has one at his fingertips — to collect info on everyone in the Marseille office of Renand, Baham and Cabut as a basis for getting familiar, and then go to work. What do you think, Rick?"

"For myself, I would jump on it tomorrow. But, I'm not sure that I support the idea of exposing Chandra to the dangers of Marseille."

"Oh really," shot back Chandra. "I may be young, 'buster', but I have completed four years of investigative reporting exposed to the dangers of Jacksonville, and I probably could introduce you to a couple of guys who still regret trying to manhandle me."

"Bravo," chimed in Patrick. "She also has experience in reporting that gives her a solid edge in manipulation; that is, in addition to any physical capabilities she may exhibit. I vote in favor, Mike. Let's make something happen."

"Okay Dad, I'm nervous, but sold. If you younger folk want to give it a try, I will sponsor it and contact Nigel for assistance."

"Count me in," said Chandra, "just as soon as I can get some time off from my boss."

"Right, let's do it," agreed Rick.

TWENTY-FIVE

Washington, D.C.
September 14, 1977

Jordan Hale was having a very busy day receiving confidential email reports from his colleagues in FBI field offices in Birmingham, Huntsville, Jackson and Atlanta. Two contacts could not be reached and the FBI was waiting on a court order for search warrants. One other spouse was interviewed, but the information echoed that already received from Mrs. Mason in Jackson. The most useful information was coming from the interviews of the two demolition team members not included on the Broward Yard incident.

Although the two excluded demolition men were not privy to the assignment involving their former army companions, they did provide background on other jobs, some of which appeared to be illegal. Their confessions were prompted by the news of the fishing boat explosion within two weeks of the Broward Yard blast. Although they had no personal information about the Broward Yard explosion, other than news media accounts, it had the professional footprint of their colleagues. The fishing boat incident sounded equally suspicious, especially since they have been unable to contact any of their four friends. They were eager to repay the sponsors for apparently murdering their friends.

Agent Russell Edwards from Birmingham actually phoned Hale on a secure phone to deliver his information. "Jordan, my suspect here in Birmingham told me that these six men were all part of an army demolition team within the Corps of Engineers. They all received honorable discharges at about the same time, around 1967, but there were few job openings for their skills.

"So, one of their number, a man named Blakeley, now apparently deceased, started researching building demolitions and, through a number of new contacts, began to call upon his army

81

buddies for assistance on contract work. Most of the jobs were relatively straightforward building demolitions, but a few involved illegal bombs for thefts and questionable activities—he has already solved three cases for us here in central Alabama. We have not arrested him because of his cooperation thus far."

"My best recommendation for you is to search their team coordinator Blakeley's apartment in Atlanta for explosion sponsors. He never revealed them to the rest of his team members, and he lived alone for the past few years since his wife died of cancer. Our guy believes that he kept records at home.

"One other point worth your attention is that there was a supervisor of a couple of the illegal jobs—a big African-American of about age 40, who went by the nickname of 'Big Moe'. Our guy figures that he represents one or more illegal sponsors. I'm sorry that we do not have any more identification on him for you."

"Not a problem, Russ; we know about Big Moe, and he is a key player. But, so far, we cannot locate him. You have done a very thorough interview on your man in Birmingham, and I am truly grateful. We will keep you posted on results. Many thanks."

Hale immediately phoned the Atlanta FBI office to inquire about the status of the search warrants. He learned that the judge had signed off on both of them and two search teams were mobilized and on their way to the two target apartments. He breathed a sigh of relief and decided to call it a day. He phoned home to tell his wife to expect him for dinner.

The call came just as Jordan Hale was finishing his dinner hour. He stepped away from the table and picked up the new wireless phone. "Jordan Hale."

"Agent Hale, this is Suzan at the office. Some terrible news just arrived from Atlanta which I believe that you should have. An apartment on the sixth floor of a midtown building just blew up killing six FBI agents at the scene—no survivors. The fire department has evacuated the building. The FBI Agent-In-Charge of the Atlanta Station has postponed a second apartment scheduled to be searched, pending a City Police Bomb Squad examination. The Atlanta Station has closed its phones until morning."

"Thank you, Suzan. I appreciate you letting me know."

TWENTY-SIX

Jacksonville International Airport (JIA)
September 14, 1977

Rick O'Shea made the telephone call from the Jacksonville Airport to his father's office where Mike's longtime secretary answered the phone. "Michael O'Shea Law Office, Maryanne speaking."

"Maryanne, this is Rick calling from the Jacksonville airport. There must be some error. The tickets you gave me earlier today are for two first-class seats. My father never purchased first-class seats in his life . . . "

"That's right, Rick . . . up until this week; that is, when he told me to do so for you and Miss Jones. I believe that his exact words were: 'this couple is going on a dangerous assignment, Maryanne. See that they travel first-class all the way.' So, Mr. Patrick M. O'Shea IV, that is exactly what I did. Bon voyage!" And she then hung up, emitting a slight giggle to herself.

Therefore, still somewhat embarrassed at the expenditure, Rick handed the airline tickets reserved for Patrick M. O'Shea IV and Chandra M. Jones, along with their passports, to the Delta ticket agent who checked their luggage through to Marseille. The smiling agent said: "Actually Mr. O'Shea, you should have checked in at the no-wait 'First Class' counter, but I am pleased to go ahead and print these boarding cards for seats 1A and 1 B on the flight to Atlanta, connecting to the overnight Delta flight to Paris with a final connection to Marseille, France. Have a pleasant flight."

After completing the forty-five minute flight to Atlanta, they were ushered to the VIP Lounge by a cordial attendant and offered drinks and snacks. Prior to the listed boarding time, the same attendant ushered them to the appropriate gate, showed their boarding passes to the gate attendant, and turned them over to a flight attendant inside the plane. She showed them to their seats and offered French champagne to toast their journey to the wine capital of the world.

Chandra leaned over from her window seat on the wide-body Boeing 747 airplane to whisper in Rick's ear: "So far, this is one of the most difficult jobs that I have ever encountered. Thanks for including me."

Rick replied in his normal voice: "Let's get one thing perfectly clear, Miss Jones. I had absolutely nothing to do with these travel arrangements. Furthermore, I had nothing to do with retaining you for this assignment. So, if you wish to convey thanks, please speak to my father and grandfather. But, in the interim, please enjoy yourself. Bon voyage."

"Rick, I can understand that you are a bit miffed at the unexpected extravagance of the travel arrangements. But, since we are working together for the next several days, I propose that we accept our fate and enjoy each other's company to the extent possible. Wha'd'ya'say big fella?"

Her companion suddenly turned to her and smiled. "You are absolutely right. I was miffed at the first-class expenditure and took my annoyance out on you. I apologize and promise to be nicer from here on." He turned to the flight attendant. "Plus champagne, s'il vous plait!"

And they then took off for Europe.

TWENTY-SEVEN

Polar Star, Mediterranean Sea
September 12, 1977

The freighter, Polar Star, was making good headway in a following sea toward its re-fueling port in Gibraltar, when the captain was interrupted by his radio man arriving on the bridge. He spoke in Russian.

"Please excuse this interruption, Captain, but I have a radio message addressed to you from a Mr. Dimitri Chekov in Gibraltar. He wishes to speak to you personally. Would you like me to contact him at the number he left?"

"Yes, I will join you in the radio room in ten minutes," replied the captain. He then summoned the first mate to the bridge to take control, and informed him that he would only be gone for a brief time. The captain then proceeded directly to the radio room to take the call in the Russian language.

"Captain, this is Chekov speaking. Are you having a safe trip?"

"Yes, indeed, Mr. Chekov. We are ahead of schedule in light seas. I expect to arrive in Gibraltar tomorrow, one day ahead of schedule."

"That is good news, Captain, but we must revise your schedule slightly. I have examined the berth reserved for you here and it is not satisfactory because of its proximity to an oversize British naval ship. I have reserved an alternate berth for you on the following day at El Puerto de Santa Maria in the Bahia de Cadiz on the Spanish coast north of Gibraltar. Are you familiar with this port at Cadiz?"

"Yes, I took on cargo from that port several years ago. I assume that it has not changed much since that time. I recall sailing north of the city of Cadiz and picking up a pilot at the outer edge of the bay. Is that correct?"

"Yes, that is your instruction. Please notify the harbormaster in Spanish or English when you have visual sight of the old city on the peninsula and he will direct you to the meeting position for taking on the pilot. Please advise your crew that we will host a welcome reception for you and them upon arrival. A guide will meet you at dockside to lead you to the reception hall, regardless of the time of landing."

"Well, thank you, sir. I am certain that they will be most happy to attend. Signing off!"

The captain then directed his radio man to contact the Gibraltar harbormaster and cancel their berth reservation and fuel request as they had been re-routed to Cadiz. He personally was pleased by the change because the Cadiz area contained restaurants and bars at a lower price than the "tourist-traps" at Gibraltar.

Chekov departed the communications office in Gibraltar and proceeded to walk across the airport runway, currently open to vehicle and pedestrian traffic with no immediate airplane use, and to pass through Spanish customs and immigration. He then strolled casually along the waterfront street full of tourists until he located the side street tavern where he had agreed to meet his Corsican assassin leader. He spotted him in the same rear booth where they had met the previous evening to agree on the change of ports where there were better arrangements for the murders. He greeted his new accomplice in Italian, but then switched to Spanish with which he was more familiar.

"Ciao, Victor," he greeted the Corsican as he took a seat across from him. "All the arrangements have been made. The ship will be docking in Cadiz on the day after tomorrow, and then you can earn your exorbitant fee."

"Excellent, my friend," replied the Corsican in Spanish. "You will be pleased with our efficiency."

TWENTY-EIGHT

Cadiz, Spain
September 13, 1977

The Polar Star freighter nestled quietly into its berth 9A at the El Puerto de Santa Maria on the Bahia de Cadiz. The pilot shook hands with the captain and was the first man to leave the ship as soon as the gangway was secure. He passed a young man with a sign on a stick held above his head stating "Polar Star Crew Party" in both Russian and Spanish. It attracted crew members leaving the ship to gather round him eagerly awaiting their first shore leave since leaving Poti, Georgia.

Three Corsican onlookers stayed in the shade of the adjacent warehouse ready to follow any crew members not interested in the party, but it seemed like the full complement of officers and crew— seventeen total— assembled behind their young guide and strolled beyond the docks to a recently vacated tavern a block from the waterfront. The three onlookers then bribed the hired security guard and proceeded to search the ship from stem to stern for any overlooked crew members, but they found none to execute.

The party-goers were met at the front entrance by three pretty young Corsican girls dressed in colorful native costumes who handed a frosty stein of beer to each arriving crew member—some men even took two. They took a seat at one of the four round tables set with checkered red and white tablecloths. Each table was adorned with a centerpiece of a liter of Cadiz sherry, billed as the world's finest, ringed with small wine glasses and plates of pastry, cheese and crackers. When everyone was seated, a trio of native musicians playing an accordion and two guitars appeared from the rear of the hall and pranced around the room playing native folk songs. The three waitresses soon joined in the dancing and some of the crew members even jumped up to accompany them. Four bartenders kept the steins full from kegs of beer behind the bar.

It appeared like a gala party for the entire crew. The captain was so impressed, he attempted to ask where he might find Mr. Chekov to thank him, but none of the party staff seemed to understand any of his languages.

After thirty minutes of revelry, one of the sailors fell to the floor unconscious. His mates thought he was drunk and let him alone. But then several others followed suit and the remaining crew members realized that there must be something amiss. But, it was too late to repent. Within ten more minutes, all seventeen crew and officers were on the floor either dead or in the final stage of life. The Corsicans broke out a large package of body bags and proceeded to bundle up each of the lifeless guests while the three waitresses changed into work clothes and began to clean up the remaining food and drink. All of them wore plastic gloves to guard against the poison in the beer and sherry. By the time that the body bags were all full, a large covered rental van backed up to the front door and the three former onlookers jumped out and helped load the vehicle with bodies, garbage bags and beer kegs. When all remnants of the fateful party were loaded, the truck quietly drove away and the other Corsicans followed in rented cars. By evening, after leaving the stolen truck at the city dump and being driven to the airport and boarding their charter plane, they were safely back on their island home of Corsica, considerably wealthier from their assignment.

Within two hours of docking, all of the Polar Star crew had completely disappeared and the ship's quarters were being cleaned by hired maids. It was soon ready for its new occupants and re-fueled for its new journey departing Cadiz, Spain for Port Everglades, Florida.

First thing the following morning, the professional sign-painting team arrived to change the identity of the Polar Star. Before noon, the ship had become "Empress IV" with a home port of Liberia. No sign of the former identity remained and Chekov had newly-forged papers to support its fresh identity and cargo.

The new crew, hired through a human resource firm in the Philippines, had a captain of thirty years' experience and deckhands from several nations who appeared strong and healthy. They all arrived in early afternoon and Chekov put them to work exchanging shipping labels with the new ones reading the outgoing port as Cadiz and applied with very strong adhesive on top of the old Poti labels.

The captain estimated a six-seven day crossing to South Florida. This meant that Chekov had to have his railway arrangements in place by September 20 in order to receive the five main shipments for the proper destinations, according to the plan endorsed by Prince El Saud (now Henry Stanton).

Nevertheless, the Russian was optimistic as he boarded his flight back to Jacksonville, and from there to his luxurious oceanfront condominium. His new career was in good condition.

TWENTY-NINE

Marseille, France
September 13, 1977

After a direct Delta flight from Atlanta to Charles de Gaulle Airport outside Paris, Rick and Chandra transferred to a regional airline for arrival in Marseille before noon, European time. They quickly picked up their bags, exchanged dollars for Euros, and caught a taxi to the recommended Hotel Dieu InterContinental, where the office secretary, Maryanne, had arranged adjoining rooms. It was an elegant structure of grey limestone overlooking the Vieux Port (Old Port) in the city center.

Although neither Rick nor Chandra spoke French, the pleasant desk clerk quickly recognized them as being Americans and addressed them in English. After requesting their passports for safekeeping during their stay, she had them sign the registration already listing their home addresses, and then handed keys to a bellman assigned to conduct them to their adjoining rooms on an upper floor. The bellman placed their single bags in each room and handed each of them English guides to the room features and hotel amenities as well as a welcome brochure and map of the city of Marseille. Rick tipped him appropriately and the bellman bowed politely and left closing the door upon the two of them standing silent in one of their double rooms.

"Well," began Rick, "here we are, then."

"Yes," replied Chandra somewhat hesitantly, "here we are. I vote that we nap for a couple of hours before strolling down to the 'Old Port' and selecting a restaurant for dinner."

"Sounds like a good plan to me," replied Rick, as he picked up his suitcase and walked into the adjoining room, closing the door softly behind him. Rick set his watch alarm for two hours, removed his clothes and hopped into one of the two double beds.

About three hours later, after he had phoned Chandra's room to awaken her, followed by a long, hot shower and dressing in casual tourist clothes, Rick knocked loudly on Chandra's door and suggested that she meet him in the bar as soon as she was dressed. After a relaxing drink and a review of the city map, they set off for initial orientation, beginning with a walking tour of the "Old Port." The late afternoon sun bathed the harbor and its pleasure boats in golden hues and the historic waterfront buildings framed the entire scene in postcard splendor. They selected an outdoor table at the restaurant suggested by the English-speaking desk clerk and enjoyed a wonderful baked fish-for-two platter with local vegetables accompanied by a refreshingly chilled local white wine.

"Wow," said Chandra, after completing her final bite, "this foreign research is fantastic. I am ready to start a new career."

"Not so fast, my friend," replied Rick with a smile. "We haven't even started work yet. How be we discuss that little item over coffee back at the hotel?"

"Oh, very well," she replied with a pout, "providing that we can return here tomorrow for more tourist experience."

"Absolutely," laughed Rick, as he paid the check and rose to leave. "It is a definite date."

The hotel bar turned out to be noisy, with a mixture of tourists of various nationalities all speaking and laughing in a cacophony of sound. At Chandra's suggestion, they decided to order coffee and a selection of French pastries sent to Rick's room instead of braving the noise at the bar. Rick picked up a Fax message at the desk from a nondescript Washington address which stated "All principals are squeaky clean with no questionable connections. Full report will follow by express mail overnight."

After entering his hotel room, he immediately began selecting background material from his attaché case. Chandra went to the other room for her own research material. No sooner had they got prepared than the coffee and pastries arrived. So, they set their documents aside and enjoyed their dessert.

"Rick, I must admit that this venture so far is more like a vacation than a research assignment. I am really enjoying myself. Thank you for including me."

Her companion smiled back at her. "Believe me, Chandra, let me be clear that it was my respected grandfather who proposed that you join me on this venture, and I am certain that he did not arrive at this idea for my romantic enjoyment. Rather, he believed that a man and woman traveling together are less suspicious than two men, and he also perceived that a woman of your beauty and charm has a much better chance of extracting information from French lawyers than a mere male. Furthermore, he believed that your news-reporter training would be perfect background for this assignment. All I did was nod agreement."

"Well then," she smiled back at him, "thank you for your nod of agreement. I am truly thrilled to be here with you," and she reached out her hand to cover his emphasizing her pleasure.

This brief show of affection caused the stalwart Harvard lawyer to actually blush, and he quickly stood up to clear the dishes from the table, and recover his work papers. Chandra also stood and followed his example. The two of them began to concentrate on the task at hand.

By ten o'clock, they had drafted a program schedule for the next two days which would begin at nine o'clock the following morning with Chandra phoning the targeted law firm seeking an immediate interview with a senior partner. She would represent an

American firm planning to retain a legal firm for services in Marseille. At the same time, Rick would visit the Marseille Chamber of Commerce to inquire about legal firms under the same pretense. They would meet for lunch at the hotel to compare findings before making appointments with other legal firms.

THIRTY

Marseille, France
September 14, 1977

Chandra returned to the hotel after one o'clock to find Rick in the dining room nursing a soft drink. She immediately rushed over to take a seat across from him.

"Sorry to take so long," she said apologetically, "but I had to wait until an English-speaking partner returned from an appointment at another location. After almost two hours, M. Jacques Chartreau, one of the younger directors, was able to see me. And then . . ."

"No problem," interrupted Rick. "I have been sitting here watching all of the beautiful French ladies parade past. It has been most educational. How about relaxing and ordering lunch before we exchange information on our morning adventures?"

After consulting the menu and guessing the meaning of the French lunch offerings, they both ordered a "Croque Monsieur" which Rick had learned earlier was a ham and cheese sandwich baked in pastry. The waitress already had served water to Chandra, which suited her preference.

During their wait for the sandwiches, Rick told her of the information he had gathered during the morning. The law firm of Renand, Baham and Cabut was a relatively young legal entity, having been chartered only three years prior by six young attorneys from other firms. The group had apparently secured clients in advance or had private financing, because they established offices in the high-rent district of the city and quickly hired a support staff. The new firm positioned itself as experts in civil law and, due to the partners' absence at local professional gatherings, evidently conducted most of its business with clients from out of the city. Other than the fact that all six partners were raised in Marseille, the local Chamber of Commerce executives appeared to know very little about their activities. They were much more conversant about other legal firms in the city and they highly recommended two such older firms with well-founded credentials.

After concentrating on eating the very tasty Croque Monsieur sandwiches, Chandra lightly patted her lips with the napkin, or serviette, as she learned to call it from the waitress, and opened her notebook.

She wasn't surprised to learn that Rick's account of the founding and positioning of the law firm was identical to her own notes. But she did express surprise that the elegant young lawyer, Jacques Chartreau, asked her if she was originally from Algeria. Since her American education had not taught her that Algeria was a former French colony, she never realized that her copper-colored complexion was shared by many French nationals, and she responded with a simple "no." M. Chartreau appeared somewhat embarrassed by her answer and she quickly took advantage of his response by delving into his own background as a stepping-stone to the firm's origin. However, even though he openly discussed his own upbringing and education in Marseille, he only provided very slim details on the firm's founding with its six partners three years ago. He also said nothing about their connection with Castle Rock Investments, Inc. in Baltimore, even when she deliberately asked him about any experience with American clients. In fact, the only positive outcome of the interview was his invitation to discuss further details over dinner that evening. Of course, she accepted with pleasure.

"Well," responded Rick after she finished, "you made out better than I, at least wangling a dinner invitation with a handsome lawyer. Your former date will be lonely without you."

"I certainly hope so," she countered with her very best smile. But then she remembered asking Rick to confirm a dinner date with her for that evening. "Oh dear, I completely forgot about the date you promised last night."

"No problem, my dear. You can entertain me with a blow-by-blow account in the morning."

"Don't worry, there will be no blows exchanged."

"I didn't plan to worry, but I trust that you will keep our objective firmly in mind," Rick replied somewhat authoritatively.

"Absolutely!"

"Good, now let's move on to our afternoon appointments."

Just in case anyone might be paying attention to their actions in Marseille, the two of them had scheduled two appointments a day with major law firms under the same pretext of interviewing on behalf of a confidential American client. However, on this first day, they agreed that Rick would follow Chandra's interview at Renand, Baham and Cabut and schedule an interview with one of the senior partners, Claude Renand, on the pretext that a fictional American colleague had personally recommended the French lawyer. Rick also had business cards printed prior to the trip that identified him as Richard P. Stanford, Attorney, from Boston, Massachusetts, a city that he knew well from his college days at Harvard University.

While Rick waited for the senior partner to return from a client luncheon, Chandra was busy meeting an English-speaking partner of a much larger firm a few blocks away. She was successful in asking a question about other law firms in Marseille, particularly about the recent success of Renand, Baham and Cabut which they had been asked by their client to check out. Her interviewee expressed nothing but praise for their competitors, especially for the rapid launch of the Renand, Baham and Cabut firm.

Rick was sitting in the bedside chair reading a novel when the knock came on the connecting door at just after ten o'clock that evening. He started to rise when the door opened and Chandra entered in a low-cut black gown delicately tailored to her perfect body.

"Wow, the lawyer didn't stand a chance with you in that get-up," exclaimed Rick.

"Well, thank you kind sir. I am flattered. Would you like to de-brief now, or defer it until morning?"

"Let's get right at it. Come and join me at the table where we can take notes."

"Okay, just wait until I get my own notes," whereupon she disappeared into her room, only to emerge within a minute carrying her document bag. She sat down across from her fellow investigator, put both elbows on the table and looked him in the eye before speaking: "Do you want to go first, or shall I?"

"By all means, ladies first," he replied.

"Right! My new friend Jacques . . . "

"Your new friend?" he interrupted.

"Well, of course. I assumed that you prefer me to make friends with everyone I meet."

"Sure, but . . ."

"Or would you prefer me to leave a trail of annoyed people in Marseille?"

"No, of course not, but . . ."

"Good! My new friend Jacques proved to be a charming dinner companion, but a lousy information source. It seems that his charm was directed solely at me, and never included any useful information about the firm. He reminded me of my unsuccessful interview with your grandfather at his birthday party. Every time I asked a question, he would ignore it and respond with one of his patented list of compliments about me. So, I must apologize, Rick, for a poor performance from a professional reporter."

"Not at all! Being a reasonably normal male, I can well understand Monsieur Chartreau's fascination with you, especially in that dress. May I humbly suggest that you tone down your appearance for the next guy. Perhaps a high collar and even a pair of glasses would be appropriate."

Chandra wrinkled her brow at her companion's remarks, but responded appropriately. "Right, I will slip out to the shops in the morning and buy some more conservative attire. Now, how about your afternoon?"

Rick smiled before responding: "Believe it or not, I experienced a similar situation to your own, but not with my target interview. Rather, the lawyer was delayed with a client meeting so I spent an hour alone with a vivacious, and rather forward, English-speaking receptionist. Taking your cue from your new friend Jacques, I acted charmed by her advances and asked her to join me for dinner. But, she frowned and reported another engagement, but then looked up cheerfully and informed me that she had been given a long lunch break tomorrow and she would love to spend it with me. So I arranged to meet her at Le Detour, a popular luncheon spot recommended by our friendly front-desk clerk. Although her mind may be on sex, mine is directed solely at useful information, and I am optimistic that I will succeed."

"That's great, Rick. I just wish that I could join you to learn some of your techniques," she replied with a mischievous grin.

"Bah! Humbug! I'm sure that you can spin rings around me in that category. But, I will look forward to seeing you in the morning, shall we say seven-thirty for breakfast in the dining room?"

"That sounds fine," replied Chandra, somewhat haughtily, as she gathered up her notes and disappeared through the adjoining door.

THIRTY-ONE

Marseille, France
September 15, 1977

When Chandra returned to her hotel room the next day, after a non-productive morning interview, followed by a solitary lunch in a small café, she immediately knocked on the door to Rick's room, but no reply. So, she decided to take a relaxing bath prior to his return. After a half hour in the tub, she toweled and dressed in casual clothes prior to reviewing her notes. Another half hour elapsed before Rick came rushing through the adjoining door without knocking. She rose from the table just as he grabbed her in a crushing embrace and danced her around the room.

"We did it," he exclaimed loudly. "She gave it to me without my asking. I don't believe it."

"Hold it a minute, Rick. What did she give you?"

"The name of the owner, Prince Hassad El Saud, a rich Saudi prince living in Monte Carlo. There seems little question that he is our man."

"But why, why did she give it to you?"

"Just because she wanted to impress me. It's as simple as that. We were on our second bottle of wine and I was being pleasant and attentive, when suddenly she blurted out that she was given a long lunch period today because she had to stay late and tidy the office before the prince arrives in the morning. Dumb me! I thought that she was referring to a wealthy client. It took a few more minutes before she proudly told me that she really worked for a rich prince. After that, we chatted about the prince and his massive real estate holdings in several countries, including Castle Rock Investments in the United States."

"Can you let go of me now?"

"Oh, sorry, I got carried away."

"Don't be sorry, I enjoy being hugged, especially for this kind of celebration. Let's break open a bottle of wine."

"No! We have work to do. I must advise our CIA friend immediately by public phone. I just came up to get his private number. So sit tight. I will be back in a flash." Then he rushed into his own room and retrieved his case prior to heading out the door.

Rick forced himself to walk sedately across the hotel lobby, so that he wouldn't draw attention to his impatience. Use of a public phone was mandated by JD (Joshua Dempsey), his friend from college, and now his CIA contact. The public phone box that he had located the previous day was less than a block from the hotel. Rick closed the door and glanced through the windows to ensure that he had no visible watchers. Seeing none, he dialed the direct line to JD and received a message instruction — after all, it was still night-time in the Washington area.

"JD, we have an ID, courtesy of the legal firm's receptionist, on a Prince Hassad El Saud of Monte Carlo. RSVP further instructions."

He then replaced the receiver and returned slowly to his hotel room where Chandra was waiting impatiently. They decided to cancel all other appointments on the assumption that they had completed their objective, so Chandra returned to the telephone in her room in order that Rick's phone would be free to accept a return call from JD.

Rick's hotel phone rang about an hour later. He quickly picked up the receiver and said "hello." An answering male voice said "Monsieur LeGrande, s'il vous plait?" Rick replied in English: "I am sorry, there is nobody here by that name. You must have a wrong number." He then replaced the receiver and left the room, stopping only to wave to Chandra with a thumbs-up gesture.

After returning to the public phone box, he once again viewed his surroundings for suspicious-looking characters. Seeing none, he dialed the number for JD's direct line.

"Josh Dempsey here, may I help you?"

"Hi Josh, Rick here. I am on a public phone in Marseille."

"Okay, my friend, please listen carefully. Prince Hassad El Saud is indeed a wealthy prince of age forty-nine residing in Monte Carlo with a wife and three children, but our files indicate no illicit activities connected to him and no connection to either the Marseilles law firm or the Baltimore investment firm. He appears clean as a whistle . . ."

"Darn, I thought my information was valid. I guess that we had better resume . . ."

"Not so fast, Rick. Please listen. My friend, Nigel Harris of MI6, contacted an acquaintance who is a ranking official at the French Sûreté in Paris to inform him of our activities. He was officially notified that our amateur sleuths in Marseille could be in immediate danger.

The Sûreté official requests that you leave Marseille immediately. In fact, an official police escort will pick you up at your hotel at five o'clock and transport you to the airport with tickets for the evening flight to Paris. You will be met there by another police escort to convey you to the Georges V Hotel where two rooms are reserved for you. Under no circumstances are you to leave those rooms until Sûreté agents with identification knock on your doors at nine o'clock tomorrow morning. You will then be escorted to a face-to-face meeting with Georges Paissant, Deputy Director of the French Sûreté for an informal information exchange. Also, before you leave Marseille, send flowers to your female source with a note that you must leave town immediately on urgent business, but you look forward to contacting her upon your return. So, please pack up and meet your police contact in the lobby at five. That is all. Be safe."

THIRTY-TWO

Paris, France
September 15, 1977

The George V Hotel is one of the most elegant hotels in Paris. It was constructed in grey limestone in the 1920s and named after the King of England, no doubt to attract English visitors. After being escorted by the police to the airport in Marseille, Rick and Chandra were met by two Sûreté agents in Paris who escorted them and their baggage to a pair of adjoining rooms in this hotel. During their rush trip from Marseille, none of their escorts were able to provide any clarification for the rapid move. The Sûreté agents did register strong insistence that the two Americans remain in their rooms and be packed and ready to leave when picked up by other agents at nine o'clock in the morning for their scheduled meeting with Deputy Director Paissant.

"Rick, I am really at a loss about what is happening. Can you make any sense out of all of this movement by police escort? "The beautiful Chandra sat slumped on the edge of the bed and seemed near tears.

Rick came over and sat down beside her, placing a consoling arm around her shoulders. "I'm truly sorry that I dragged you into this mysterious quandary, Chandra. I have already told you everything that I know. But this personal meeting with France's second-ranking policeman escapes me. I am certain that we have done nothing against the law, but the care that they are providing us implies that some bad guys may be after us for some reason, probably related to our discovery of Prince Saud. But, his lily-white credentials certainly do not match the "bad guy" image, so I cannot fathom the connections. I assume that we will just have to wait until tomorrow morning to find out."

"Well," she exclaimed, jumping to her feet. "I do not intend to just sit here and mope. I am going into the bathroom and wash up, followed by a drink from the mini-bar, and then a tasty meal from room service. So there!" And she marched off to the bathroom with head held high.

"Good for you," called Rick with a smile. "I will do the same in the adjoining room." But, just as he started to move, Chandra uttered a piercing scream and came dashing out of the bathroom, with wet feet dripping water. "Rick, the bathroom is flooded and the water is seeping into the bedroom. Please do something."

Without replying to his distraught companion, Rick dashed to the phone and attempted to explain to the operator in a mixture of French and English that the plumbing was broken. Within five minutes, two maintenance men appeared at the door and headed for the bathroom. They were followed by the night manager and his chief of security, who no doubt were both acutely aware of the sponsor of these two Americans.

"Monsieur et Mademoiselle, please accept my deepest apologies," he stated in English. "This kind of failure just does not happen at Georges V. We will find other accommodations for you immediately." And he marched to the room telephone to carry out a spirited conversation with an obvious subordinate, which ended with him exclaiming "excellent." He then turned to the unhappy couple and stated, "Please follow me. Your bags will follow in a few minutes."

The American couple looked at each other in bewilderment, and then turned and followed the diminutive night manager down the hall to the elevator, or 'lift' as the French preferred. The elevator stopped on the top floor, and their guide continued his march to a pair of ornate double doors, which he quickly unlocked and opened to reveal a lavishly decorated living room with adjoining bedroom suites on either side.

"Welcome to our Royal Suite" he exclaimed proudly, waving his short arms in both directions, "and it is yours to enjoy with the compliments of the management. A waiter will appear momentarily with suggestions for dinner which he will serve personally just for you. He also can take your breakfast order. Here is my card. You can reach me any time at this number. Please enjoy the Royal Suite." Then he bowed ceremoniously, and left the room just as the waiter entered to discuss their dinner plans.

"I can't believe that the two of us just finished a fabulous dinner served by our personal waiter in the Royal Suite of the George V Hotel in Paris. This is really a lifetime event to share with your grandchildren." Rick then rose from the dining table and sat on the sofa with the snifter of brandy poured by the waiter as the climax of an extraordinary feast: cold lobster salad, poached haddock with marinated asparagus, a bacon-wrapped filet of Spanish-bred steak adorned with grilled mushrooms and pearl onions. And white wine from Bordeaux followed by a full-bodied red from Burgundy. As if this wasn't enough, the waiter then flamed bananas foster at tableside with an exquisite French brandy of which ample was left over for quiet post-meal reflection.

"Do you think that my grandchildren will give a hoot about an ancient Paris hotel dinner? They will more likely want to hear about the romantic details of an apparent honeymoon suite."

As she spoke, Chandra, rose from the table and plunked down beside her fellow investigator. "So what am I going to tell them big fella?"

"Well, golly me, ma'm, I'm just a small town boy who has no experience with such affairs. Shall we begin on this couch with all our clothes on, or strip down and meet in the bedroom?"

"Frankly, Mr. Patrick Michael O'Shea the fourth, I don't give a hoot how we start, but I do know that we have been avoiding this topic for the past week and this is the right place and the right time to more than start."

"I cannot imagine how any sane man could resist that offer, Miss Chandra Matilda Jones," as he carefully set his brandy glass on the end table and turned to face her with clear intent to caress her body.

"Where on earth did you learn my middle name? I never reveal it to anyone," she whispered as she moved her body into the crook of his arm and looked up at him expectantly.

"I never take on a partner without thorough investigation. And since you are clearly the most beautiful creature that I have ever shared hotel rooms with, my investigation will now proceed way beyond your middle name." With that said, he proceeded to kiss Chandra's welcoming lips as he moved his arms to begin explorations of her fantastic body. She responded with experimentation of kissing motions as well as her own explorations of his muscular body. His gentle caress of her lips with his tongue inflamed her desire to the point that she ripped his shirt off his body and pulled him down upon her using both hands to grab his enlarged member and thrust it inside her exploding vagina. Rick responded by grabbing her rear in both hands to ensure his complete insertion and consequent mutual climax. He then rolled off her body to the floor gasping for air before rising to his feet where he stood staring down at her in awe.

"Lady, you are more beautiful naked than fully clothed. Most women are just the opposite. I could just stand here and stare at your perfect form all night."

"Not a chance big fella! We are about to seek a better playing field."

The couple's love-making on the sofa had begun slowly and deliberately with acceleration as clothing was discarded, ending in mutual frantic haste. Neither one exercised patience for moving their climax to the bedroom, but found each other simultaneously on the sofa with pieces of clothing entwined about their now-perspiring bodies. She rose slowly from the sofa and took him by the hand as she whispered, "I don't know about you, but I would like to try that again in a large bed."

"I'm your man. Let's do it." The two of them then walked hand-in-hand into the nearest bedroom, where they pulled off the bedspread and climbed beneath the sheets of the oversize bed for further exploration of a new-found relationship.

The thunderous explosion occurred at four o'clock that morning, a massive noise which caused both of them to sit up and exchange stares of wonder as the bed continued to sway from the shock waves.

Rick jumped up and looked out the window to witness clouds of smoke and flames billowing up from a lower floor. There seemed no question that it was a blast within the hotel itself. Sirens soon shattered the formerly quiet night and water hoses began spewing their liquid deterrent within another ten minutes. As the smoke began to dissipate, Rick could count the floors below the blast. There seemed little question that the explosion came from the two rooms on the fourth floor that they had initially occupied.

"Oh my god!' exclaimed Chandra. "That bomb was for us."

"I'm afraid you're right, my love. Somebody doesn't like us."

"Yeah, but it's quite clear that we like us, and that's much more important." So, she snuggled up to her big companion and they managed to keep busy until dawn signaled time to get dressed and ready for breakfast.

The two policemen knocked on the suite entrance doors at two minutes before nine o'clock. After presenting their credentials, they wasted no time in grabbing the luggage and hustling the young couple down the freight elevator to the rear entrance and into their unmarked car for the brief trip to the garage under the Sûreté headquarters building. From there, the agents directed Rick and Chandra into an elevator and up to meet Deputy Director Georges Paissant on the top floor. He greeted them both in perfect English and expressed his concern about the "spot of trouble" at the hotel during the night.

The deputy director then led them to a small conference room that was completely sound-proof for confidential discussions. They were offered drinks by a pleasant lady who served and disappeared within five minutes. A blue light appeared above the entrance door, apparently indicating that the room was sealed, and the deputy director began speaking about an extraordinary set of circumstances.

The two hours spent with Georges Paissant—who spoke fluent English—constituted the most astounding meeting ever experienced by Patrick Michael O'Shea IV. But neither he nor Chandra were permitted to record it either electronically or by hand. In fact, at the end of the meeting, Paissant informed them that American CIA agents would meet them outside his office and escort them to a private airport outside Paris where they would board a charter jet to return to Washington. They would be met at Andrews Air Force Base and escorted directly to a secure meeting at CIA headquarters in Langley, Virginia.

The two Americans were to be the only source of the message being relayed by Paissant. They were, in fact, couriers of top-secret information that they had helped generate from their interviews in Marseille.

The two of them were in a state of shock as they were hustled out of the police office building to a basement vehicle exit where they were introduced to two CIA agents from the American Embassy who drove them to a private airfield south of Paris. They were then introduced to two marines in uniform who would accompany them across the Atlantic.

The Gulfstream jet was cleared for takeoff immediately after they were aboard. Along with their marine escorts and two pilots, they were served drinks and in-flight meals by a male steward who attended them throughout the flight.

THIRTY-THREE

Washington, D.C.
September 16, 1977

As the Gulfstream IV settled into a perfect landing at Andrews Air Force Base in Washington, DC, Rick and Chandra each awakened from a sound sleep. It seemed like only minutes ago that they were hustled out of the Sûreté headquarters in Paris and into an unmarked Peugeot for a rapid trip to a small airfield south of the city. They must have been in shock, as they barely remembered meeting two American Embassy marines in full uniform who were assigned to accompany them across the Atlantic Ocean.

As soon as the four of them were seated inside the well-appointed interior of some wealthy sponsor's private airplane, the co-pilot immediately advised them to fasten their seat belts while the captain requested clearance for departure. A rapid takeoff was followed by an efficient flight steward appearing from the rear of the plane. He served them drinks and then in-flight meals; after which he attended to any need throughout the flight, although they only remembered part of it as they both drifted into deep sleep.

Once on the ground, the Gulfstream IV taxied to a secure military reception building where the couple was handed over to the CIA's JD Dempsey—a familiar face that they were happy to see through sleepy eyes. He welcomed them both and requested in a quiet voice that they not discuss any aspect of their trip to France until they were safely inside the secure CIA headquarters meeting room.

He then ushered them to the rear seats of a black SUV, where he joined them in the front seat with a non-uniformed driver. Rick noticed an identical vehicle carrying four men followed them out of the airport and stayed with them on the drive to the CIA headquarters in Langley, Virginia, some eight miles north of central Washington.

They entered the spacious (258 acres) and park-like grounds of the CIA headquarters through gates opened in advance. The driver wasted no time in following the main drive to the underground reception area of the enormous headquarters building (1.4 million square feet). JD helped them out of the vehicle and accompanied them past armed guards to an elevator that whisked them to the top floor. They were then ushered into an internal meeting room by a pleasant grey-haired lady of executive bearing who introduced herself as Janet Cochrane, special assistant to Director Malone.

Ms. Cochrane introduced each of them to both Director Charles Malone and Deputy Director Thomas Sebastian of the United States Central Intelligence Agency, prior to directing them to seats directly across the conference table from the two white-haired executives. JD took a seat farther down the table, but nobody else joined them except a uniformed steward who entered and offered light refreshments and a selection of soft drinks.

The director waited until they both were served and tasted the food and drink, before opening the discussion. "Miss Jones and Mr. O'Shea, I first of all want to welcome you back to the United States. I understand that you have experienced a rather hectic time over the past couple of days, and I want to assure you that you are now in one of the safest buildings in the entire world. So, please relax and enjoy the snack while I banter on.

"I also want to apologize to you for rushing you out of Marseille and then Paris, but as you know by now, you are privy to what the French believe to be some very delicate and disturbing information. We will be learning about it from you for the first time, because Deputy Director Paissant believed it too sensitive to transmit by even the safest of our electronic or written communications. Yes, we could have had him brief one of our own people and send that person back home, but Monsieur Paissant was uncomfortable about a possible leak in our own Embassy, so you two became eligible messengers. Unusual? Absolutely, but, after examining all of the options, he preferred the use of "virgin" messengers. Please excuse my use of that term, but it is the adjective that Paissant deemed most appropriate under the circumstances. I note that you are actually smiling, Mr. O'Shea."

"No offense taken, Director Malone, but at first I thought that the expression referred to our young ages rather than our experience. I now understand that it could have double meaning."

"Absolutely, Mr. O'Shea, a double entendre, if you will. But, enough of my small talk. I see that you both have apparently satisfied your possible hunger—and we will offer more substantial sustenance after our meeting—so I would like to begin. First of all, I should advise you that you are about to be recorded in three different ways: audio microphones in the middle of the table, video in the ceiling, and, perhaps most accurate, Mrs. Cochrane with her own mastery of the lost art of shorthand. May I assume that you have no objection to these recordings?"

"I have no objection."

"Miss Jones?"

"I have no objection."

"Good, let us proceed. Just for the record, I should state that these two American citizens are carrying a verbal message of confidential nature from the Deputy Director, Georges Paissant, of the French Sûreté in Paris, which they have agreed to convey to us to the best of their recollection.

Chandra motioned to Rick to take the lead, and he did so without hesitation.

First, after receiving confirmation from Dempsey that his superiors had been briefed on the purpose of their trip to Marseille, he revealed that he had managed to become friendly with a receptionist in the Marseille office of the attorneys serving as directors for the Castle Investment Group Inc. of Wilmington,

Delaware. During a luncheon with her, she mentioned that the real owner of the firm, Prince Hassad El Saud of Monte Carlo, was due in their office for an important meeting the next day and that she was requested to work extra hours on preparations for transferring a large amount of money that was to be packaged into several separate parcels to be sent to the United States office of Castle Investment Group.

She did not specify the exact amount but we assume that it is cash to complete the purchase of the Florida East Coast Railway that was contracted a week ago in St. Augustine.

After their luncheon date ended later that afternoon, he immediately phoned Agent Dempsey at a public phone outside the hotel, as he had been instructed. He informed Agent Dempsey that a man by the name of Prince Hassad El Saud of Monte Carlo was the apparent sole owner of Castle Investments Group, Inc. JD instructed him to return to his room and not discuss this fact with anyone, including Chandra, until he received further communication. Neither of them was to use the phone for anything other than room service, and, of course, no further communications of any kind should be conducted with anyone in the Marseille law firm.

At this point, Agent Dempsey interrupted Rick to acknowledge that he had received the phone call—actually two calls because the first one was prior to his arrival that morning.

"Yes, I must apologize for that oversight," interrupted Rick, "first of all in calling before office hours on a direct line, and second, for leaving out mention of the double calls from my report."

"Not a problem," smiled Director Malone. "Please continue. And, Ms. Jones, please don't hesitate to jump in if you note that he has missed a salient point."

"I will do that, sir, although I must admit that I did not think that the double call was important."

Director Malone smiled gently at her before speaking: "That is exactly why we have three sets of recordings, Miss Jones. Because we really cannot be sure what is important in these matters. But no harm done! Please continue, Mr. O'Shea."

At this point, Dempsey intervened to remind his superiors that, after briefing the Deputy Director on O'Shea's call, he immediately contacted MI6 Agent Nigel Harris in London. Harris, in turn, contacted Deputy Paissant.

The French policeman was astounded to learn that his fellow agents had collected this information and urged them to sit tight until he learned more. He contacted Harris again the following afternoon to instruct O'Shea to send flowers to the secretary at her home with a note saying he must leave Marseille on business immediately, but looked forward to calling her upon his return. Then, Harris requested that they pack their bags, check out by phone, and be ready for a police escort to arrive and transport them to Paris for a secure meeting with Paissant. Harris delivered this message to Dempsey who passed it on to O'Shea by public telephone.

O'Shea then passed the monologue to Chandra who described the defective plumbing in her room at the Georges V hotel in Paris followed by the manager arranging a two-bedroom suite on an upper floor. Both she and O'Shea were shocked by the explosion before dawn and further distressed to learn that it was their former rooms that had been bombed. They were contacted by Paissant who sent a police escort to transport them to his office in a seemingly secure meeting room. She then turned back to O'Shea and gestured for him to continue.

O'Shea had condensed his recollection into precise points which he delivered in slow and concise fashion, after explaining that the Sûreté had acted with amazing speed to break into the Renand, Baham and Cabut law office before morning and place recording devices in the key meeting rooms prior to the arrival of Prince Saud for his early meeting that same morning. The information that they received was combined with prior information from other undisclosed sources in the following summary considered to be too sensitive for communication other than by personal messenger:

- "Prince Hassad El Saud is a citizen of Saudi Arabia residing in Monte Carlo who is suspected by the French Sûreté of financing terrorism training in Libya and financing Al Qaeda recruitment programs in France; however, the Sûreté have no concrete evidence for prosecution;

- "The Marseille law firm of Renand, Baham and Cabut is owned by Prince Hassad El Saud and provides policy management for the Castle Investments Group, Inc. of Wilmington, Delaware, which has a purchase agreement for the Florida East Coast Railway (FECR) signed by Chairman Edward Ball of Jacksonville, Florida;

- "El Saud has engaged in current negotiations with Carlos Esperanza of Colombia (now reported to be living in Matanzas, Cuba) for the delivery of street-grade cocaine packaged as fresh vegetable produce from Miami to several northern cities via the Florida East Coast Railway and its contracted connections with other railroads (no apparent evidence of FECR collaboration);

- "Unbeknownst to Esperanza or any of his colleagues, El Saud has financed the creation of very large bombs by an Al Qaeda group in an undisclosed Asian location to be shipped by sea to an undisclosed seaport in the United States for trans-shipment to center city destinations in selected United States cities within the next three months. The American trans-shipments are to be managed by Hassad's accomplice, Dimitri Chekov, who currently resides in Atlanta and sub-contracts with a known assassin named Mohammed "Big Mo" Abdullah. Abdullah is believed responsible for the recent rail yard explosion in Jacksonville, Florida and a sport fishing boat explosion off the coast of the island of Providenciales in the Turks and Caicos Islands (details from Nigel Harris, UK MI6);

- "El Saud is aware of the research being conducted by Patrick O'Shea IV and Chandra Jones in the United States and Marseille. He has contracted for their immediate execution (note George V Hotel bomb blast described by Ms. Jones);

- "All of the above issues were discussed by Prince El Saud and his three business partners, Renand, Baham and Cabut, as recorded by Sûreté in Marseille on the basis of information supplied by Patrick O'Shea IV."

THIRTY-FOUR

Langley, Virginia
September 16, 1977

Rick and Chandra were enjoying dinner courtesy of the CIA via JD Dempsey in the CIA Guest House a short distance from the headquarters building where they had conveyed their oral report to Director Malone and Deputy Director Sebastian. The two senior officers had thanked them for their concise report and dismissed them under the care of Agent Dempsey while they adjourned to prepare their own report to the President on the following morning.

JD had escorted them back down to the basement garage where a car and driver waited to take them to the nearby Guest House, a rehabilitated large white farmhouse from the historic property, boasting three floors of accommodations for select guests of the CIA. Needless to say, despite its location inside the gates, this facility displayed its own armed guards on the perimeter and front entrance.

As the waiter cleared the main course dishes, JD explained the protocol for the next few days. "Tomorrow morning at ten o'clock, the two of you are requested to meet with our legal staff in Meeting Room A adjacent to the dining room. Then, the three of us are scheduled to have lunch in this room with Deputy Director Sebastian at noon. There is nothing planned for the afternoon, so I booked you into the Fitness Center on the lower level of this building. Gym clothing and swimsuits are provided, and they have an excellent massage staff who I can recommend to you. I will report any further events as they are scheduled. Now, I am ready to plunge into this delicious dessert."

Each of the three enjoyed their dessert before Rick and Chandra bid JD good-night and retired to their "sleeping" rooms.

The first signs of daylight could be seen in the eastern sky when Rick awoke with a start to discover Chandra missing from their bed. He sat up quickly and surveyed the room. He spotted her wrapped in the bed cover and sitting curled up in the upholstered chair staring out the window at the semi-darkness. He jumped out of bed naked, and knelt beside the chair.

"Chandra, what on earth is wrong? Why are you sitting up looking so sad? Is it something I said or did that is making you unhappy? Speak to me."

"Oh, Rick, I am so sorry to wake you at this early hour, but I cannot sleep." It was then, when she turned to look at him, that he noticed a tear stain on her cheek.

"So what is making you feel bad?" he asked.

"It is difficult to explain, but I'm afraid that we must terminate our relationship before we go back to Jacksonville. I believe that our separate racial ancestries will cause career hardships for both of us that we cannot overcome."

"Is that so?" Rick queried. "Well, we need to discuss this issue in a logical manner. I propose that I get guest robes for each of us and then make some coffee. You go wash your face and I will serve coffee for two at the table. Okay?"

"Alright, just give me a few minutes to freshen up."

Ten minutes later, the two lovers sat across from each other at the table, with full coffee cups steaming between them.

"Now Miss Jones, the jury will hear your testimony. You have my undivided attention."

"This is very hard for me, Rick, because my feelings for you run very deep, and our love-making has been the greatest experience of my life. But, I must face the fact that you are an ambitious lawyer in a southern city and I am a reasonably well-known news reporter. Our relationship will be instant news as an inter-racial affair in a city that is still full of racial tension. People you want as clients will disdain you for having an affair with a black girl from the wrong side of town, and I will be downgraded in my profession as an upstart hussy with loose morals attempting to improve my lot by peddling my sexual favors to an upper-class white man. Both of us stand to lose our career positions."

"Wow, those are pretty tough words, my love. I cannot deny that Jacksonville society is full of bigots, many of them with ancestry in the KKK and beliefs in white supremacy. And there are many African-Americans who feel equally strong. The physical violence of 'ax handle Saturday' in Jacksonville was only fifteen years ago, followed closely by the St. Augustine motel sit-in. These are terrible atrocities that will never be wiped from our history, despite Ed Ball's successful efforts in the past to keep them from being reported in his newspaper.

"However, I believe very strongly that keeping these terrible incidents sheltered from our young people will only prolong the long-awaited reconciliation among races. We must face them head on and strive to overcome them, to paraphrase Martin Luther King. In fact, although you may have acted in self-interest, you are already a symbol of class equality by climbing out of poverty and representing your multi-cultural heritage as a popular television personality. I am certain that teen-age girls of African-American heritage look up to you as a model for success. The question is whether your relationship with a white man will strengthen or weaken their admiration. I don't know the answer, but, from an academic viewpoint, I would like to find out."

"Well, Rick, you are a very persuasive guy. But my career is not an academic exercise. I believe that it is fragile insofar as I suspect that it is a trial for the station. So far, so good, but I must admit to some considerable concern about my position. The station hires an independent survey company to measure ratings, and mine have been consistently high ever since I was a field reporter. I attribute this to a combination of always looking my best and carefully trained elocution. Frankly, this job is all that I am trained to do, and I am scared of losing it."

"Okay, I believe that you should do whatever you feel is best for you. I will support your decision. But, at the risk of sounding foolish, I would like to present one other argument."

"Frankly, I cannot imagine you sounding foolish, Rick, but I am willing to listen to anything that you believe worth saying."

"Right, then, I will give it a try. Although I have only known you for about three weeks, I have become very attached to you; not in terms of physical attachment, although that has been a magnificent experience too; but in terms of companionship. Simply put, I love being with you as a business partner, regardless of our sexual pleasures. Now, I am only twenty-six years old, and my close encounters with women are relatively few. But, the companionship I feel with you feels a lot like what novelists define as love. Furthermore, it grows stronger each day. The thought of you leaving me is beyond my comprehension at this point. I even thought of inventing an African ancestor to make myself more presentable. But, I cannot lie to you, so that's out of the question. What I could promise is to sit you down opposite the two wisest men and one very wise woman (all white, I'm afraid) and discuss this topic in depth. I promise that I will abide by their majority opinion. Could you hold off on your termination decision for another week until we could organize such a meeting?

"Rick, you're going to make an outstanding courtroom lawyer. Of course, I accept. Who are these three wise people, anyway?"

"Fantastic! They are, first, my great grandmother who grew up in the slums of Dublin, had one child out of wedlock, and never married in her ninety-eight years; second, my grandfather who grew up in the luxury provided by his father courtesy of Henry Flagler, who some claim was his rightful father; and third, my own father, an attorney who helped raise seven children during his thirty-year marriage and has consistently provided me sensible advice on a wide variety of topics."

"Wow, that is impressive, but I would like to propose another woman, just to add a little more color to the gathering—my own mother, who has been an active campaigner for black freedom all of her life. She truly understands the depth of bigotry in Jacksonville."

"You're on! I will schedule this session at a neutral location as soon as possible."

"Now, can we have breakfast, I am starving.

"You bet! I'll race you to get dressed."

The following day began with a leisurely breakfast before Rick and Chandra appeared at ten for the scheduled session with three CIA attorneys in Meeting Room A in the Guest House. Each of

118

the attorneys gave them a pleasant greeting, but the Senior Attorney was the only speaker. He went over each of the points in Rick's summary of information given to the two senior CIA officers on the previous evening. He probed for more particulars on Prince Hassad El Saud and the law firm of Renand, Baham and Cabut, but neither Rick nor Chandra had anything to add except the complimentary remarks about the firm received from other attorneys.

The Senior Attorney then showed them a copy of the confidential report prepared for President Ford and asked for their edit and corrections. They had none, as it was essentially the summary that Rick had delivered orally the night before.

The Agency's Senior Attorney then asked Rick to meet JD at the Guest House entrance at eleven the next morning and they would fly to Richmond to present confidential evidence of foreign ownership of Castle Investment Group to the Fourth Circuit Court Judge and then return. He told Chandra that Agent Rebecca Johnson had been assigned as her companion and that she would touch base with her the next day.

Finally, the Senior Attorney impressed upon them the importance of secrecy about everything they had experienced and reported both in France and at the CIA headquarters. They were aware of Chandra's profession and insisted that she pledge secrecy with her editor and colleagues in Jacksonville. At some future point after the current issues were settled, she could apply to the CIA to be released from this pledge.

The Senior Attorney reminded them that they were still in possible danger, so each of them would be assigned an experienced CIA agent as companion for the duration of the case. He could not project how long that would be, but he was hopeful, with their information, that they could wrap it up in days rather than weeks.

Rick and Chandra went directly to the dining room at the conclusion of their meeting with the legal staff and met JD and Deputy Director Sebastian who had reserved a table for lunch. After being seated and decided on menu items, Sebastian addressed them both.

"First of all, I prefer to be called Tom by non-company people. The deputy director title is too long and formal. Second, I want to express the sincere thanks of President Carter, in addition to the gratitude of Director Malone and myself for the vital surveillance work you did in France. It produced invaluable intelligence for a very important case. Third, we appreciate the fact that you are still in danger from the very people you revealed, and we have assigned experienced agents to accompany you both—JD will stay with Rick and Agent Rebecca Johnson has been assigned to accompany Chandra. Both of them will attempt to cause minimum interruption to your professional and private lives, but their surveillance training will assure your safety until we close this case, hopefully within days."

"Tom, sorry to interrupt," said Rick, "but may I ask what prospects you have for rapid closure?"

"Yes, I know that you would like to know the answer. Frankly, so would I. But, no, I cannot even venture a guess. This is a very complicated piece of business and we are acting with great caution, as I am sure that you can understand."

They paused a few minutes to enjoy their lunch, before Tom continued.

"There is another important matter that I must discuss with you. Chandra, I realize that you are in the news business and I am certain that your editor is eager to learn about your adventures and probably about the inside of CIA headquarters and the people you have met here.

"However, I must insist that everything you have discussed, seen, or heard over the past week remain secret information. Our business is all about secrecy. We cannot operate successfully without it, and that is especially true in this case. So, I must insist that each of you sign the pledges of secrecy that JD has for you. Chandra, if you are pressed to produce something by your editor, you may petition the agency through me, after this case is closed, for release from your pledge. Even then, we will require an advance edit."

"I understand," she replied.

"Now, I must run to another engagement, but please stay for dessert. And, once again, our sincere thanks. I have enjoyed meeting you both."

He shook hands with both Chandra and Rick, before quickly making his way to the exit.

After lunch, JD produced the secrecy pledges for their signatures, and then he returned to work while Chandra and Rick returned to their rooms for a change of clothes and an afternoon of relaxed enjoyment in the Health Center. After all of the fine dining they had enjoyed courtesy of the CIA, their exercise followed by a light dinner was a welcome change.

THIRTY-FIVE

Langley, Virginia
September 17, 1977

Chandra was right on time to meet CIA Agent Rebecca Johnston at the entrance to the dining room in the Guest House. As soon as the agent saw Chandra, she extended her identification card and smiled: "Hi, you must be Chandra. I'm Agent Rebecca Johnson."

"Chandra Jones, but I'm afraid I do not have an ID card to show you."

"It doesn't matter," replied Agent Johnson. "Only we federal agents are required to display our cards at every introduction. Now, let's have lunch."

The dining room steward showed them to a table by a window which looked out onto the immaculate lawns and gardens surrounding the Guest House.

"What a lovely work environment you have here," remarked Chandra.

"It really is, but I'm afraid we rarely have time to enjoy it. The bulk of our time is spent within windowless rooms in that massive headquarters building. So, I am really pleased to be selected for this assignment to accompany you." She paused to allow the waiter to take their luncheon selections, before asking Chandra about her career as a journalist.

The waiter had no sooner returned with lunch when the dining room steward appeared with a portable telephone to announce a call for Agent Johnston. The CIA agent apologized for the interruption and stepped away from the table to take the call. She returned in a few minutes to announce a slight change in travel plans. Whereas they had previously planned to fly down to Jacksonville with Rick and JD that evening, now for some unexplained reason, they requested that Agent Johnston drive Chandra to meet them in Richmond that afternoon.

"So Chandra, please take your time to finish lunch, and then go up and pack your belongings as quickly as is convenient. They would like me to get down there as soon as possible."

"No problem, I am almost finished here. I can be up and back in fifteen minutes."

"Great. I'll get the car and meet you at the front entrance."

Within twenty minutes the two women were settled in the front seats of the black SUV and on their way to the front gate. Rebecca smiled at the gate guard and handed him a copy of the official release for Chandra before driving out to the highway and heading for I-495 south to its junction with I-95 and on to Richmond.

"Just one thing, Chandra: I didn't plan on such a long trip, so I will need to stop at the first service station on I-95 for gas. It won't take long.

"That's fine," responded Chandra brightly. "I can slip into the variety shop and get us both a bottle of water."

"Great! Oh, here it is coming up now." And she quickly pulled up to an empty pump, after which Chandra slipped out of the big car and headed for the shop. Just as Chandra was about to enter the shop, she felt a large arm extend around her shoulders and she glanced up in surprise to see a very large African-American man turn her away from the entry toward a dark blue Chrysler van with the rear passenger door open.

"Stop! Who are you? What are you doing. I'll scream." She turned her head back toward Agent Johnston to cry for help, but Johnston and the black SUV had disappeared.

The big man clamped a hand over her mouth and picked her up with his other arm and set her down in the back seat where a very large black lady stuck a syringe in her arm. Chandra started to fight with both of her captors, but to no avail. The last thing she remembered was the two of them lowering the back of her seat and fastening her safety belt.

Within seconds the big man had climbed into the front passenger seat and the quiet driver had accelerated away from the station and on to the ramp headed south on I-95.

"KIDNAPPED! WHAT DO YOU MEAN, KIDNAPPED?" shouted Rick O'Shea. You guys told me that the CIA was the safest place on earth. How could she be kidnapped?"

"Take it easy, old buddy," urged JD. "Sit down in this chair and have a drink of water. We'll find her, but for the moment, these unknown bastards have the upper hand."

The five men were in a small meeting room in the Richmond courthouse waiting on the Judge to see them, when a special delivery envelope was delivered to Patrick M. O'Shea. It had no markings on the envelope and a single sheet of white paper inside with pasted newsprint stating "MS CHANDRA JONES WILL REMAIN WITH US UNTIL THE FECR SALE IS COMPLETE." Nothing else was in the envelope.

The senior attorney pulled out his handkerchief and grabbed the paper before inserting it back into the envelope, being careful not to add more fingerprints. He asked his assistant attorney, Tony, to search for a wrapper to cover it until they could get it to the laboratory. In the interim he was notified that the Judge was available to see them.

"I will see the Judge alone," he announced, "and revise our strategy accordingly. JD, phone the pilot and tell him we have a change in plans. We will fly to Jacksonville this afternoon. Then phone Michael O'Shea and tell him that we would like to meet with him in his office at five o'clock. When I return from the Judge's Chambers, we will phone Jordan Hale at the FBI. Perhaps you should brief him in advance. Yes, please phone him first and brief him prior to my return.

THIRTY-SIX

Jacksonville, Florida
September 17, 1977

The CIA Gulfstream IV gained clearance to land at Jacksonville's Cecil Field Airport, relatively close to the central city. The five passengers were picked up by Rick's brother-in-law who had the dual advantage of living in Hidden Hills Country Club Golf Community close to the airport and owning a large seven-seat van. He was happy to assist a member of the family. Besides, it was only a fifteen minute drive to downtown and the Jacksonville Bank Building where the Michael O'Shea office was located. Mike was standing at the open door to welcome each of them and offer refreshments in the conference room carefully prepared by his loyal secretary, Maryanne.

The CIA senior attorney seated himself at the end of the table and proceeded to open the meeting. "Gentlemen, I decided to fly down here today in order to bring the most knowledgeable people about this kidnapping face-to-face. Clearly, this is a blatant attempt to keep us from blocking the pending sale of FECR to the Castle Investment Group. Why? What is so vital about ownership of this railway that motivates a capital crime? The fact that they pulled it off in one of this country's most secure headquarters is disturbing, but not our main issue. By the way, Tony, would you brief everyone on how they pulled this off—a rather clever ruse, I must say."

"Yes, sir," began the young attorney from the CIA. "Upon learning that Agent Rebecca Johnston had apparently abducted Ms. Jones, our security team at the agency immediately went to Johnston's apartment and found her securely bound and gagged in her living room. It seems that the kidnappers had discovered a woman who closely resembled Johnston and coerced her to assume Johnston's identity, which she did with such skill that our regular gate guards and the Guest House dining room steward—all of whom

125

professed to be familiar with Johnston—were fooled by her impersonation. My personal view is that the scarcity of African-Americans on the CIA staff tend to lull our staff into a lower level of perception about people of color.

"Are you suggesting that the distinguishing traits of people of color blend into an illusion of sameness for unsuspecting observers," asked Mike O'Shea.

"I am indeed, sir, and I intend to submit a brief on this precise topic recommending more intense training on facial observation. Our agency is behind the times on this subject."

"Please carry on, Tony," interjected the senior attorney somewhat impatiently..

"Yessir, the vehicle requisitioned by Johnston was found by Virginia State Police relatively quickly at a service station stop on I-95 south where the transfer to another vehicle apparently took place. It was wiped clean of any fingerprints or other identity clues. Even the small suitcase containing Ms. Jones personal items—which the dining room steward witnessed her placing in the car prior to the two women leaving the Guest House— was missing.

Extensive interviews by police produced no witnesses, which is not surprising since most people do not stay long at these facilities. The police will use their influence to gain a prominent announcement on the evening television news of all channels— admittedly a long shot, but the best chance we have for a witness. However, at the direction of the CIA Director, we will not use her name or picture, or any mention of the CIA. It will be treated as a kidnapping of an unidentified woman."

"Okay, thank you, Tony," stated the senior attorney. "Of greater import for this meeting is the reason for the kidnapping. That is, we know that it is vitally important for someone that this sale of FECR be consummated, and I suspect that they will attempt to move the schedule up. I believe that alleged drug smuggling by rail is not the primary reason that they want this railway—something more important."

"It seems quite likely, to me at least," suggested Mike O'Shea, "that they need the management of the company rather than just the rolling stock. They were quite clear on that point during the press conference. If that is correct, then I assume that they may be considering one or more major explosions like the one here in Jacksonville. A possible reason for retaining management is to ensure that their bombs get delivered to strategic locations for maximum terrorism impact."

"Thank you, Mike, that makes a lot of sense," replied the senior attorney. "So, JD, what strategy should we pursue?"

"Well, sir, we already are pursuing actions on several fronts. First of all, we have the personal attention of FBI Senior Agent Jordan Hale directing the kidnapping case. He, in my opinion, is the best there is at this type of case. If we can identify the kidnappers, there is a good chance that they will lead us to the principal. Second, thanks to Rick and Chandra's investigation in Marseille, we have the identity of the alleged key principal—Prince Hassad El Saud of Monte Carlo—who is the outright owner of the Marseille law firm that manages Castle Investment Group, and who is bankrolling the purchase of FECR. However, he has thus far eluded the best efforts of Interpol to locate him. His home is empty and his yacht, Cleopatra, is anchored in Monte Carlo Bay with an idle crew. Other than guest identities, the Sûreté people have no reason to believe that any of the crew members are guilty of any criminal activity.

"Through our liaison with MI6 Senior Agent Nigel Harris, we have confirmed the presence of Mohammed Abdullah, aka Big Moe, on the island of Providenciales at the time of a fishing boat explosion killing four unidentified Americans presumed to be the arsonists of the Broward Yard explosion. But, I'm afraid that we have not been able to locate him either.

"However, on the positive side, an interview by the French Sûreté with a crew member of El Saud's yacht confirmed the presence of the international criminal Dimitri Chekov on the yacht some ten days ago conversing with the Prince. From historical agency records, we know that Chekov frequently hires Big Moe to do his dirty work. In fact, airline ticket records confirm that the two of them flew from Atlanta to Jacksonville and return two days prior to the FECR sale announcement.

"In short, sir, all of these incidents can reasonably, although not conclusively, be assumed to be linked together in some unknown scheme with presumed criminal intent. Our strategy, to return to your original question, is to find and detain Prince Hassad El Saud."

"That is an excellent summary, JD, responded the senior attorney. But, I'm afraid it doesn't give us specific actions that we can launch today."

"Perhaps not, sir, but since I am on protective assignment with Rick O'Shea here in Jacksonville, it occurred to me that an interview with Mr. Ed Ball might be helpful. His decision to sell FECR appeared rather hasty, and it may not be coincidental that it occurred within two days after a round-trip by Chekov and his enforcer from Atlanta to Jacksonville."

"Indeed! Another excellent thought, although, given your assignment, you had better take Mr. O'Shea along with you. In fact, just the presence of an O'Shea in his office might incite him to irrational actions. Yes, I rather like the idea.

"Tony, please notify our pilot that we can leave for Washington within the hour and order us a taxi. Mike, it has been a pleasure to meet you, and thanks for the use of your conference room. I believe that it was a useful meeting."

"My pleasure, sir. You are always welcome."

THIRTY-SEVEN

Near Darien, Georgia
September 18, 1977

Chandra Jones awoke very slowly in a strange bed in a strange room. She had a nasty headache and her mouth badly needed a toothbrush. At last, her memory revived and she remembered the big black man picking her up and seating her in the car where a seriously overweight black lady injected a syringe into her arm. She remembered shouting for Rebecca, her personal protector, who disappeared along with her CIA car.

She had handcuffs and a seat belt restraining her in the car, but these restraints were now gone and she was free to move about the small bedroom with attached bathroom. A window with blinds was on the other side of the bed, but no light was filtering through the edges of the blinds. It was dark outside. They must have driven for many hours to this destination; they were probably a long way from Washington. She remembered that they had been heading south when she was abducted, so they now could be hundreds of miles south, perhaps even back to Jacksonville if they had stayed on I-95.

Chandra tried to sleep again but the pounding in her head was too annoying. So she ventured into the bathroom and washed her face with cold water, then took a wet washcloth back to the bed to put on her forehead. She dozed off again for a while until the first light of dawn began to brighten the room and she noticed that the window opening was secured with iron bars. But a comfortable upholstered chair was by the window and a round table with two straight chairs at the end of the bed. A bedside table held a sturdy lamp. She was on the second floor of a house apparently in a rural area—no other houses or other buildings were in sight, just farm fields and dark evergreen trees. No clues appeared as to where she might be.

Finally, the lock turned in the door and it opened to reveal the large African-American woman who had put her to sleep in the van. This time she carried a tray with a mug of coffee and buttered toast on a plate.

"Now, don' ya get angry with me, young lady. I was ordered to put ya to sleep in the van, so I had to inject ya with some tranquilizer. You probably have a headache, so I brought ya some pain pills with a glass o' water, and some coffee and toast. There's cream and sugar if'n ya use it, and e'en some jam for the toast. I'll put it on this table for ya. Later on, I'll fix ya some real breakfast, but this will get ya' started. Your suitcase is in the closet if'n ya want to change clothes.

"My name is Mandy and I'll be lookin' after ya for a week or so, until they decide to give ya back. Please don' give me any trouble, 'cause these two men with me are rough, tough fellas who might hurt both of us. Ya' must stay in this locked room for the time bein'. There's no television or radio, but there are a bunch o' books and magazines to read, and the chair by the window is comfortable. If ya' need anythin', ya' can ring this bell on the tray, and I'll come. But don' be ringin it too often, 'cause I don' climb stairs as well as I use' to."

"But, Mandy, where are we? Do you know why they kidnapped me?"

"No, Ma'am. I don' know nuthin'. I'm jus' hired help ta cook and clean house. If ya'all have questions, you'll have to ask the big fella. He 'peers to be in charge."

Then she left and locked the door from the outside. Chandra faced the boredom of more quiet time than she needed or wanted.

THIRTY-EIGHT

Amelia Island, Florida
September 18, 1977

The noise of his children playing on the weekend was too much stress for Saud (now Stanton), so he phoned Mr. Chester (Chostek) and told him that he was coming up to visit him in his rented condominium. He and one of his bodyguards hopped in the electric golf cart and drove over to Chester's building. The other guard would stay with his wife and children—customary split duties when the family traveled. Lalonde and his bodyguard took the elevator up to Chester's floor and he told the bodyguard to wait outside as he had personal matters to discuss with Chester.

"Good morning Mr. Stanton," greeted Chester as he opened the door. "Please come in." would you prefer to sit inside or out on the balcony?"

"Inside will be fine."

"Would you care for a drink?"

"Just water will be fine."

Chester brought him a tall glass of ice water and freshened his own glass of juice.

"Now, Mr. Chester, let's review our progress thus far, and plan ahead. First, the purchase of the FECR is not proceeding fast enough. Our decision to kidnap the news reporter did block the O'Shea bid to delay the sale. The necessary cash to pay for the sale will be transferred within the next few days to Castle Investment Group. We need to move ahead with a closing date as soon as the money has arrived. Please take care of this next week."

"Yessir! Consider it done," replied Chester.

"Good! You have successfully handled the change of crew and the new registration of the Polar Star to Elizabeth IV. That appears to be complete."

"Yes it is," smiled Chester, "and now on its way across the Atlantic."

"However, we are not yet ready to receive and trans-ship the cargo items. I was waiting on the FECR purchase closing to conscript railway monitors for each shipment, but now we are running out of time to have each shipment in place by Colombus Day. I believe that you must move ahead immediately to retain these five persons and get them in position at Port Everglades. Do you have a plan for immediate action?"

"Yessir, I do. Big Moe's cousin, a resource that we have used successfully in the past, is in Fort Lauderdale at this minute, screening candidates. I expect to join him in the morning to make final selections and instruct them in how to proceed on the train as well as how to trigger the explosion device from a remote location."

"Please keep in mind, my friend, that your retirement fund, as well as your life, depend on the performance of these monitors. Nothing can go wrong at this late stage."

"I understand completely," replied Chester immediately. "Nothing will go wrong. I even have received reliable information from inside FECR that trains will be running through Broward Yard by next week.

"Good! Now, what about this young woman we have in custody? She has seen Big Moe, although briefly when he grabbed her outside Washington.

"Yes, she is dispensable, but I recommend that we keep her alive at the farmhouse until the FECR purchase is complete. It is conceivable that we might have to produce her at the last minute to make the sale complete. I don't expect that to happen, but it might be wise to be ready for possible contingencies."

"Your point is well taken. Instruct Moe to keep her well fed, although we may need him in the interim to back you up in Port Everglades. Can the other two operate without him?"

"I believe so, sir. After all, she is locked into a secure upper bedroom, and only seen for meal delivery."

"Very well, then, leave her be for the time-being. Let's turn to your vulnerability in Fort Lauderdale. First, I don't want you, Big Moe, or any of our team to remain in Port Everglades. Contact Moe's cousin and ensure that all five are re-settled in five Fort Lauderdale hotels. Then reserve a conference room in a sixth hotel for your training meeting. Have all of them, including Moe's cousin, show up at the conference room at nine o'clock tomorrow morning. Have lunch sent in so that not a single team member is seen outside that hotel. By the time you leave late that afternoon, every single man should be able to recite his in-transit duties and how to ignite his bomb with the transmission equipment. Any questions? "

"No sir. I understand the program."

"Good! Now, the day after tomorrow! Each man is to travel separately by bus from separate terminals in Southeast Florida. You and Moe's cousin—by the way, I am tired of calling him that, what is his first name?"

"Alfred!"

"Okay, Alfred, it is. The two of you can rent a car under your new identity —something plain like the one you have now—and drive to Savannah. Rent rooms for each of them in separate hotels in Savannah. Have Alfred pick them up from the bus station and deliver them to their hotels. Tell them that we will connect them with their target trains at the right locations when the cargo is ready to ship. Have Alfred keep the rental car for transporting them when we are ready. You keep your current rental for back-up. Are you comfortable with all of that?"

"Yessir!"

"Now, we both will be gone for the next few days—you to Fort Lauderdale and me back to France to ensure that our money transaction has been processed smoothly. You can contact me through the law office if absolutely necessary. We will meet here again when we both return in three days time. Good-bye."

"Good-bye sir, safe flight!"

THIRTY-NINE

Near Darien, Georgia
September 19, 1977

Chandra had been sitting in the chair by the window most of the day—the rest of the time she was pacing aimlessly in the small room. It seemed quite clear to her that she was being held for ransom of the FECR sale to Castle Investment Group. If the CIA/FBI capitulated, then her life would lose its value. Rather than assume what she might have heard or seen, it would be simpler to just kill her—an ominous, but realistic, conclusion. So, if she was to live, it was up to her.

She began to focus on potential weapons that she might use to free herself. Of course, she could overpower the overweight housekeeper, but either one or two armed guards in the hall would be her undoing. Nose-to-nose combat was out of the question. She had to be smarter. Tying the bed-sheets into a rope was a good idea, but the bars on the window were firmly implanted and too close together for even her slim body. "Damn!" she muttered. "There must be something I can use. She began her search again, not missing a single inch of space.

Then, suddenly, there it was, right in front of her. How on earth did she miss it before? The plaster ceiling in the closet was collapsing close to the outside wall. It must be a leak in the roof that had been festering for years without repair. Indeed, as she positioned one of the straight table chairs below the bulge to stand on, a solid poke with one of her high-heel shoes caused a major collapse of dry plaster all over her. Being bright white would never do in the darkness, but she deferred a change of clothes until she tested the roof planks. They were completely rotten, held together only by the ancient wood shingles. The shingles turned out to be a more difficult challenge—each one required all her strength to pry loose—but her determination overcame the problem and she eventually had a hole big enough to squeeze through. She climbed back down into the bedroom and relaxed in the chair.

When was the best time to make the break? Probably right after their dinner which she had learned was served immediately after hers. She always heard the television sound after that, implying that security was lax. Of course, she would need to wait until Amanda came up to take away her dinner dishes for washing—always backed up by one of the men with a weapon.

In the meantime, she could strip the sheets and bedcover to begin making a rope. She took them off the bed and then covered it with the bedspread so that Amanda wouldn't notice. She ripped each sheet in three strips, using her nail scissors to make the initial cuts. The strips were not equally wide, but she could tie the six strips together with knots that she had learned from her father for extending fish lines when she was a youngster. She tested each knot for strength by looping it over the bed post and pulling with all her strength. The result was a rope over thirty feet long. She was quite proud of herself.

Next, she stored the rope in the closet and carefully looped the end over an exposed attic rafter and applied her very best knot. Then, she cleaned up for dinner, before carefully selecting her clothes for the journey. Walking shoes with her thickest wool socks to guard against blisters—she had no idea how far she was from I-95, but there was a nighttime glow in the lower eastern evening sky, which intimated a cluster of lights implying a town, or at least a service station. Although it was summertime, she chose warm underclothes and her dark blue windbreaker, envisioning lying flat in a ditch when a vehicle passed by. She would wait until she saw people walking before she revealed herself and sought help. Even a police car could be compromised by these villains. Mandy had left a couple of extra plastic bags for the two wastebaskets. She took them in her windbreaker pockets for possible rain protection. Finally, she would wear her jeans for long-term wear and warmth. She didn't have a hat, but would put her hair in a pony-tail before she left and then, with some reluctance, wear the old peaked hat she found in the closet. She stuffed her essential toiletries in the jacket pockets with her plastic bags, in the hope that she would have a rescue bathroom.

She then tucked all of her escape clothes under the bed on the window side away from the door, and kept her light blouse and shorts on for dinner. She barely finished everything before Amanda and the shorter security guard appeared at the door with an appetizing meatloaf with mashed potatoes, gravy and fresh vegetables, along with a slice of apple pie—perfect fare for a long hike.—she ate every bite in anticipation of a long night ahead. She was ready.

Amanda turned up again with the same companion to collect the dishes and smiled when she noticed all the food was gone. The door closed and locked indicated that it was time to go.

First, she dressed very quietly and then threw the rest of her clothes in the bathroom clothes hamper, made the bed look occupied with use of the pillows, and left everything else in neat order.

Obviously, she would need all of the lead time that she could manage, so she turned off all the lights, carefully closed the closet

136

door, and then wedged it shut with a coast hanger to delay its opening. Then, she had to use all of her arm strength to lift herself up to the edge of the hole in the roof. After a brief rest to catch her breath, she hauled up her homemade rope and dropped it down the outside of the house. It did not reach the ground, but looked close enough to drop without injury. So, she squeezed her legs out ahead of her and wrapped them around her rope. The secure knots that she had tied proved to be handy brakes on her descent. In fact, the entire trip down was a "piece of cake" or as "easy as pie" she thought, with her first smile of the day. She left the rope creation with a touch of sadness and proceeded to the next stage of her plan—to disable the two vehicles.

Disabling the vehicles depended on two factors: (1) if they were parked in the light from the front porch where she could easily be seen, and (2) if they were they locked to prevent a silent disabling (slashing tires could be noisy). It was her lucky night. The porch light was off and the cars were not locked. So, having learned a thing or two from a former mechanic boy- friend, she very quietly raised the hood on each car and stole the distributor cap from each, thereby disabling each vehicle for potential pursuit. She then lowered the two hoods very quietly—no need to latch them—and quietly walked away down the entrance lane to the paved road. She kept the distributor caps until she found good hiding places in thick bushes off the road.

Chandra's plan was to walk at a strong pace on the left side of the road facing potential traffic and jump into the dry ditch and lie flat covering her face at the first sign of a vehicle from either direction. Luckily, this part of Georgia was relatively modest rolling terrain, so the walking was easy and she could see a long distance ahead for approaching headlights. She stopped every fifty paces to look behind her for any lights. She stumbled a few times at first—vowing to carry a flashlight in her luggage on future trips—but soon learned to step higher for better control.

She could not erase the sense of panic that gripped her for the first hour, but eventually learned that it disappeared when she concentrated solely on her hiking. So, with this new revelation, she overcame the panic—or at least she overcame it until headlights appeared and she dove for the ditch, anticipating all sorts of critters being angry at being driven from their sleeping places—but no critters appeared and renewed concentration on hiking overcame the panic until the next headlights occurrence.

One hour, two hours, and then three hours passed by with no incidents when she noticed that the former glow in the eastern sky was growing stronger. The excitement of reaching some form of civilization caused her to increase her speed, and within twenty minutes the glow actually turned into individual lights. It was more than a way-stop—a substantial tourist Mecca with a couple of gas stations, restaurants, fast-food outlets, two motels and a discount shopping center with attractions for children (already closed for the night). Chandra was undecided as to which facility that she should approach for help. Finally, she picked the larger of the two motels which featured a grey-haired lady at the reception desk.

"Hello, may I help you?" questioned the receptionist.

"Yes, I do need help. Could you please phone the state police for me. Please excuse my muddy clothes, but I have escaped from being held captive in a farmhouse a few miles from here and I walked here because of the lights. You looked like the friendliest person I could see . . ." and then she began to cry as the pent-up emotion of her escape became overwhelming.

"Now, honey, don't you worry none. We'll look after you. C'mon over here and sit down. Would you like some coffee?

"Just a glass of water, please."

"You bet. Oh good, here comes Martin, our security man. Martin, please call 911 and tell them we have a kidnap victim just walked into our lobby. Here's your water dear. Just relax, the state police are on their way."

Chandra was so overcome with relief that she could hardly answer the policeman's questions. Between frequent tears, she did manage to give her name and that she was from Jacksonville, but that she had been kidnapped outside of Washington from the Central Intelligence Agency. She knew that she wasn't telling a coherent story, but her mind did not appear to be working properly.

While Chandra was unsuccessfully attempting to be coherent, a second state police car arrived and the second policeman seemed to know something about her. He asked her if she was a news reporter from Jacksonville and she immediately brightened up and acknowledged that she was, and then she attempted to describe the farmhouse from which she escaped.

Martha, the night clerk, overheard and said to the policeman, "That sounds like the old Connover farm that sold fully furnished after he died a couple of months ago—five or six miles down this road—poor baby, she walked the whole way. The two policemen conferred and then told Chandra that a female officer was on her way along with an EMT vehicle.

"As soon as they arrive, Officer Hunt and I are going down to check out this farmhouse. Now, don't you worry Miss Jones. You are in safe hands here. We have notified the federal authorities."

Chandra must have dozed off in her chair, when she suddenly awakened with a female voice addressing her. "Hi, Miss Jones. I am Officer Harriet Winston of the Georgia State Police. You will be perfectly safe with me here. These two men are emergency medical technicians from the local sheriff's office. Please allow them to check your vital signs. That's it. Good!"

"Harri, her vital signs are good except for a fast heartbeat. I would like to take her down to Brunswick Hospital for a more thorough check-up, but she might prefer riding with you."

Chandra overheard and spoke up: "Yes please. I would sooner ride with Officer Winston."

"Okay, we can do that. Can you stand and walk out to my patrol car?"

"Yes," and she stood up without assistance and headed toward the hotel entrance.

In the interim, the two first-responder state policemen decided to ride in one car to examine the farmhouse. They had informed the dispatcher that they were approaching the identified farmhouse which was reported to contain two armed kidnappers as well as a housekeeper, so they requested backup of two additional officers before entering the premises. Dawn was beginning to light the eastern sky as they drove their car up to face its headlights on the front door and turned on the blue flasher lights and the loud speaker.

"OCCUPANTS INSIDE THE FARMHOUSE. STEP OUT ONTO THE FRONT PORCH WITH YOUR HANDS RAISED AND NO WEAPONS. DO IT NOW."

The front door opened slowly allowing the housekeeper to step out with hands above her head. "Please don' shoot. I've got no guns. I'm all alone here. I'm just the housekeeper. The two men ran out the back door when they saw you coming down the road."

"OKAY, PLEASE SIT IN ONE OF THE PORCH CHAIRS AND DO NOT MOVE UNTIL INSTRUCTED. OTHER TROOPERS WILL ARRIVE IN A FEW MINUTES."

The police car then followed the lane around to the rear of the house shining its high beams and its spotlight on the pasture field behind the out-buildings. Seeing no movement in the field they turned the spotlight on the outbuildings and radioed dispatch that two armed black fugitives are on the run in fields adjacent to this farmhouse. They requested a search helicopter and further search directions.

Within a few minutes, the headquarters dispatcher responded that a helicopter was on its way and Captain Murray Brown was the search coordinator. He had requisitioned troopers from other districts to establish a cordon on side-roads surrounding the escape route. The first- responder troopers will return to examine the farmhouse and interview the housekeeper. Other troopers should be arriving now to search the outbuildings and establish a cordon perimeter in the reported escape fields. Brown advised them that this is a federal kidnap case and FBI agents will be on-site within the hour to assume leadership coordination. He directed them to cooperate with FBI instructions.

The Southeast Georgia Hospital in Brunswick is located in central Brunswick, Georgia. It is a general medical and surgical hospital with full surgical and care facilities for trauma as well as in-patient specialties. It is a short drive south on I-95 from Darien and Officer Winston accompanied Chandra Jones into the emergency entrance just twenty minutes after leaving Darien. Chandra was led into the trauma room and immediately examined by a resident and the staff psychiatrist before being sedated in a private room. At Chandra's request, Officer Winston phoned the law office of Michael O'Shea in Jacksonville to report her escape and current examination at the Brunswick hospital.

Brunswick is approximately seventy miles north of downtown Jacksonville where the Michael O'Shea Law Office is located. Rick was working in his office when the phone call was received at nine o'clock from Officer Winston that Chandra had escaped her kidnappers in good health and she was being examined at the Brunswick hospital.

The young attorney immediately vacated the office and ran to his car parked in the building garage. It is possible that he set a new speed record from Jacksonville to Brunswick of forty-nine minutes, but fortunately no such records are maintained. Of equal good fortune is that the state police of both Georgia and Florida were focused on finding the kidnappers rather than catching speeders on that morning.

Rick turned up at the hospital reception before ten o'clock looking for Miss Chandra Jones. He was directed to her room where Officer Winston was sitting outside waiting for replacement officers from the City of Brunswick to take over her guard duty. She welcomed Rick O'Shea, about whom she had been briefed by Miss Jones. She informed him that Chandra had been up all night and that she was currently sedated to regain her strength. But, other than that, the doctors reported no health issues. She then summarized the account of her night escape from the kidnappers and the now-massive search being conducted to find them.

The city police arrived and Officer Winston took her leave.

Rick positioned himself by Chandra's bedside and waited for her to wake-up. When she did awake, he summoned the doctor to examine her for release. Then the happy reunited couple settled into Rick's car and enjoyed a leisurely drive south to Jacksonville where Rick was to pick up JD for their appointment with Edward Ball.

FORTY

Jacksonville, Florida
September 20, 2015

Mid-week was the best time to seek a meeting with Ed Ball. He usually stayed in his Jacksonville condominium apartment and read or watched sports on television. Thus, he agreed to Rick Shea's request to bring his friend JD for a brief visit. They were met in the building lobby and ushered up to the apartment by Ball's regular security companion, Richard. He took them through the apartment entrance where Ball got out of his chair to shake hands with Rick and JD Dempsey. Richard served them soft drinks and then disappeared to allow them a private visit.

"Mr. Ball," began Rick, "I don't recall that we have met before, but, of course, everyone in our family is familiar with you and your many management positions. My former college room-mate, Joshua Dempsey, has been in Jacksonville for the past couple of weeks investigating the Broward Yard explosion for President Ford's Explosion Task Force and he expressed a desire to interview you personally. So, here we are."

"Welcome, Mr. Dempsey," replied Ball. "How can I help you?"

"Thank you for seeing us on such short notice, Mr. Ball. As you may know, I am seconded from the Central Intelligence Agency in Washington to serve the Task Force, and I am here today on behalf of Chair Margaret McBride and the members of the Task Force. First of all, I should ask you if you have any ideas about who may have committed this crime?"

"No, I do not. I discussed this issue with my senior staff and nobody revealed an idea, either objective or subjective. Some suggested that it might be a carryover from our union disputes of the past few years, but the court settlement and jail terms for the ringleaders seem to have put that issue to rest. Some others suggested that it might be members of the O'Shea family unhappy about their trust fund termination by the courts, but I have never known them as violent persons in the past, despite our disagreements. Your own investigations have ruled out accidental causes, so that leaves senseless terrorists as the only other option in my mind."

"Thank you, your thoughts are similar to our own. Are you acquainted with a man named Dimitri Chekov, sir?"

"I believe that I have met that man briefly, but I cannot say that I am acquainted with him. Do you believe that he might be connected to the explosion?"

"According to our records, he and an associate named Mohammed Abdullah came to visit you last Wednesday evening and the next day you announced the sale of FECR to an investment firm located in Wilmington, Delaware. Is that correct, sir?"

"I'm afraid that I cannot discuss any aspects of a sale in process, Mr. Dempsey."

"But Chekov and Abdullah were here in your apartment last Wednesday evening, sir. Are they connected with the Castle Investment Group?"

"Once again, I cannot discuss that topic, Mr. Dempsey."

"Mr. Ball, we have reason to believe that Chekov is involved with the Castle Investment Group and that he represents a wealthy sponsor from outside the United States who may finance terrorism activities. If so, your sale would be disallowed under federal law and you, yourself, may be subject to collusion charges on proposed terrorism activities."

"Mr. Dempsey, I have been a leading businessman in Florida for most of my adult life. I am now almost eighty years old. I doubt very much if anyone will bring personal charges against me. So, don't bother threatening me."

"Very well, sir, but I must give you fair warning that we have strong evidence in the records of Florida courts concerning your relationships with Senator Ebeneezer McCloud and Judges Samuel Coburn(now deceased) and John Mason (now Justice Mason of the Florida Supreme Court). The federal government has no interest in these people, although my friend Rick here certainly does have an interest."

"Well, now, Mr. Dempsey, those are a lot of unconnected allegations that you are throwing around. I am confident that my legal team can handle them satisfactorily."

"Yessir, you do have a fine legal team, although I doubt if it can match the legal staff in the combined FBI and CIA. But I am not here to argue that point. I am more concerned about maintenance of your lifelong reputation, if you spend the final years of your life in court, or perhaps even in jail."

"Hmm! Does that mean that you have a publicity-free alternative, Mr. Dempsey?"

"Well, I am only a small cog in a large wheel, Mr. Ball, but if, for example, you would like to bring some substantial information about Mr. Chekov and his foreign sponsor or sponsors, I would be willing to become your advocate for an unpublicized clean bill of health."

"Really, you would switch your allegiance?"

"Not at all! I believe that my director would support my advocacy for your reputation if your information was both valuable and timely."

"What do you mean by 'timely' Mr. Dempsey?"

"Sir, I personally believe that Chekov's foreign sponsor is planning to use your railway to launch a multi-target act of mass-murder. I also believe that we have very little time to stop him or them. Finding him after the act will mean harsh sentences against those who assisted. Finding them in advance means celebration for all. As the Realtors say: 'time is of the essence'."

"You would make a fine courtroom lawyer, Mr. Dempsey—very convincing. Last week, I was threatened with physical harm if I did not cooperate. You have offered a much more valuable reward for an aging man of sterling reputation—preservation of my honor. I am convinced. Tell your director that I know the name of Chekov's sponsor and I used to know his home location—he may have moved. What is this worth in terms of cleaning the black side of my slate? Come back tomorrow about the same time with your certified answer and we can possibly make a deal. Good-day gentlemen."

The two visitors found Richard waiting outside the entrance to usher them back to the building lobby. Neither one of them uttered a sound until they were safely seated in the car. But then, they both let out a resounding howl of victory.

"JD, you were magnificent. I cannot recall a better debate argument. Thank you."

"I must admit," replied his friend, "I was pretty proud of myself. But now we have a major document to draft. Full speed back to your office, my boy."

FORTY-ONE

Near Darien, Georgia
September 20, 1977

The sound of a police siren in the pre-dawn caused the three occupants of the Georgia farmhouse to wake up in a hurry. Big Moe dressed quickly and instructed his shorter companion to put some clothes on and start up one of the two vehicles. He rushed upstairs to check on their prisoner. Unlocking the bedroom door and turning on the overhead light revealed no sign of Miss Jones. But the tail of the improvised sheet rope hanging from the closet ceiling provided clear evidence of her escape.

Big Moe wasted no time investigating his prisoner's escape route. He rushed to the bottom of the stairway to be met by his companion, William, waving his arms and yelling: "Moe, the distributor caps are gone from both vehicles. We are screwed!"

"Sonofabitch," yelled Moe back at him. "Tell the old lady to sit in a chair and wait. Then grab two flashlights from the kitchen and meet me at the back of the house. Do not turn on any lights. Tell her that we are leaving by the back door."

The state police car was speeding up the driveway toward the front of the house when the two black men, now wearing dark pants and windbreakers, crawled from the back of the house west to the windbreak of pine trees leading down to the road. As the police ordered Mandy out to the front porch and then searched the house, Big Moe and William ran down to the road in front of the house and crossed to the pasture field on the other side. As an experienced criminal, Big Moe felt certain that the police had Chandra Jones in custody, and that they would soon be joined by reinforcements to catch the kidnappers. He assumed that the police would expect the two kidnappers to run north through the fields and woods behind the farmhouse. Therefore, he and his sidekick would head due south as fast as they could travel in the dawn's faint early light.

Moe's assumption proved accurate. Within the next twenty minutes, as the two criminals peered out from a woodlot at the rear of the pasture across the road, they witnessed two helicopters with floodlights circling north of the farmhouse. They could hear the sirens of additional police cars approaching from the east.

"Okay, my man. Keep that flashlight off and follow me as fast as you can. We are getting out of here due south until we find a vehicle to steal or a building where we can hide. After we get transport, we'll find that sneaky broad and kidnap her again." Big

Moe's long legs soon forced the smaller man to a trot in order to keep him in sight.

As the new day was about to spring morning sunshine across the south Georgia farmland, Moe urged his companion to move faster. He had spotted his target straight ahead up the grassy lane they had followed since emerging from woodland an hour earlier. It was a large vehicle shed with a metal roof and sides right on the edge of the lane. When they finally stumbled into the shed, Moe was astonished to see two pick-up trucks parked within the open doors next to a large tractor and several implements for cultivation, seeding, fertilizing, and harvesting. It was exactly the reward he had imagined. Better yet, the doors of both trucks exhibited the name of the farm and its owner: "Sunny Acres, John Mathews & Son."

While William stretched out on the dirt floor in apparent exhaustion, Big Moe carefully examined each of the trucks to decide which one he would steal. Neither one contained ignition keys, but that was not a problem for an experienced auto thief, an occupation that Moe had pursued in his teens. About the only real difference he could ascertain between the two vehicles was that one was extremely dirty from recently acquired mud splatters covering most of the painted portions of the exterior (including the license plate). "Perfect," muttered the big man, as he grabbed a half-empty pail of gasoline and proceeded to pour it into the tank. "We have transport— at least out of this dirty farmland."

The next trick after wiring the ignition and starting the truck was to drive it to the road without being seen by the owner. The two men, now somewhat rested in the vehicle shed, hopped in and Moe then drove very slowly to avoid raising a trail of dust. He soon encountered a further bit of luck. The lane intersected a second lane which appeared to be directed away from the farmhouse and out-buildings toward a public roadway that was paved with asphalt, but lined with a fence and swing gate at the lane entry. However, the gate appeared designed for retaining animals rather than humans as the latch did not contain a lock. Upon a brief order from Moe, William exited the vehicle and opened the gate. He closed it after Moe drove the truck through and he quickly regained his seat in the truck.

Now, right or left? Moe chose to turn right on the assumption that there would be more police in the I-95 corridor that must be a few miles to the east. A right turn would lead west, farther into the rural part of the state where he could trade the truck for another vehicle left in the open for an enterprising thief.

Within twenty minutes, the side-road came to a stop at U.S. Highway 84. Big Moe turned left on the highway, which soon became Plant Street entering the historic city of Waycross. Although the entrance sign showed only a population of 11,000 residents, it contained everything that Big Moe needed to continue their escape. First on his list was food. He spotted a roadside Kentucky Fried Chicken and pulled into the back of the lot behind a couple of parked cars. Moe then gave William a ten dollar bill and asked him to order chicken, sides and drinks for four persons. Moe would use the public telephone and check in with his cousin in Port Everglades and then find a fresh vehicle for transportation.

When William emerged from the KFC thirty minutes later, he found no sign of either Big Moe or the pick-up truck. He paced nervously in front of the entrance for ten minutes before a car horn attracted his attention. It was Big Moe in a late model blue Dodge sedan. He picked up the bag of food and drink and rushed over to open the passenger door. Big Moe waved him in and drove away at a moderate speed. Whenever William began to speak, he waved him to be patient while he navigated from Plant Street to turn left onto U.S. 1 at the city center. He continued at a modest pace until stopping at a service station south of the city and topping off the gas tank.

Upon returning to the driver seat and then driving to the highway, Big Moe explained that he found this car a few blocks from the KFC. It was being parked behind an office building by its assumed owner when he happened by; he quickly subdued the driver and bound and gagged him with materials that he had procured at the farm for this purpose. The prisoner is enjoying the ride from the trunk and will be released when they vacate the car. "Now, let's have at the chicken."

It was after nine o'clock when the phone rang at the Ware County Sherriff's office and answered by Deputy Nancy Stone.

"Nancy, this is John Mathews out at Sunny Acres Farm."

"Hi John; good to hear from you."

"No, it's not good. Somebody stole my pick-up truck last night, a blue Ford 150 with my name on the side and License GH 63785. I need you folks to find it for me so we can put it back to work."

"John, do you know when it was taken?"

"Hell, no! The drive shed is a half mile from the house and there is an alternate road entrance. My son Dean drove it out there last night about eight, took the key, and drove home with me. We did not see or hear anyone out there."

"Alright, John. I have your information, and I will post an "All Points Bulletin" to police units throughout Southeast Georgia. I will phone you when they find it."

"Thanks Nancy, 'ppreciate it."

Captain Brown of the Georgia State Police received the "all-points-bulletin" on the stolen truck almost thirty minutes after it was issued by the Ware County Sheriff. "Dammit all to hell, men! Who held this up? Our kidnappers have outfoxed us and headed south; probably headed over to Waycross to trade the truck for a plain-looking car."

"Richard, get this message out to all police in southeast Georgia. I want a roadblock on every federal, state and county highway within fifty miles of Waycross in all directions, right now. We are looking for any, repeat any, vehicle with two African-American men in it. They may be armed and dangerous. Approach with caution and apprehend. Notify me immediately."

Daniel Chester, as he was now known, had been parked at the entry toad to Jacksonville's International Airport for over thirty minutes waiting for a blue Dodge to show, but to no avail. "Dammit, Walter!" he exclaimed to his companion. "Your cousin must have stopped for lunch. He should have been here by now."

"Well now, Mr. Chester, I don' ever recollect Moe to be late unless he got a good reason. Let's jus' hope that reason isn't wearin' a uniform."

"You got that right, Walter. Because if he's leading a police car, then we are out of here pronto."

Just as he stopped speaking, an old pick-up truck pulled up behind him and Big Moe got out of the driver seat. "Sorry to be a mite late, Mr. Checkov, but the state police had the highway blocked off and I had to find me some sideroads. While I was at it, I snared this old truck just in case they had a line on the Dodge."

"First of all," replied Chester, "my name is Chester and don't you forget it. Second, go park that thing inside the parking lot and walk out. I'll pick you up outside the gate. Hurry up. We are late.

William, you come over and drive this car; I can sit in back with Moe."

The two men followed orders, and within a few minutes the four men were out of the airport headed south on I-95 toward Jacksonville.

"Okay, here is what is happening," spoke Chester from the rear seat. "William, I want you to drive at the speed limit right through Jacksonville on I-95 and keep going at the same speed until you get to Daytona Beach about ninety miles south. Then, Walter, you take over and drive to the airport turn-off at West Palm Beach, keeping to the speed limit all the way. Then Moe can take over and drive us to the Fort Lauderdale hotel that he booked for the meeting tomorrow. We can eat after we get there, except that I will eat in my room, the men tomorrow will only know me in my 'Don' disguise. None of you are to call me anything except 'Don.' Is that clear?" The three men all replied "Yessir."

"Okay, let's move. It's a five hour trip and the tank is full."

FORTY-TWO

Jacksonville, Florida
September 21, 1977

Chandra Jones had to request her editor's assistance to secure an interview with State Senator Ebeneezer McCloud and State Assemblyman Edward Cosgrove. But, when she turned up at the Senator's office in Saint Augustine, both men were sitting in the Senator's inner office. They rose as one to shake hands with Chandra and acknowledge her cameraman, Jimmy Brozovitch.

"This is a great pleasure, Miss Jones," stated the senator. Although I watch your weekend show frequently when I am in St. Augustine, this is the first time I am privileged to greet you in person. Welcome to our small office." The tall senator turned on his finest smile from the creased, but still handsome, face under his full head of well-groomed hair.

"Allow me to echo the Senator's remarks. I am pleased to meet you," stated the much younger assemblyman. He was a handsome, but rather short, man with naturally curly blonde hair and a ready smile.

"I assure you, gentlemen, that the pleasure is mine. Both of you have strong voting records in the State Legislature which deserve far greater publicity, and we are here to make that happen." And she then sat down in a guest chair across from both men. The cameraman focused on her for the introduction of her two guests and then focused on the guests before Chandra began her statement.

"Senator, you are the senior legislator not only here, but in the Legislature, with over forty years to your credit. For most of that time, you have been a known friend of Edward G. Ball, the chairman of the Alfred DuPont Testamentary Trust. Is that correct?"

"Yes on both counts! I am the oldest State Legislator and I am proud to have Ed Ball as a friend for many years."

"Has Mr. Ball influenced your legislation support on some cases?"

"I wouldn't put it that way. I have sought his advice on legislation about which he is knowledgeable, but my voting record is clearly my own."

"Do you also consult the opinions of Florida State Judges, in particular, the late Justice John Mason or sitting Judge Daniel Coburn?"

"Well, I certainly knew John Mason when he served the Fourth Circuit Court here in Jacksonville, as well as during his brief tenure as Justice of the Florida Supreme Court. He was a fine man and a competent jurist. So is Judge Coburn. I had lunch with him just last week."

"Did you ever have occasion to discuss with Judge Mason or Justice Mason any particular case or cases?"

"Absolutely not! I would consider that to be an infringement of my legislative position. As you know, the American system of law consists of three components operating independently: legislative, executive, and justice. Discussing issues privately between members of each of these bodies of law would be contrary to the Florida Sunshine Law which mandates transparency to the public on any issues coming before these bodies."

"In particular, sir, do you recall the case that Mr. Ball brought before the courts with respect to the status of the O'Shea Family Trust in 1970?"

"I certainly recall the Trust. I believe that it was funded by the Florida East Coast Railway. But I do not recall being involved in it in any way."

"Thank you Senator. Let me now turn to Assemblyman Cosgrove. I understand that you only have been in state government a couple of years. Is that correct?"

"Yes, it is. In fact, you interviewed me on the eve of my election."

"I do recall that interview. Prior to that, I believe that you were an investigative reporter for the Jacksonville Times-Union. Is that correct?"

"Correct!"

"I believe that you were working on an article about the legal suit between Edward Ball and the O'Shea family. Is that correct?"

"Correct again!"

"My research indicates that you implicated Senator McCloud and Judge Coburn and Justice Mason in this litigation . . ."

"Now, just a minute, young lady," interjected McCloud. "Are you trying to implicate me in this affair? If so, I will sue you and your station for unsubstantiated fraudulent character assassination. This interview is over."

"Excuse me Senator. I am not trying to implicate you. You are already clearly involved in bribing a public official. I would not be here otherwise. I am offering you an opportunity to make a statement, but if you wish to remain silent, we will move ahead without your cooperation. However, I can assure you that the FBI will listen if you would like to cooperate.

"Jimmy has turned off the camera, but both of you are invited to make cooperative statements of your own choosing. Thank you for allowing me this time with you." She rose from her seat and exited with Jimmy holding the door for her. After she stepped out the front door onto the street, Ed Cosgrove came hurriedly in her footsteps. "Excuse me, Miss Jones. Please understand that I am not linked with Senator McCloud in any way. I was present by his invitation. I want you to know that, if you are picking up the cause for the O'Shea family, then I would like to offer you substantive assistance with information from my reporter days. McCloud and Coburn are certainly involved along with Ed Ball, and I relish the opportunity of presenting a bill in the legislature to correct this wrong. By the way, please call me Eddie."

Chandra stopped in her tracks and listened to Cosgrove. "Eddie, do you have evidence of bribery in this law suit?"

"I believe that I do, although Justice Mason is now deceased. But his colleague, Sam Coburn, is still on the bench and the good senator McCloud back there was the money man."

"Would you be willing to meet with the O'Shea attorney?"

"You bet I will. I still have my notes from my reporter days, but my editor refused to run the story, so I quit in disgust. But count me in. Here is my card. Call me any time."

Two hours after completing the Senator McCloud interview, Chandra Jones was sitting at Michael O'Shea's conference table briefing Mike and Rick on her response from McCloud and Ed Cosgrove.

"It sounds to me like you uncovered a real gold mine in Eddie Cosgrove," spoke Mike O'Shea. "From your prior summary of his notes, he has time, place and people for tracking the Ed Ball bribery of public officials."

"He does," echoed Rick. "But, I am wondering if we might be able to short-cut this legality through our package for delivery by JD and me tonight? After all, Ball did alter his usual tough-guy stance by suggesting he would deal upon a pardon for past misdeeds. What if we raise the ante? Since JD is a better arbitrator than I am, we should get him in here to voice an opinion. Do you both agree?"

Both Mike and Chandra nodded their agreement and Rick picked up the phone to call JD who was at Rick's apartment studying his script for the evening meeting. "Hey JD, Rick here." Chandra interviewed the two politicians earlier today with somewhat surprising results. Can you hop over here and review the results. They could change the tone of our discussion tonight . . . Okay, see you shortly."

Twenty minutes later, the lanky figure of JD Dempsey barged into the O'Shea conference room. "Okay, here I am. What's up?"

Chandra once again summarized her interview with Senator McCloud and her later conversation with Eddie Cosgrove. She ended with Rick's thought that you might weave this revelation into tonight's meeting with Ed Ball, and possibly kill two big issues with one stone. "What's your reaction?"

JD jumped from his seat and uttered, "I like it." Then he sat down and began to doodle on his sketch pad. "But the payoff may rest with how it enters the conversation. It is not Ball's favorite subject, but a lawsuit against him for bribery is not a pleasant prospect either. Mike, how would you address it?"

"Well JD, my old Daddy, a pretty fair salesman in his day, would remind us that we should only sell one thing at a time. Don't confuse the issue by putting two deals on the table at the same time. Solve one first. Then, while your subject is feeling relaxed about the settlement, quietly address the second deal."

"If you can get agreement on both deals, you will have a bunch of happy people (even Ball may break open a bottle of champagne). However, and I kind of hate to say this, if he balks at the second deal, do not push. Let him sleep on it and we can bring it up again prior to a court ordeal, which I feel certain that he does not want. Does that sound like a reasonable plan?"

"Mr. O'Shea," smiled JD, "that is why you are a successful lawyer and I am just a new boy on the block. I believe that your plan is exactly the right way to go. What's your view, Rick?"

"I am in full agreement, old buddy. Let's do it. How about you Chandra? Do you agree?"

"I do, and furthermore, I am impressed with the talent around this table. You guys make a great team. I am thrilled to be working with you."

FORTY-THREE

Fort Lauderdale, Florida
September 23, 1977

The Hampton Inn meeting room reserved by Big Moe's cousin, Walter, was set up with coffee, juices and water, along with a platter of small pastries for the men invited to the briefing: five monitors in addition to Walter, William, Big Moe and The Don. The monitors were given numbers to protect their identities and thus wore number one through five rather than name tags. Big Moe and his cousin Walter wore no identities, as did The Don when he entered in his elderly disguise at exactly nine o'clock.

"Good, everyone is here," said The Don. "Please be seated with numbers one, two and three on the right side and numbers four and five on the left side. As you have heard, I am known as The Don. I am in command of this operation. Big Moe and William at the end of the table carry out my orders; therefore, you are to consider an order from one of them is an order from me. Do each of you understand?" Each of the five nodded their understanding.

"Despite the fact that each of you is being paid a large sum of money to perform this task, the operation is relatively simple. You will learn all of the details today and then be shipped immediately to the embarking location. You will make no contact with anyone from this minute until the task is complete. Let me repeat that: no contact with anyone outside the people in this room until the task is complete. The penalty for disobedience is immediate death. Do you understand?" Each of the five nodded their understanding. "If this rule is too difficult for anyone, you may leave now. Anyone?" Not one man moved. "Good, then we can begin."

"First of all, let there be no doubt in your minds. We are about to commit a major act of terrorism against the United States in five large cities on Columbus Day, October 8. Your act is murder, and, if caught, you will be subject to the death penalty. However, if you follow our exact directions, there will be nothing to fear on that point. We have tested the escape mechanism and it works perfectly. Furthermore, you have been given numbers rather than names, so nobody can identify you by name. On the good side, each of you has been given one thousand dollars deposited into a bank account of your choosing. You will receive another five thousand in cash the moment that your bomb goes off successfully. There are no strings attached to these funds.

"Your bomb is very large. It is in a container that will be loaded on a single freight car along with a smaller container that is equipped with a single mattress, a pillow and two blankets, portable toilet and refrigerated food supplies to last ten days, as well as bottled pure water. It contains a water supply and small basin for washing. It contains a heating and cooling element in the ceiling that you control to your comfort. You will not be required to perform any labor. You may take reading material with you as the container does have battery-powered electricity. However, alcohol and smoking are prohibited for obvious reasons."

"Some of you will reach your destination in less than five days, but everyone will be in place in less than ten days. The freight car carrying your bomb will be shunted to a specific destination at the center of one of five selected large central cities. You will set the timer at twelve noon on Columbus Day and the bomb will detonate at five o'clock when we estimate the largest crowds will be within killing range. After setting the bomb timer—as we will show you shortly—you will use the periscope to ensure that nobody is watching and you will walk away from the freight car carrying a small hand-bag which contains a change of clothes and a back-up detonator.

"Each of you will be given a map of your city to indicate the safe distance away from the blast as well as public transport stations and a hired car for your use in leaving the city. If for any reason, the bomb does not detonate at five o'clock, you will arm the back-up detonator to explode immediately. It has a range of fifty miles. Your suitcase will contain five hundred dollars to pay for transportation out of the city, if, for any reason, that your rental car malfunctions. We recommend that you take a taxi beyond the blast zone, before accessing public or private transportation, as a safeguard.

"Are there any questions on what I have covered thus far? No! Then we will take a twenty minute break before explaining the technical aspects. Please do not leave the hotel and return on time. Thank you."

The five monitors left for the hotel toilets while the three terrorists sampled the drinks and snacks on the side table. Nobody engaged in casual conversation. The Don began drawing a sketch on the whiteboard attached to one wall of the meeting room.

Within twenty minutes, everyone had returned to their places and appeared to look forward to The Don's further lecture. He did not disappoint them with his sketch of the bomb and living cube on the whiteboard.

"Now gentlemen, if you are all settled in, I will resume our lecture. On the board behind me, I have drawn a crude sketch of the apparatus that you will be traveling with. First, the larger sketch depicts the ordinary container that most of our goods are carried in for national and international transport. The same container fits on ships, trains and trucks. Within one of these containers is a cleverly-sealed aluminum tank full of liquid gas which is highly volatile when ignited. You can see that it only occupies about two-thirds of the container. The living module is placed immediately behind the liquid gas container. It is a two meter cube, or in American measurement, over two yards. The remaining space at the rear is filled with wooden boxes of machine tools, labeled as such for customs inspection when they arrive from a foreign country, ostensibly to fill the entire container and so registered for customs officers. But, my smaller drawing indicates the placement of each of these items in the interior. Unlike most containers, this one is equipped with inside latches on the doors for exit and a revolving periscope for inspecting the immediate terrain.

"When you finally reach your destination—you can be sure by the detachment sounds of de-coupling the car from the train and check it by the time itinerary we will provide at the end of the day— you can use the periscope to ensure that you are in place. Then you must be patient until the noon of the blast day to arm your bomb before your departure. Your instructions will include a map of the local area showing the location of your rental car. The glove compartment will contain a map of the regional area with the shortest route to beyond the blast area. It will also contain your remaining $5,000 plus your $500 in expenses. There will be no need to contact us again. However, we will keep your current address in a locked file in the event that we may have another job to offer you.

"I hope that each of you agree that we have made this operation as simple as possible for you to operate. Now, do we have any questions?

"Yes, Number Three?"

"Sir, I am concerned about finding the hired car. How will I recognize it?"

"Excellent question Mr. Three. You will have a map in your tote bag that will note the location and street address where the car will be parked at the curb. The car will be a Toyota Corolla model with a sticker on the side of the rear window which states 'Reserved for Number 3" and the keys will be in the center console. Does that ease your mind?"

"Yes, indeed, thank you."

"Number Five?"

"Yessir, I am curious about ventilation in the cube?"

"Another excellent question! In my description, I failed to explain that the cube has a three-speed ventilation fan with a heater supplement in the upper corner which attaches to a removable plate in the top of the container. It is battery-operated with sufficient supply for several weeks, plenty of power to fulfill your needs during the trip. Does that ease your mind?"

"Absolutely! Thank you."

"Okay, let's have lunch which will be served here in a few minutes, and then we will have a brief questionnaire to ensure that you received my information adequately. "I will be leaving ahead of you with Big Moe. William and Walter will accompany you in their van to a hotel close to the final rail yards. You may draw lots for seats in the van. Bon voyage."

"But Don, where is each of us headed to complete our assignment?"

"Ah, that, my friend, you will find out when you are ready to leave with your cargo."

FORTY-FOUR

Jacksonville, Florida
September 23, 1977

The time scheduled for CIA Agent Joshua Dempsey and Rick O'Shea to meet with Edward Gresham Ball was eight o'clock on the evening of September 23, 1977. They rode up the private elevator to his apartment five minutes early, and they were met at the entrance by his manservant, Richard, who welcomed them and ushered them to the magnificent living room overlooking the St. Johns River. He then departed through the entry and the elevator.

Both Dempsey and O'Shea stopped abruptly when they discovered another guest seated in a chair at an angle to the chair occupied by Ed Ball. Both men rose to greet them.

"Good evening, gentlemen," said Ball. "May I present our company's general counsel, George Atkins. George, this is Agent Joshua Dempsey and Attorney Rick O'Shea."

"Yes indeed, my pleasure," spoke Atkins, as he shook hands with both men. "I believe that I met Agent Dempsey when I addressed the President's Explosion Task Force."

"That is correct, sir, you gave us a very concise and factual summary of the history of the Florida East Coast Railway. It reduced my research time substantially."

"Good, I am glad to know that it was helpful." Atkins then pointed to the vacant two chairs facing the ones occupied by him and Ball. "Why don't you be seated and we can begin. As I understand it from Mr. Ball, your prior meeting came to an oral agreement over an exchange of his private information about the proposed new owner of FECR in return for documents signed by ranking government officials exonerating Mr. Ball from any wrongdoing with respect to the railway management or his private affairs. Does that sound right?"

"Yes sir, it does sound about right," replied JD. "We have such documents with us, signed by the directors of both the CIA and the FBI. Our purpose is to free Mr. Ball from any concerns about possibly embarrassing publicity that might harm his reputation in his later years."

"All-right, good, let's have a look at them." responded Atkins.

"Yes, but prior to showing them to you, we have encountered some additional information that we believe you might like to discuss in tandem with the oral agreement we reached at our last meeting."

"And what might that be?" asked Atkins.

"Yesterday, a news media associate of ours interviewed State Senator Ebeneezer McCloud and Assemblyman Edward Cosgrove about irregularities in legal actions undertaken by Mr. Ball involving the senator and Justice John Mason of the Florida State Supreme Court."

"Now, wait a minute, Dempsey," interjected Ball. "You are off on another track altogether. Justice Mason is dead and McCloud has no involvement with the FECR whatsoever. What possible topic could he have discussed that would have any bearing on the FECR activities?"

"Sir, I'm afraid that there is no delicate way to introduce this topic, so I will just blurt it out. It appears to me, as an active attorney, that a strong case can be mounted against you for bribery of court officers in your petition to dissolve the O'Shea Family Trust. It appears that the good senator was your bagman in negotiating the court decision on this issue and he has indicated to us that he might like to turn state's evidence in order to avoid a potential jail term. It seems to me that we might be able to resolve this issue in tandem with the FECR issues."

Suddenly, George Atkins rose from his chair and looked down at Mr. Ball. "Ed, I believe that it might be useful for you and I to have a word in private. How be we step out onto the terrace for a breath of fresh air?"

"Very well," muttered Ball as he rose from his chair and led Atkins to the doors leading to the terrace. The two men closed the doors after them and proceeded to a part of the terrace not visible from their young guests.

JD turned to his college friend and raised both hands palms up in a symbol of silence. Rick nodded his understanding after which the two of them sat in solitude waiting for the older men to return.

About fifteen minutes of silence passed before Ball and Atkins returned. Ball resumed his seat while Atkins stood behind his chair somewhat in the manner of an attorney about to make a statement before the court. But, the two young lawyers were his only audience.

"Gentlemen, as counsel for the FECR, I also serve as legal counsel to its officers. In that capacity, I have advised Mt. Ball to reveal all the information he has on the proposed buyer of the FECR. From my knowledge of this information, I believe that it will deny the sale and possibly result in a serious jail term for the principal. This action will return the management of FECR to Mr. Ball. At that point, he will be in a legal position to negotiate your second issue.

"Now, assuming you have concerns about delay, I would suggest to you that the irregularities, as you have defined them, will not disappear. Although, I must admit that Senator McCloud may get a bit anxious. I will volunteer to speak to Senator McCloud and urge his patience until the far more serious issue of pending terrorism is settled. I believe that he will agree. In the interim, assuming that your declarations of non-action against Mr. Ball are in order, I have advised Mr. Ball to divulge any and all information that will prove useful to you in halting any terrorist acts."

JD acted immediately in pulling out the two declarations of implied innocence to Edward G. Ball signed by the directors of the FBI and the CIA and handed them to Mr. Atkins. After a quick perusal of the virtually identical documents, Atkins nodded to Ball that they were in order and that he should proceed. Both Atkins and JD pulled out small tape recorders to ensure accurate recollection of Ball's statement.

Ball sat up straight in his chair and spoke without notes.

"Gentlemen, I was born in 1888 in Northumberland County, Virginia, to Thomas Ball and Lalla Gresham. I am now almost eighty and approaching the end of my life. I feel the need, with the help of my attorney, George Atkins, to straighten out certain portions of my life that may be misinterpreted by others.

"I freely admit that, for a man with only an elementary school education, I have been very fortunate to have my older sister marry the very wealthy Alfred I. DuPont in 1921, a man who took a liking to me and gave me a management position in the DuPont empire of business enterprises.

"In 1926, I followed Alfred and my sister, Jessie, in their move from Wilmington to Jacksonville, Florida. Alfred proceeded to develop their Epping Forest estate on the St. Johns River as the centerpiece of a large community including what is now the Bolles School on the river and the San Jose Golf Club across the street. By then, Alfred had made me his business partner and we began purchasing large tracts of timberland in northern Florida, as well as several existing business enterprises, including the St. Joe Paper Company and the Florida National Bank.

"After Alfred's sudden death in 1935, his large estate was bequeathed to Jessie. She immediately asked me to manage the Alfred I. DuPont Testamentary Trusts, which I have done faithfully ever since. These trusts have multiplied in value several times under my management, a fact that I admit with considerable pride. All net profits are assigned to the Nemours Foundation dedicated to caring for sick children and the elderly. In addition, since my sister's death in 1970, I have managed her estate with annual awards to the Nemours Foundation. Since I have no heirs, my own personal estate will also be deeded to the Nemours Foundation.

"During the 1930s, the Florida East Coast Railway was in court-ordered bankruptcy, and I was able to purchase a majority share of the ownership as mortgage bonds selling at very low prices. I might add that Patrick Michael O'Shea Junior, Rick's grandfather, followed my lead in purchasing these bonds for the Patrick Michael O'Shea Family Trust established by Henry Flagler in 1897. This investment multiplied during the past fifteen years since I was appointed manager of the railway by order of the federal court in 1961.

"During my fifty years as Trust Administrator, the Testamentary Trusts have increased in value many times to well over a billion dollars, and they continue to increase as we speak. Now, with that brief summary of my career to date, I will turn to the issue at hand.

"After the divorce from my wife of sixteen years in the 1940s, I suffered for two or three years from loneliness. During this depression period, in 1953, I attempted to cure myself with a packaged two-week nightlife adventure in Paris and the French Riviera. The lovely lady assigned to my pleasure encouraged me to drink and gamble heavily in Monte Carlo. The result was a devastating debt of some five million dollars. I don't even remember spending most of the money. When I did not pay the total bill promptly, the package company put it on auction and it was purchased by an investment firm and re-sold with a number of other debts to a wealthy Arab named Prince Hassad El Saud. I learned all of this only after I paid a collection agent to investigate that unpaid debt and the current owner, Prince Saud.

"Last year, some twenty-three years after this foolish vacation escapade, I received a contact from this prince requesting a meeting to discuss my debt. I felt obliged to agree, so he scheduled an appointment in this very room. He attended with the same three unsavory-looking associates. Instead of demanding money, the very erudite Arab, speaking in perfect English, told me that he didn't want my money. He wanted to buy Florida East Coast Railway.

"Prince El Saud was prepared to pay more than the full market value for the railway in addition to cancelling my French debt and causing the story of my wild venture to disappear forever. I replied with confidence that I had no concerns about my reputation and that he should look elsewhere to buy a railway. He stood up and stated that I would be hearing from him further on this matter. All four men left without another word.

"During this past month, the shortest man of the escort group, later identified as Dimitri Chekov, returned unannounced with his tall negro companion to show me a full-color magazine insert, totally devoted to my 1953 escapade, complete with bedroom scenes featuring sexual entanglements with my former companion. Chekov advised me that they were prepared to go to print in a national American magazine within sixty days. He would return for my answer in two weeks time. I told him to get lost.

"Within two weeks, I found the same two men sitting right here in my so-called high-security apartment, when I returned alone from an evening meeting. They presented me with a full set of documents for the purchase and sale of the FECR at a price above market value according to a seemingly bona fide appraisal of current property, equipment and financials at a date two days from that night. I protested that I needed time to have our accountants and attorneys review the documents. He responded that the purchase agreement contained a sixty day due diligence clause for that purpose.

"The short man, named Chekov, then invited the big black man to take me out to the terrace for some air. But, I refrained from assumed physical violence by agreeing to the sale. The deposit and signed agreement were delivered to me by the close of business the next day and the sale was announced the morning after. I have not confessed this blackmail to anyone else, but your offer of clemency was too good to refuse."

"Have you heard anything from Prince El Saud or Chekov since then?" questioned JD.

"Nothing from either of them, but daily communications with the executives of the purchaser, Castle Investment Group, Inc.," responded Ball."Their latest message is that their due diligence is complete and the cash is on-hand ready for closing this week.

"I should also like to throw in a couple of other comments that Chekov let slip. First, they are expecting five metal containers of explosives by freighter in Port Everglades ready for trans-shipment to identified sites in five major cities in the United States by early October. I did not learn the name of the freighter, but I gathered that its arrival is imminent. Second, they have trained five men to accompany the shipments to arm them on the target day. I learned that he plans to have all five bombs blow up simultaneously on the afternoon of Colombus Day. Chekov went so far as to boast that the five explosions would impact over fifteen million persons and become the biggest terrorist attack in U.S. history."

"Mr.Ball," stated JD, as he rose from his chair, "you may have given us enough information to halt the most devastating one-day terrorist attack in history. I am only sorry that we cannot publish your role for fear of potential harm. But I am certain that you will sleep better because of your statement. Mr. Atkins, I see that you have drafted a brief consensus agreement which I will sign on behalf of the United States Government. Then we will schedule a follow-up meeting with you to discuss the O'Shea Family Trust. Thank you both gentlemen. It has been a very good evening for our country. Goodnight."

Within twenty minutes of leaving Ed Ball's apartment, Rick was unlocking the entrance door to the recently re-named "O'Shea Law Firm, PA." The two men immediately went to separate phones to notify their seniors that they had uncovered new and valuable information that needed to be communicated personally as soon as possible. They suggested a group meeting of key officials in the O'Shea conference room in Jacksonville the next day.

Forty minutes later, they had confirmation from all senior participants except Margaret McBride—who did not return the phone call yet— for a meeting on the following day at the O'Shea Law Firm in Jacksonville.

FORTY-FIVE

London, England
September 23, 1977

In a corner office on the top floor of the MI6 building in London, the wall clock indicated seven o'clock in the morning, British Summer Time. The two men sitting down with their early morning tea were Senior Agent Nigel Harris reporting to the Director-General of Middle East Affairs, Sir Alfred North.

"Good morning, Nigel. What fascinating new issue calls for my attendance at this ungodly hour? I certainly hope that it will merit my full attention."

"I do apologize for the early hour, Sir Alfred, but I'm afraid our American brothers need our help with minimum delay. A cooperative effort between our combined agencies has uncovered a potential terrorist threat of unmatched ferocity in several large cities in the United States. I have been concentrating on the source of the large bombs currently in transit across the Atlantic to their unidentified target cities. Our research team estimates that each of these bombs could be of greater strength than the American bombing attacks on Hiroshima and Nagasaki in 1945.

"About three hours ago, I received a communication by coded telex from my reliable source in Tashkent stating that she believes that she has located the bomb factory. I would like your approval, sir, to requisition an Air Force fighter jet to take me out there immediately. Time is of the essence for the Americans."

"Hmm, perhaps I have a better idea. Hold on Nigel." Sir Alfred then looked up another number in his notebook and dialed. "Good morning, Harold; Alfred here. Sorry to ring you so early, but last night at dinner you mentioned that you are headed east today in one of your government's jets. Do you have an extra seat? . . . No, not me, but one of our senior agents who has a very hot situation in Tashkent. I remembered that you Yanks have an air base in that general area and this is an American issue that we are assisting with . . .You do? Splendid! I believe that we can have him over there in forty minutes. Does that sound doable? Great! Thank you, Harold. Have a safe flight."

After hanging up the phone, Sir Alfred advised Nigel to hurry and rustle up his baggage; "a car and driver will be waiting at the rear entrance. It will be my personal driver and he knows the fastest route. Off you go, safe trip."

Nigel rushed down two floors to his office and grabbed his "ready" satchel from the closet, along with his attaché case. He took a minute to take his service pistol out of the case to avoid an issue with Uzbekistan customs and immigration officials. It took another five minutes for him to reach the rear exit, just as Sir Alfred's Jaguar was pulling up to the door. The driver hopped out to hold the door open, but Nigel gently moved him aside: "Save that for the big brass, Tony. I can handle myself."

"Yessir, Mr. Harris. Off we go." And the black Jaguar accelerated through the gate and on to his waiting flight.

As MI6 Senior Agent Nigel Harris was enjoying his ride in the Jaguar, Sir Alfred was greeting the customary early arrival of his personal assistant. "Good morning Susan. I wonder if I could bother you to place a personal call to Charles Malone, Director of the Central Intelligence Agency in Langley, Virginia?"

171

Susan smiled brightly at her aging boss, and replied, "Right away, sir. Remember that it is still night-time over there."

"Of course it is. Well, give it a try anyway. One never knows." He wasn't completely surprised when she popped back into his office: "Director Malone is on the line, sir."

"Charles, good morning! I do apologize for calling you in the wee hours, but we have a new event in the potential American terrorist case, and I wanted to report it to you at the earliest possibility; although I must admit that I didn't expect you to be available at this hour."

"Good morning to you too, Alfred! I suspect that you are enjoying your morning tea about now, while we migrants are overloading on strong coffee. Seriously, though, your call is always welcome, even when I am putting in extra hours on the very case you are calling about. We have just received some additional information which may be the key to breaking it open."

"Good show, old chap! Maybe I can add some fuel. By the way, do you have any reliable assets in Tashkent that we might use?"

"As a matter of fact, we do; depending, of course on what kind of help you need."

"Right! Here is the situation. You may recall that your chaps have been interacting with one of our best men, Senior Agent Nigel Harris . . ."

"Absolutely, the chap who discovered the origin of the fishing boat victims. I met him briefly when he was in our office a couple of weeks ago; an impressive agent."

"That's the man. He brought me in at seven this morning to report that an asset of ours in Tashkent believes that she has discovered the bomb factory that made your trouble. We put him on a military jet—one of yours actually—to explore this lead. The purpose of my call is to find him some back-up in case these folks over there turn out to be less than cooperative."

"I take your point, Alfred, and I am requesting that information as we speak. I will phone you back when I get an answer. Have a great day."

"Thank you, Charles. I will await your call."

FORTY-SIX

Washington, D.C.
September 23, 1977

President Carter welcomed Margaret McBride into the oval office. She immediately began mutual greetings with the top security directors of CIA, FBI. NSA, and her own boss, the President's Security Advisor. Upon completing the circle, she took a seat as the only female in the group; a position that she found normal in the White House.

"Margaret," began the President, "these gentlemen have been discussing with me the frustratingly slow pace of progress on the terrorism threat that looms larger every day. Last night, we received word that the target date for possibly multiple explosions is October 8, Colombus Day, only a little more than two weeks from now. We still can't find the alleged leader, Prince Hassad El Saud, despite apparent help from Interpol as well as individual nations, even including his home country, Saudi Arabia. This scoundrel and his Russian sidekick, Dimtri Chekov, have not surfaced anywhere. We know that the bombs are on a freighter headed for Port Everglades, but we cannot define the ship's identity or where it may be. We know that Chekov has recruited experienced train personnel to monitor the bombs into position, but we cannot identify them. Our people have stopped all train traffic out of Florida and they are searching container cars, but we cannot find anything dangerous either on the trains or in transit from ships in port. In short, although none of these able men are anxious to admit it, we need your coordinative help once again. Are you willing to jump back into the saddle?"

Margaret drew a deep breath before responding. "That is a very succinct summary, Mr. President, and I am certainly complimented that you have singled me out from all of the professional security people here in Washington. However, this is no time for a group of advisors, regardless of their impressive resumes. If I am to become involved, I want a select team of action-oriented persons who are already oriented to the case and who have direct access to the chief executive of each agency in this room, plus the military, for instant decisions. I would prefer to not have any debate about my team choices, but if any should arise, I request that they be sent immediately to this office for instant decision. Those are my terms, sir, and I require unanimous consent of the men in this room in order to proceed."

"Wow," exclaimed FBI Director Tindale. "That sounds pretty dictatorial, Margaret. We are accustomed to collegial rather than unilateral decisions. I would like to think that this group could come together on short notice to achieve consensus as you progress."

Margaret immediately rose from her chair. "Thank you for inviting me, Mr. President, but one dissident is one too many. I decline the offer." And she turned and headed toward the door.

"Whoa back, Margaret," shouted the President. "I do not believe that Aubrey intended to oppose your methods—only to suggest keeping us informed. Is that correct, Aubrey?"

"Wel'l'l'l, Margaret. I believe that I spoke too hastily. Let's do it your way . . . but grant me one small concession on reporting daily progress?"

Margaret paused, but remained standing by the exit door. "I will not concede any group decision-making—two weeks is not enough time for the slow wheels of government bureaucracy. However, with due respect to Director Tindale, I agree to retain one publicist to sit in on all dialogue and send a confidential summary report to each of you on a daily basis. But, I request the FBI Publicist, Barbara Clements, for this position, not because she works for Director Tindale, but because I believe her to be the best publicist in the Federal government."

"Gentlemen," said the President. "I want to get this settled and move on. Please register your opinion to Margaret's proposal: yeah or nay. "All four men said yeah. "There you are, Margaret, full consensus. Please move ahead and select your team. I would like your selections in twenty-four hours."

"Yes sir, Mr. President. You will have them." She then went around and shook hands with each of the men, as well as President Carter.

FORTY-SEVEN

Tashkent, Uzbekistan
September 24, 1977

Although Nigel Harris had never been to this part of the world before, he had been reviewing travel books in preparation for his self-imposed assignment. As the very comfortable Gulf V executive jet began its landing approach, he glanced at the large urban center spread out between impressive mountains guarding the green valley. The scene was highlighted by two rivers flowing through the expanding city—over a million residents in this former key rest stop on the venerable "silk road" linking east and west. It already had adopted many western ways, with large and impressive hotels and office buildings in refreshing oriental architectural designs gleaming in the early afternoon sun.

The plane landed softly and taxied to the executive lounge where his fellow travelers, six American government officials, hurried in to freshen up, before taking off again after re-fuelling. His presence apparently had reduced cabin talk to sports and current news events, so he had no idea where they might be headed, but he was happy to have reached his destination. He shook hands all-around and wished them a pleasant journey. Then he picked up his single suitcase and headed for the government officers at the customs and immigration counter. They checked his British passport and welcomed him to Tashkent, then directed him to a taxi waiting outside.

Sir Alfred's secretary had registered him at the five-star Grand Mir Hotel in the city, a twenty minute drive through humble residential neighborhoods. When he reached the city center, it became clear why this city is promoted as good value. One of his flight companions told him that a British pound would make his driver happy. The driver even offered change, but Nigel waved it off with a cheery smile. He presented his passport at the registration counter and was astounded to hear perfect English in response: "Welcome to Tashkent, Mr. Harris. If you need any assistance, please do not hesitate to contact me. My name is Sonya. Here is the key to your room and a note left for you earlier this morning."

Harris responded that he needed advice on how much local currency he should carry for sightseeing excursions? The lovely Sonya replied by offering him a small booklet for English-speaking tourists which listed average prices for a wide variety of services and goods, and then suggested that his money was worth much more in Uzbekistan than in England. He settled on one hundred pounds and proceeded to the cashier.

He then took the lift to his upper floor and unlocked the door to his room with a dramatic view of the mountains—a lovely place to enjoy ones-self if he didn't have work to do. The note was from the MI6 asset named Tarina: "Lunch is good at the Kazak Kabin just down the street."

Although he had no idea how to recognize Tarina, he assumed that she would pick him out of the crowd. So he strolled down to the restaurant, which took up the entire sidewalk with tables and chairs. As he began to look around, a small, skinny waiter approached him, "Meester Herrice"? Harris nodded the affirmative. "Pleez to come to courtyard, much nicer, okay?"

"Okay," he replied, and followed the little man through a very busy mid-day meal crowd to a corner table partially concealed by a palm tree. A single woman in Arabic attire with her head covered jumped up from her seat: Nigel Harris, welcome to Tashkent. I am Tarina Moomtaz. Happy to meet you." And she stuck out her hand with a firm shake. She was of medium height with an olive complexion and large brown eyes. His first guess from her face alone was that she was under thirty.

"Well, I am happy to meet you as well, Tarina. I do apologize for my failure to learn Arabic. I'm afraid we must communicate only in English."

"Not a problem, my friend. I will enjoy the opportunity to practice. I learned the basics in school and improved with a job as hotel receptionist; and then, of course, my past five years employed by your company. Besides, even if you did speak Arabic, people in Uzbekistan would not understand you. Our dialect is quite different from the Mediterranean Arabic. Anyway, why don't I order lunch for you and then we can talk. Okay?"

"Okay," he replied.

The skinny waiter returned and they exchanged phrases with each other, before he bowed politely and hurried away. He soon returned with a pitcher of brown-looking liquid that was cold and refreshing, a plate of unleavened bread and a dip that appeared grey, and tasted like sesame. But that was just for starters. The waiter brought a wonderful hot broth, somewhat oriental in flavor, then a sizable bowl of white rice and a lamb stew to mix with the rice.

"Is good?" she asked.

"Very good," he replied, and kept on eating. Harris was amazed at the quantity of food that he consumed, and still had room for the pastry dessert and delicious mint tea.

Finally, the Englishman leaned back in his chair and said "Enough, I cannot eat any more. We must stop."

His antics caused peals of laughter from his new companion. Of course, she had eaten much more modestly and spent most of her time watching him enjoy his massive meal.

"Now," she said, "there are two men who have been waiting to meet you. They didn't want to interrupt you meal, so they have waited until you were finished. May I call them over?"

"Wait a minute, Tarina, I don't know anyone in Tashkent, other than you, of course."

"But, Mr. Nigel these are Americans from the 'Company' who are instructed to assist you. They are here today just to meet you."

"Oh-h, those kind of Americans! Yes, by all means, please invite them to join us." Upon Tarina's beckoning hand, two fit-looking men if average height dressed in western attire came over to meet Harris and discretely display their CIA credentials as they shook hands and introduced themselves. "Welcome to Tashkent, Nigel," greeted the first agent. Don't bother with your creds. The company wired us your picture. I am Jack Tulley and this is my partner Al Golding. I suggest that we walk a short distance to a safe house we have down the street so we can chat in private."

"Excellent idea," replied Nigel as he rose and gave Tarina some local currency to cover the lunch cost. She caught up with them outside and returned most of the money to him, explaining that food is very low cost in Uzbekistan.

178

A few minutes later the four of them were seated at a table in a room overlooking a courtyard just a block from his hotel. Nigel led off the discussion by asking the two CIA agents how much information they received about his mission. Jack explained that they had just received a "top secret" dispatch through the embassy courier to provide you optimum assistance on a high priority mission. "MI6 Senior Agent Nigel Harris would reveal all after arrival."

"Very well," replied Nigel. "I assume that first names are appropriate among us"—the other three nodded their assent—"so I will be equally concise with my explanation. It appears that a wealthy Saudi is bankrolling a planned act of terrorism in five U.S. cities by igniting five gigantic bombs being delivered in freight containers by ship from the Port of Poti on the Black Sea. We believe that their arrival at a Florida port is imminent, and a multi-agency force is now at work searching for the containers. They are due to be trans-shipped by train to the designated target cities that they have not yet identified. I was instructed to investigate the possible source of the bomb's manufacture to learn what we can from the bomb-makers. Yesterday, our local asset Tarina informed us through her embassy contact that she believes she has located the source. I managed to get a ride on one of your executive jets coming this way and here I am eager to hear Tarina's information." With that, he turned to his new friend who now had the full attention of all three agents.

"Gentlemen, you please will accept my apologies for my poor English, but I will do my best. My cousin, whose name is unimportant, lives in the small town of Charjew, just across the border in Turkmenistan, south of the ancient Uzbekistan fortress city of Bukhara, about six hundred kilometers southwest by road from here."

"I am familiar with that beautiful city," interjected Al. "We have an informal asset living there who may be helpful."

"Excellent," replied Nigel. "Please continue, Tarina."

"Yes, my cousin is an engineer on the railway that runs from the junction at Charjew northwest along the border of Uzbekstan with Turkmenistan all the way past the Aral Sea to Kazakhstan and on to the Black Sea port city of Poti in Georgia. His general cargo is ore from the mines south of Charjew around the mountain town of Mary. Before you ask, I do not know the origin of this name, but I do know that he hauls trainloads of ore from this town twice per week all the way to Poti.

"When I received Nigel's request about unusual freight containers traveling to Poti, I decided to pay a visit to my cousin. Although it was against the rules, he let me ride with him in the engine up to Mary. About 20 kilometers south of Charjew, we passed a small village that has a large metal building with a side track from the railroad running into it. Adjacent to the building was a large sealed vessel tank similar to the small ones that we use for holding butagas to burn for cooking. I counted four large freight containers sitting outside the building which, according to my cousin, are similar to the five that he had picked up from this factory and hauled to Poti with his regular ore shipment about one month ago. He told me that this factory and the metal houses for workers were built here about one year ago, and that this was the first shipment he had taken from it. He tried to speak with one of the workers, but they could not understand each other's language.

"My cousin's wife added that some of the wives of workers come to the Charjew market each week in an old bus along the railroad maintenance road to buy food for all of the workers. Other than that, none of their neighbors seem to know anything more about the factory. At the beginning of the summer, that road is used by kayakers to haul their boats up the river to ride down on the rapids from spring melting of snow. Other than that, it is rarely used.

"So, gentlemen, I thought that this building might be the factory you are seeking. Was I right in contacting Mr. Nigel?"

"Absolutely, you were right, Tarina," replied Nigel. "I will submit a request for your bonus as soon as I return to Britain. But, tell me, did you or your cousin see any soldiers or guards with weapons around the factory?"

"Yes, we saw two in a tiny building near the entrance, and my cousin's wife told me that two with guns always ride the bus to market. All the other men that we saw appeared to be workers."

"Jack, Al, is either of you a linguist?" asked Nigel.

"I'm afraid not, Nigel. We get to learn enough of the local language to get by at just about the same rate that we get moved to a new posting—one of the issues I will put in my book after I retire."

"Well, we could just get permission to put a couple of rockets into the factory at night with limited human loss, but we wouldn't learn anything that way. First of all, we need to confirm Tarina's information with photography. I'm thinking of a potential kayak exploration in a four-wheel drive vehicle."

"Now, that is an area of potential expertise," replied Jack. "Al, here, has cameras of all shapes and sizes as well as the ability to use them covertly."

"Don't go overboard, Jack, but yes, we probably could work up some pictures, perhaps even get inside if we had a linguist."

"How about the university?" asked Tarina. "It has a well-regarded language department."

"Good thought, Tarina, but I had better brief my superior first. It's still morning in London, so I will go over to the British Embassy and communicate our knowledge to date and seek further guidance. How be we all meet back here at eleven tomorrow morning?"

Each of his new companions nodded in agreement, and Nigel asked Tarina to help him find a taxi.

Nigel was able to reach Sir Alfred on the secure line from the British Embassy. He summarized his connections and intelligence to date, and he requested his director's guidance on how to proceed. Sir Alfred responded that the Service maintained a multi-lingual expert in the Istanbul Embassy and he would check immediately on his availability to join Nigel for a couple of days in Uzbekistan. He would have a note delivered to his hotel within a few hours.

"Nigel, your first objective is to verify this location as the bomb factory and, if so, to ascertain the source of its support. The second objective may require capturing one of their management team for interrogation. I like your kayak scheme and suggest that you and your companions fly over to Bukhara and rent a suitable vehicle for ground transportation. Upon completion, see if you can rent a helicopter or small plane for aerial pictures. Send everything you get to me personally by courier and have your American friends send copies to Margaret McBride through the CIA priority transmission. Good luck and play safe."

Nigel immediately requested assistance from the Embassy staff to phone his CIA colleagues to make arrangements for travel and necessary gear, including informal hiking apparel and weapons. He then contacted Tarina to ascertain her cousin's schedule for the next two days and plan to accompany them to Bukhara and beyond in the morning. Then he returned to the hotel for a light dinner and to bed.

FORTY-EIGHT

Bukhara, Uzbekistan
September 25, 1977

The commuter flight from Tashkent to Bukhara had taken just over an hour and the Range Rover rental vehicle was waiting with a full tank of fuel. The four travelers, with Tarina in traditional Islam covered local attire, the two Americans in their full length gallabayas, and the Brit in jeans and a T-shirt. If asked, the three locals were exploring potential sites for a British kayaking club and Nigel was the advance man. Tarina was to be their spokesman as well as guide. And a Turk named Samir, a multi-lingual American government staff specialist from the United States Embassy in Ankara, joined them at the airport where his flight from Istanbul landed shortly after theirs.

Al, having been to Bukhara in the past, became the designated driver with Samir in the passenger seat to navigate, and Tarina, Jack and Nigel in the rear bench seat. They first drove to Al's asset's home who had rented the equipment they had prescribed: a single two-man kayak with paddles to go on the roof for appearance, light back-packs for the three men containing emergency supplies, cameras, and light weapons (the latter being banned on airplanes flying out of Uzbekistan airports). They also each brought a carry-on bag with a change of clothes if necessary. The local asset was to charter a four-passenger helicopter for late in the afternoon for Al to photograph the target site from the air.

With everything loaded, Tarina directed Al onto the paved road south to the border with Turkmenistan and the town of Charjew where they would lunch with Tarina's cousin and receive instructions to the unpaved maintenance road up the river valley. The border crossing proved to be a non-event as the lonely immigration officers were delighted to welcome visitors to their sparsely settled corner of Turkmenistan. Samir had no difficulty displaying the five passports and describing the purpose of their trip, an apparent frequent recreation earlier in the spring when the river filled with melted snow runoff.

Tarina supplied simple instructions to her cousin's sturdy house on the edge of Charjew and the group enjoyed a typical lunch with the family of five children all involved with their mother cooking and serving the meal, eaten around a wooden table in the neatly landscaped terrace adjoining the house. At the end of the meal, Nigel presented the local family with a number of gifts that he had requested Tarina purchase the previous evening.

After leaving his home, the railroad engineer led them to the unimproved vehicle track beside the train tracks up the river valley, and they moved uphill at a slow pace. Although Al was a careful driver, the terrain proved a rough ride. It took them the better part of an hour before they came abreast of the large metal building described by Tarina the previous evening.

An apparent security guard emerged from a tiny guard house and approached the Range Rover. As previously agreed, everyone sat tight except Samir who emerged from the front seat with a smile and handshake for the guard. He then addressed him in salutations from several nomadic languages before the guard reacted in a friendly manner and responded to a welcome that he understood. The two men then conversed for several minutes with the guard becoming more animated as they progressed. He beckoned Samir over to view a welded tank resting on a flat rail car, which gave Al the opportunity to snap some photographs on one of his smaller cameras. He quickly hid it as Samir and the guard walked back toward the Range Rover.

Samir asked everyone to emerge from the vehicle and he proceeded to introduce each one to the guard who shook hands and smiled at each new introduction. Evidently, Samir had explained the kayak skills of the men, because the guard invited them to follow him across the rail tracks to view the river west of the rail track. Samir cleverly instructed the men to examine the river more carefully, allowing Al to photograph the metal containers in the yard and the large tanks of what appeared to be liquefied gas. Soon a few workmen emerged from the metal building to meet the visitors. Samir quickly translated for the newcomers the same story he had related to the guard and introduced them to the sportsmen from Tashkent and their visitor from England. Additional workers emerged, a few of whom appeared to have some ability to converse with Tarina in her native language. She learned that the men were skilled metal workers from Kyrgyzstan to the east who were recruited for relatively handsome salaries to bring their wives and small children by train to work at this location for two years building the welded containers that contained internal tanks as well as miniature living quarters for guards to travel with them by train to blow up hated infidels in western countries. They did not appear to relate the two Americans or the Brit to these enemy infidels. These were deep mountain men with no education other than the metal skills they had learned at a factory in Kyrgyzstan. The rest of the world was a mystery to them.

Suddenly a loud siren sounded and a former military vehicle roared into the gathering outside the factory building. Several security men with automatic weapons appeared and began separating the workers from the visitors. A small, bald man in western clothes appeared and walked up to Samir. He appeared to be a manager of some sort and engaged in loud discourse with the gentle, always-smiling Samir. In the interim the guards herded the workers back into the factory and assembled behind their manager with guns held menacingly toward the visitors.

Samir paused in his spirited conversation with the manager and walked over to Nigel. "How much cash do you have with you? He wants to hold us for ransom, but I believe that we can make a deal on the spot."

Nigel admitted that he had about one thousand British pounds, but he suggested that they were just working men looking for a vacation, but they would be pleased to pay five hundred pounds as a gift to the workers so that they could bring their friends next spring to kayak down the river. He counted out the five large bills slowly into Samir's hands and was left with one additional hundred pound note that he returned to his pocket. Samir returned to the manager and related that story, whereupon, as Nigel expected, he demanded the additional bill that had returned to Nigel's pocket. Samir asked for the last bill and Nigel slowly gave it up as though it was his last money in the world. He then hurriedly turned and demanded that everyone get in the Range Rover. They did as he asked and Al turned the big vehicle around and headed north back down the track as the manager and guards looked stunned by the rapid action. Not a shot was fired.

The trip back down to Charjew and then on to the border crossing toward Bukhara was substantially faster than the trip up. Everyone congratulated Samir for his language skills and Nigel for his payoff strategy. But Samir protested that their language was a rather simple dialect of Farsi inherited from ancient Persian conquests, and Nigel claimed that he could have saved money if he had lower-price bills in his possession. He believed that these people had little knowledge of monetary values. "Anyway, my friends, we accomplished our first objective. This is the bomb factory, but there was no sign of the investment source. Jack, I would be grateful if you could document our day and send it off with Al's pictures to both our countries. Al, I would be pleased if you could hop into the helicopter we reserved and take some aerial pictures to complete our task. Then we can catch our evening flight back to Tashkent where I will spring for dinner prior to catching a morning flight to Poti.

Nigel was amazed at the scale of the railroad yards and freighter berths that he could see from the air as his flight approached Poti the next morning. He promised himself to read more about this part of the world in future.

Once on the ground, he discovered exceptionally helpful harbor officials and local police to help him with his quest for the armed freight that left this port a month previous. He learned that a short Russian man was the owner agent, who inspected the cargo very carefully before it sailed away on the Polar Star freighter with a mid-fueling port at Gibraltar. So, he immediately booked flights to get him to Gibraltar that night.

Although Nigel had vacationed in Gibraltar with a brief love of his life many years ago, he never spent much time enjoying the physical features. This trip was no exception. It took less than an hour to learn that the Polar Star cancelled its berth and docked instead at the port adjoining Cadiz north along the Spanish coast. So, he rented a car and drove the two hours to Cadiz, only to find that the Polar Star had actually berthed at El Puerto de Santa Maria, just north of Cadiz on the Bahia de Cadiz. But then came the surprise. Neither the ship nor its crew ever left this berth.

Further inquiries revealed that the owners apparently fired the entire crew and replaced them with a new crew that they had flown in from Italy. But a further inquiry to the immigration office reported that there is no national exit record for any member of this crew, and none have resident addresses in Spain. An ongoing investigation by immigration officers produced no information on any of these crew members, including the captain.

The owners, apparently located in Marseille, France, re-registered the ship in Liberia as the "Empress IV" which set sail for Port Everglades, Florida after every container on board was re-addressed to a fresh final destination—a total of sixty-two separate U.S. destinations for the cargo containers on board. The ship's arrival estimate in Florida was recorded as September 25, the very day that Nigel was in Cadiz.

Upon learning all of this information, Nigel Harris located the British Consulate in Cadiz and prepared a summary brief to be wired "top secret" to Sir Alfred in London, with the suggestion that it be forwarded to Margaret McBride in Washington as soon as possible. He reported in the cover note that he planned to catch a flight from Gibraltar to Fort Lauderdale that afternoon to provide background information to the Americans. He received an immediate wire in return advising him that virtually every freighter destined for Port Everglades in the past twenty-four hours had cancelled its Port Everglades berth and was re-routing to Charleston, South Carolina. Most of the search team was in transit to the new location. However, Margaret McBride has set up her new task force in the Federal Building in Jacksonville. Sir Alfred suggested that Nigel report directly to her. So, he quickly changed his travel plans to Jacksonville and drove his rental car back to the Gibraltar Airport.

FORTY-NINE

Port Everglades, Florida
September 25, 1977

The combined task force of FBI and CIA agents, as well as a contingent of Florida State Police, had swarmed into the terminal and off-loading freighters at Port Everglades at eight o'clock in the morning. They were equipped with magnetic detectors and sniffer dogs as well as carpentry tools for opening interior cargos in metal containers. The team had already inspected trainloads of containers halted south of Jacksonville, where a single track was open through the Broward Yard to cross the St. Johns River for destinations throughout the country. As of the current date, no trace of combustible cargo had been discovered and the team was of sufficient size to examine every cargo arriving at Port Everglades next to Fort Lauderdale.

The team was scheduled to move on to Miami docks on the following day. After that, if nothing was discovered, they would work their way north through other Atlantic ports in Florida, Georgia and South Carolina. If contraband cargo was in transit through one of these ports, they were determined to locate and destroy it. The only identification they possessed was that the cargo was in five custom-designed freight containers that looked like normal containers.

The joint task force was under the overall direction of FBI Senior Agent Jordan Hale with agents from both federal agencies organized into platoons of twelve, each targeted to specific cargoes both off-loaded and still on board. Florida state and local policemen also were assigned to many of the platoons in order to enlarge the team and expedite the inspection process. Each container received a bright green spray of paint upon clearance.

At noon, when the team stopped for an on-site delivery truck lunch, Jordan Hale was surprised to see Margaret McBride enter the site seeking him out.

"Well, this is a surprise, Margaret. Welcome to our playfield. It's great to see you again."

"Thank you, Jordan. I apologize for arriving unannounced, but President Carter has just appointed me manager of an inter-agency emergency anti-terrorism group and I need your skills. We report only to the President and we have carte blanche to act decisively in order to find and stop this insane attack. I realize that you are fully occupied here, but if I could find an immediate replacement for you, would you consider serving with me for the next couple of weeks?"

"Wow, Margaret, that's a big question. How 'bout I offer you one of our super lunch specials and we draw up a couple of chairs to discuss it?"

"Perfect," replied Margaret with a grin. "I've always wanted to have lunch at a freight terminal. Let's do it."

Jordan led her across the entry road to one of two lunch trucks offering surprisingly diverse menus of food offerings. Most of Jordan's team had already been served so it took only a few minutes to select a sandwich and drinks from the friendly caterer. They carried them back across the road to a portable office which Jordan used as his headquarters. Margaret mounted the steps with no difficulty and found a relatively new mobile chair to pull up to the small meeting table. Jordan found a sign announcing "Meeting in Progress" to hang on the exterior of the entry door, and then took a seat across from Margaret.

After eating half of her toasted flatbread sandwich, Margaret paused to begin her recruitment pitch. "Jordan, last night two of our younger attorneys taped an amazing confession in Jacksonville from Edward Ball, Chairman of the Florida East Coast Railway. He claimed to be blackmailed into the sale of the railway by a Saudi Prince living in France, who was represented by the notorious international criminal, Dimitri Chekov. "

"Fantastic! What was the quid pro quo?"

"It turns out that Mr. Ball had a rather sordid incident of sex and gambling in France many years ago that he wants expunged from historic records, including a five million dollar note now owned by the prince. In relating this blackmail to our two attorneys, Joshua Dempsey and Rick O'Shea, he received expunction promises signed by the Directors of the CIA and FBI."

"Amazing," replied Jordan. "But, I imagine that they were coerced by President Carter."

"I cannot speculate on their actions, but it worked in our favor. Ball claimed that the prince wants the railway to ship the bombs. Your team cannot yet identify the five largest cities in the United States targeted for simultaneous explosions on Colombus Day, the second Monday in October, only a couple of weeks from now. So, you are already at the tip of the issue by searching for the initial arrival of the bombs.

"However, my concerns go beyond your search to the possibility that your team may not succeed. We need an immediate strategy with alternative tactics to resolve this threat. I need an informed small team to brainstorm and implement without wasting any time on bureaucratic niceties. Will you join me? I can fix the exchange with Director Tindale."

Hale replied without hesitation: "Yes, of course. I can pass on this task to an assistant and be out of here this afternoon."

"Excellent! Your replacement is actually waiting in my car, and my government jet awaits us at the Fort Lauderdale Airport executive terminal. I will ask him to join us immediately and we can pick up your luggage on the way to the airport."

By five o'clock that same afternoon, the first meeting of Margaret McBride's Anti-terrorism Task Force was convened in a secure conference room on the top floor of the Federal Building on Bay Street in Jacksonville. Because of her busy day, the principal participants were summoned to travel to Jacksonville immediately, as requested by McBride the prior evening by Rick and JD. The team members were already briefed by the efficient FBI Publicist, Susan Clements. She also had briefed the President and select Cabinet members on the participants of the new Task Force. All entrants to this building were subjected to electronic search by the lobby security staff.

The eight participants requested by Margaret, in addition to MI6 Senior Agent Nigel Harris, still involved in Uzbekistan, the team gathered at the Jacksonville Federal Building included FBI Senior Agent Jordan Hale, Agent Joshua Dempsey, FECR Senior Counsel George Atkins, FECR Senior Vice President Operations Mathew Cantrell, Amtrac Vice President Operations Richard Owen, and Attorneys Mike and Rick O'Shea. McBride also invited Chandra Jones because of her familiarity with the case. Non member attendees seated at a separate table for communications were FBI Senior Publicist Barbara Clements and Senior Court Stenographer Janet Sproule.

"Thank you, everyone, for interrupting your busy schedules and agreeing to join us on short notice," began McBride, " I suggest that we use no titles and only first names. My long-time secretary and court stenographer Janet Sproule has made first name tags for everyone. She will keep a verbatim record of our meetings along with the tape recording from the table microphones. Sitting at the table with Janet is FBI Senior Publicist Barbara Clements who will summarize key issues from each meeting to keep senior government officials informed of our progress. Thank you both for your participation.

"Although Chandra Jones is a prominent local reporter, she is here as a key participant in revealing this proposed terrorist plot. She has pledged to keep all meeting discussions and actions confidential.

"Like Chandra and the two O'Shea attorneys, Jordan Hale and Joshua Dempsey have been involved from the beginning of our knowledge of this activity, along with British MI6 Senior Agent Nigel Harris, who is busy tracking the source of the explosives purportedly used in the bombs. We hope to hear a report from Nigel who is planning to join us later this evening.

"Additional non-government invitees are FECR Senior Counsel George Atkins and VP Operations Mathew Cantrell— two men who are familiar with Florida operations as well as connecting routes— and also, Amtrac VP Operations Richard Owen, who is our expert on nationwide rail traffic."

Margaret then updated them on all incidents and information to date, including the Ed Ball statement. She admitted that, despite intensive bulletins to immigration personnel, as well as local police, we have no sightings of Prince Hassad El Saud or any of his known associates. She then recognized the raised hand of Mathew Cantrell.

"Margaret, just before coming to this meeting, I received a message from our Miami office that several inbound freighters have cancelled their berth reservations in Miami and Port Everglades. Evidently their owners are organizing trans-shipment schedules with the Port of Charleston, South Carolina. This is bad for our FECR business, but it may open up new search opportunities for our federal investigation team."

"Thank you, Mathew. Jordan, you might like to ensure that your replacement in Port Everglades is up-to-date on that news, as well as take immediate action to move part or all of his inspectors north to Charleston."

"You bet, Margaret. Excuse me a moment while I use the safe-line phone in the adjoining room."

Rick then interjected: "Margaret, I am sure that you are aware of the several ports north of Florida that have rail connections in addition to Charleston—Brunswick and Savannah, in particular— as well as other ports in Florida, including Cocoa and Jacksonville. We might open up a phone bank with each of them to advise us on new berth reservations."

"That's an excellent suggestion, Rick," added Mathew. "Margaret, allow me to coordinate a phone team right here in our Jacksonville FECR office?"

"Yes, Mathew, please do so . . . and thank you. Meanwhile, I am going to call upon Richard Owen to set up his projector and the pull-down screen so we can explore potential target cities and the routes and times to access them. In addition, Richard, perhaps you can use your knowledge to identify potential explosion sites in target cities?"

"I will have a go at all of those topics, Margaret. Just give me a few minutes to set up."

The team then spent the next two hours focused on Richard and his information on the largest potential target cities and most efficient routing to them. They agreed to meet at eight the next morning for further discussion and analysis.

FIFTY

Atlantic Ocean, Empress IV
September 25, 1977

Concurrently with the Jacksonville Anti-terrorist Task Force meeting, the new Daniel Chester (formerly Dimitri Chekov) was meeting with the captain on the bridge of the Empress IV container freighter (formerly Polar Star). It was now sailing north in parallel with the eastern coast of the United States, toward its reserved berth at the Port of Charleston, South Carolina. Prior to boarding his chartered two-person rental helicopter in Charleston, Chester, as chief representative of the ship owner (an obscure firm in Liberia), had confirmed the berth reservations and trans-shipment rail coordination for the Empress IV in Charleston.

During the drive to Charleston from his new condominium home overlooking the beach in Amelia Island Plantation, Chester spent two hours in Savannah lunching with the Assistant Harbormaster (the Harbormaster being in hospital recovering from a mild heart attack). In addition to the fine food at the waterfront

Hilton Restaurant, the Assistant Harbormaster received an envelope with fifty one-hundred dollar bills to ensure the coordination of an as-yet un-named container ship to berth adjacent to rail access for express rail transmission to five named cities. As arranged, the ship called in to request emergency berthing because of mechanical problems, at which time the ship's name—Empress IV— was revealed for the Assistant Harbormaster's records. He and Mr. Chester parted as the best of friends.

Later that day, after arriving safely aboard the Empress IV in moderate seas, Chester/Chekov and the captain enjoyed a couple of drinks of fine Finnish vodka in the captain's stateroom, before reviewing the plan for the next few days. The captain had duplicated confirmation of Chester's ship's berth arrangements with the Port of Charleston for September 25 prior to entering the Savannah ship channel. He contacted the Assistant Harbormaster in Savannah to secure an emergency berth requirement for his disabled vessel, the Empress IV out of Liberia, which was in the process of changing course for Savannah Harbor.

Thus, as planned, Mr. Chester was present with the captain after the Assistant Harbormaster had confirmed a berth and immediately sent a pilot and two tugs to assist the captain in docking. Chester introduced the crew to a small African-American man named William, who offered to treat the entire crew and officers at dinner in a nearby restaurant that evening as a safe trip welcome from the ship's owner. He offered to provide guide services to the restaurant once they had landed and secured the ship.

The Don's early evening meeting at the Savannah Holiday Inn small conference room once again included the five trained monitors, along with Big Moe and his cousin Walter to listen to the seemingly elder words of The Don. He welcomed them all to Savannah and reported that their ship had landed safely with their "care" packages.

Sorting and loading would take about two days before they could be smuggled into their separate quarters for their rail journeys to the target cities. He would join them again for a departure meeting at which time they each would learn their destinations and target sites. He then answered questions for an hour before driving back down to his final meeting of the day.

Once again, as Chester drove into Mr. Stanton's driveway at Amelia Island Plantation, the garage door was open for his arrival. It closed immediately after he parked inside, due to the attention of one of Stanton's security men. The big African-American then ushered Chester into the house and on to Stanton's spacious study. The older man welcomed him from his reading chair and waved Chester to a chair where a fresh drink of vodka-on-the-rocks awaited him on a side table.

"To your good health, sir," Chester raised the glass to his host. "We have completed a very successful day, and now William and the Corsicans are tidying up the remainder. William will then go on-board to direct some dockyard laborers I hired to clean out the officer quarters, while Big Moe and Walter continue to care for our five monitors. The cargo is scheduled for unloading tomorrow, when I have retained additional local laborers to replenish the supply of dock workers and missing ship's crew."

"Excellent work, Mr. Chester. Help yourself to another vodka. You have earned it. We are almost done with our work in America, after which you will be one million dollars richer. How does that feel?"

"Your Excellency, I learned as a young man never to count the chickens until they are hatched. I will feel exhilarated when five explosions have erupted as planned. Until then, sir, I am pleased to share a drink with you, but no excitement until we have reached our goal."

"Fair enough, Mr. Chester. Oh, by the way, my contacts tell me that your original name and mine are on the FBI "most wanted list," so I suggest that you get used to your new name for the indefinite future. It will serve you better than the old."

"Thank you, sir. I am growing fond of it." He then swallowed the remainder of his vodka and bid his employer a pleasant night. He returned to the garage to take his car to his own parking space and enjoy a sound sleep in his oceanfront condominium apartment.

FIFTY-ONE

Amelia Island Plantation, Florida
September 26, 1977

The two men were seated on the balcony of Daniel Chester's rental apartment overlooking the Atlantic Ocean and sand beach at Amelia Island Plantation resort in Florida. It was a cloudless morning with a gentle breeze from the ocean providing a refreshing coolant.

"Congratulations, Mr. Chester. It appears that the Empress IV has docked in Savannah successfully and unloading operations have begun. Your bribe to the Assistant Harbormaster proved to be the right amount for our priority unloading."

"Thank you, sir. It is going well, but the big issue is to find and transfer our five containers to the right trains for their rapid routing to the assigned destinations. We must bolster the warehouse crew without irritating them with non-union workers. I suggest that we make a donation to the union party fund of five thousand dollars cash with no strings attached. "

"Alright, that seems a reasonable investment. Drop into my house on your way north, and you can pick up a paper bag with that amount in one hundred dollar bills. I will add ten more bills for a tip to the warehouse manager."

"Excellent! I will be certain to transfer the major amount in full view of a couple of workers so that he will not be tempted to take a higher amount for his personal use."

"Good idea, Daniel. Your own million dollars is getting closer by the minute. By the way, how did the Corsican dinner party turn out last night?"

"It was just as successful as the Spanish affair, sir. Even more successful, when you consider that they located an abandoned quarry which accommodated the entire crew in a standing lake in the bottom. It proved to be over twenty feet deep, which is ample for the weighted body bags they used. By the way, sir, you have given me no instructions for the ship after we have unloaded. No new crew has been identified."

"Quite right, Daniel! I would have confided in you earlier, but I felt that you had enough details on your mind. Now that we are nearing the end of our assignment, I believe that we should retain an arson crew and burn it at the dock. We could use your own team if you like, with a suitable bonus, of course. The ship has ample fuel left for a good blaze, especially if we added our left-over 'Semtex' from the Jacksonville explosion. In addition to the insurance I will collect, it could create a very nice diversion for our federal agents, if they should decide to spread their search down here from Charleston."

"Very clever, sir! Your creative ideas are a major reason that I enjoy working for you. In fact, this is a good time for me to mention that I would be pleased to manage another terrorist attack for you after we complete this one—under another name of course."

"You don't like Daniel Chester?"

"Excuse me, I have no problem with Daniel Chester as a name, but I believe that adding a new one would provide an even larger shield for me in my travels."

"Good point, but I suggest that you find a quiet island resort somewhere for a few months and I will be in touch after we are comfortable that no traces have been left from this affair. But, have no fear, my associates and I are very pleased with your management skills. Your future involvement with us is almost certain, especially since our bomb-making friends are still hard at work on additional bombs for our exclusive use."

"Very well, Your Excellency. I must prepare now for my work in Savannah."

"Indeed!" replied Stanton, as he rose and waved farewell.

FIFTY-TWO

Jacksonville, Florida
September 26, 1977

Margaret McBride's task force had been meeting all morning in Jacksonville's Federal Office Building, examining a set of parameters to rank large American cities as potential targets. Central city blast sites accessible by rail were second only to damage estimates in terms of projected human fatalities as prime parameters. But such locations required extensive telephone time by the three railway experts on the team, especially when they included detailed location maps sent by special delivery and now adorning the walls of the conference room.

Over lunch, the discussion had turned to the briefs from MI6 Senior Agent Nigel Harris, first from Tashkent and then from Cadiz. The name change of the freighter to Empress IV had been pursued immediately. Not surprisingly, they learned that the ship had cancelled its Port Everglades berth and rail connections in lieu of new reservations at the Port of Charleston, South Carolina. Margaret passed this information to the new search team director who was en route to Charleston. However, they had just learned from a direct inquiry to the Charleston Harbormaster that, although the Empress IV did have a berth reserved, it had not yet arrived or even requested a pilot and tugs.

Nigel's interesting report on the recently constructed bomb factory suggested a variety of follow-up activities; but clearly, they must be secondary to finding and defusing the bombs in transit. Only then did they plan to trace the ownership and destroy the bomb factory in Turkmenistan.

When they returned from lunch, Chandra noted that she had received a phone call from Tina Jones, her cousin in Savannah who was a reporter for the *Savannah Morning News*. She returned the call, but her Tina was out of the office and she left a call-back message. Her cousin returned the call about three o'clock to report that a large container ship had docked in Savannah late yesterday afternoon and was in the process of unloading freight containers for trans-shipment by truck and rail. Her cousin had tried to schedule an interview with the ship's captain, but apparently he had disappeared along with his entire crew. Tina knew that Chandra was involved with a story about terrorist bombs being shipped into the country, and she wanted to know if Chandra would like to share a byline.

"Absolutely, Tina, it would be a pleasure to share a story with you. Do you know the name of the ship?"

"That's one of the weird things about this event," replied Tina. "The name was painted over last night, and, when I phoned the Assistant Harbormaster, he replied that the ship's name was in the process of being changed and that he could not provide the current name or the prior name."

"Really! I am on my way," said Chandra. "I will pick up my cameraman and meet you at your office in a couple of hours." She then phoned her cameraman, Jerry Brozovitch, and told him to be at the curb in front of the television station ready to go in ten minutes. She then called Rick to let him know that she was heading for Savannah and she would report to him this evening. After a brief explanation to Mary McBride, Chandra dashed out of the Federal Building to pick up her car in the building garage and then drive over to pick up Jerry. He was waiting at the curb with his equipment ready to travel.

"What's up, Chandra?" asked Jerry as she headed for the north ramp to I-95. His obviously excited reporter smiled at him and said, "We may have struck pay dirt, Jerry. My cousin, Tina, a reporter in Savannah, just called me about a container ship that slipped into Savannah last night without a name. The entire crew, including the captain, disappeared overnight, and the containers are being unloaded for trans-shipment under supervision by the owner representative. It sounds like it could be our bomb people and I want to be first to capture it on film."

"Super, let's roll," replied Jerry."Shout out if you get sleepy and I'll take over." With that, he reclined his seat and appeared to go right to sleep.

FIFTY-THREE

Savannah, Georgia
September 26, 1977

It was six-thirty that evening when Chandra and Jerry picked up Tina at the *Savannah Morning News* office and then followed her instructions to the harbor warehouse. They spotted the freighter right away where two separate cranes were unloading containers down to yard tractors that were organizing them for loading onto railway flat cars at the adjacent rail yard. The supervisor was a short elderly-looking man who was assisted by two African-Americans recording the shipping label on each container as it came off the ship. They then returned to the supervisor for train directions.

"Oh-oh," exclaimed Chandra. "The shorter of the two runners knows me. He was part of the kidnapping team and is named William. He must not recognize me." She hurried to the trunk of her car to find a shawl that would mask her facial features.

Meanwhile, Jerry organized his equipment to record the freighter and begin filming the unloading process. Tina managed to find a couple of workers that Chandra could interview about the ship and its cargo—almost one hundred containers with sixty-two separate destinations. She confirmed from the interviews that the sudden disappearance of the entire crew was a mystery and the owner representative was managing the downloading and trans-shipment assignments with local laborers. As she finished her worker interviews, Jerry drifted off and began shooting the identification signs for groupings of train cargo. Each sign contained the prime destination and code number as well as a list of secondary destinations to be switched from the primary route—a total of twelve primary routes.

Since the sun was setting in the western sky, daylight was dimming for adequate filming. Chandra decided to avoid potential recognition by floodlight interviews, although the appearance of overhead lights above the rail yard made it clear that the workforce intended to work through the night. After confirming with Jerry that he had destination labels, she decided to return to Jacksonville and report the trans-shipment. She was just about to go in search of Jerry and Tina when a large black arm wrapped around her neck and a hand clamped over her mouth.

"Ah-ha little lady, I've found you again," uttered a deep male voice which she immediately recognized as her former kidnapper, Big Moe. Her assailant threw her on the ground and pulled out a roll of duct tape which he first pasted over her mouth before binding her wrists behind her back and then wrapping her ankles. She couldn't move.

Cameraman Jerry Brozovitch witnessed the end of Chandra's binding from behind a delivery truck, but it was too dark to photograph or film and the big black man was too large for the smaller cameraman to take on. As the big man hoisted Chandra's motionless body to his shoulder and walked toward the train yard, Jerry quietly moved from his hiding place and followed. The man laid her on the ground in front of a flat car already loaded with a container and he unlocked and opened a panel on the end of the container. He picked up Chandra's wrapped body and pushed it inside. He then closed and locked the panel. All Jerry could do was copy the identification on the container—NYC3642/34—and then he silently moved back to the car-park.

Tina was waiting for him beside Chandra's locked car. He quickly told her what had happened, as he pulled out the extra key that Chandra had given him months ago to access his equipment in the trunk. He stowed his camera and accessories bag and told her to guide him back to her newspaper office. Upon arrival, she jumped out and unlocked the office, so Jerry could use the phone.

Jerry hoped that Margaret McBride was still in the office, and she was. He introduced himself and quickly recounted the events of the afternoon and evening. Fortunately, her railway experts, along with Jordan and Rick were with her studying the route maps out of Savannah, so she had Jerry hold for a moment while she briefed the others and had them contact the search team leader in Charleston to move his entire crew to Savannah with weapons. Speed was essential since the five key containers could already be loaded on train sections.

Then she resumed her phone call with Jerry and learned that he had taken pictures of all the primary and secondary route destinations. He could have them developed within the next hour at the newspaper office. He told her that Chandra was prisoner in container NYC3642/34, before he handed the phone to Tina to provide the newspaper office address and phone number.

Rick O'Shea overheard the kidnapping of Chandra and immediately jumped to his feet. "I'm out of here Margaret," as he headed for the door. "But Margaret jumped to her feet and grabbed his arm."Hold on Rick. I can get you there faster."

Margaret then picked up the phone and called Captain Brown of the Georgia State Police. He too was working evenings still tracking the Chandra Jones' kidnappers. She told him that he could find both of them at the Savannah Harbor warehouse loading bombs onto railway cars, but she urgently needed a police escort from the I-95 border to Savannah. He replied within five minutes to report that a Georgia State police helicopter would pick up four of them just north of the Florida border at the Georgia Welcome Center within forty minutes and fly them to the Savannah port. She turned and gave a thumbs-up to Rick, who momentarily relaxed.

Then she asked one of the two FECR executives to remain in the meeting room with all of the railway route reference maps to provide advisory information. She asked the others, including the Amtrac operations expert, Richard Owen, and the recently arrived (from Gibraltar) Nigel Harris, to accompany her to Savannah "right now."

The interagency search team director at the Charleston Port received the phone call from Margaret McBride just before eight o'clock, notifying him that their prior information was incorrect, and that the Empress IV was currently unloading its freight in Savannah, about one-hundred and fifty miles south of Charleston. She requested that they move every member of the team to Savannah with orders to be fully armed and prepared for well-equipped criminals mixed with day laborers in the freight yards. She would be leaving by helicopter from the Georgia/Florida state line within the hour and planned to convene with him at the state police barracks just south of the airport. Identity signs are on I-95 south. No rail movement has been detected by rail monitors out of Savannah at this time.

Margaret and her five companions—Rick O'Shea, JD Dempsey, Nigel Harris, and Amtrac executive Richard Owen— bundled into the government SUV, with JD elected driver, and headed for I-95 north out of downtown Jacksonville. Within thirty minutes, JD pulled up beside the police helicopter at the Georgia Welcome Center, where Margaret, Rick and two of the task force members transferred to the police bird. It took off within five minutes with everyone belted in and eager to view the scene ahead. JD and Nigel followed on I-95 in the SUV.

In the interim, while the federal and state officers were converging on Savannah, the disguised Chester (aka Chekov) had managed to shortcut the cargo identification and loaded his five bomb containers on leading flatbed rail cars in the railway yard. Each of four targeted engines containing the five containers was scheduled for priority routes to cities with primary switching yards where each train was labeled for quick re-routing to the target cities. Secondary trains loaded with un-prescribed containers also were destined for cities with switching yards, but their secondary routes were not given priority service. The objective was to disrupt the freight sorting process, while the priority trains surged ahead to their target sites.

In order to ensure full cooperation by engineers, three target trains were accompanied by Big Moe, Walter and William, all fully armed and exposed to their engineers with instructions to exceed all rail speed limits. The armed containers for the target cities of New York, Chicago, San Diego and Dallas were on lead rail cars where they could pass through junction yards more quickly. The New York/Philadelphia train had engines front and back for higher speed to Philadelphia and rapid detachment of the container for that target site. Then, the other engine and the rest of the train could proceed rapidly to New York. The monitor for New York City was obliged to share his on-board cubicle with the wrapped up Chandra

Jones, who was destined to remain in place after the activation site was reached. He was given extra water packs to keep her alive during the interim in case Big Moe received a change in plans.

All six trains had moved out of Savannah before dusk with instructions dispatched to all rail junctions for clear passage on their routes.

FIFTY-FOUR

Savannah, Georgia
September 26, 1977

Margaret McBride assembled her team in the Savannah newspaper office and reviewed the pictures that Jerry Brosovitch had taken. But Rick could not wait for further information. He headed out the door and headed for the dock on foot. McBride remained calm and called Captain Brown again and assured him that they had landed without incident. She described the situation to him and concluded that she needed a total of six helicopters to chase the trains before they became mired in the nation's rail system.

"I understand your request, Ms. McBride, and I can probably rustle up six copters. But all of our machines are Bell Rangers with a maximum capacity of five occupants including the pilot. What you need here is Army Chinook copters with troop contingents aboard to settle any disputes.. Let me see what I can do with the Army base just outside Savannah."

"Thank you, Captain. At the same time, I will contact the Secretary of the Army for added policy strength." She immediately dialed President Carter's private phone line and he answered personally.

"Good evening, Margaret. Do you need assistance?" She described the situation and her need for six Army units to be put under her command immediately. "Sit tight, Margaret. We'll get back to you."

Within ten minutes, the newspaper phone rang and Margaret picked up. "Margaret McBride here."

"Ms. McBride, this is Lieutenant General Mike Cassidy of the Tenth Armored Division on temporary assignment at Hunter Army Airfield adjacent to Fort Stewart in Savannah. I have six choppers leaving our base, fully equipped for combat with half a dozen armed soldiers in each chopper. We understand the urgency. Now point us in the right direction."

"Hold on General, while I link you up with Amtrac Vice President of Operations, Richard Owen." And she handed the phone to Owen.

"Good evening General, we have six container freight trains moving away from Savannah in different directions. Three are carrying massive bombs destined for major cities. The others are decoys. But we cannot tell which, nor do we know the target cities. I can give you the approximate current location of each train and I suggest that you disable each and examine it for a bomb container. I have civilian guides that you can pick up here in Savannah at the newspaper office. They know the bad containers from the good. If you will set your birds down one at a time, we will give you a spotter for each machine . . . fifteen minutes it is, sir. We will be outside at the ready."

"Okay," interjected Margaret, "Each of you six get copies of the destination label pictures of the hot cargo containers from Richard and grab a copter in front of the building. Richard also will supply you with your known current route. If you cannot find it, phone Richard at this number. Please leave the NYC label for Rick. It contains his kidnapped friend, Chandra Jones. Now, go, go, go!"

The first copter was descending as JD led the men out the door. Within ten minutes, they were all airborne.

FIFTY-FIVE

Savannah, Georgia
September 27, 1977

Richard Owen picked up the ringing phone just after midnight and transferred it to a speaker phone. "Richard Owen here; go ahead please."

"Lieutenant Crosby here, Big Bird Six. We have managed to halt a subject train at Kingsland, Georgia just south of Brunswick. It is clean of any bad containers."

"Thank you, Lieutenant. Well done. Please return to base at Savannah."

Richard pulled down some charts from his wall display and resumed his seat.

A second call came in fifteen minutes later. "Richard Owen here, go ahead please."

"Lieutenant Slobinsky checking in, Big Bird Two. We halted a subject train just east of Macon, Georgia. No bad containers on board."

Thank you, Lieutenant. Well done! Please return to base for added fuel."

The third call arrived right after the second. "Richard Owen here, go ahead please."

"This is Captain Martini, Big Bird One. We are taking small arms fire from our subject train thirty miles shy of Atlanta. Request further directions."

"You have a live one, Captain. There should only be one shooter aboard and he is in the engine cab. Suggest you shoot the last car off the tracks to cause the engine to stop, and then attack the engine on foot to subdue the shooter. Do not harm the engineer, but be sure to arrest the monitor from inside the hot container."

"Good call, sir," replied the Captain. "The disabled freight car caused the train to stop and the shooter made a run for it. Would you prefer dead or alive?"

"We prefer alive, Captain."

"Roger that, sir. We are on him."

"Good job, now please bring home the runner as well as the shipping label, and one more bad guy from inside the target container. We will notify the railway manager to collect this train."

"Well, Margaret, three down and three to go."

"Yes," she replied, "but four bombs still free—four too many."

Just at that moment Rick O'Shea slumped into the office. "She's gone, Margaret. I was too late," and he slumped into a chair.

"Hang on, Rick," said Richard Martin. "I will have personal transport for you in a couple of minutes. Go downstairs and meet Big Bird 3. They are set to head north toward Philadelphia under your command." Rick left immediately.

Finding the other three trains was much more difficult, primarily because of the dense urban development and alternate rail lines to the north. The specific rail routes, registered by the Savannah Assistant Harbormaster, ensured switch openings logged into the system. Revisions would require coordination with this individual who apparently had taken personal leave from his position immediately after the trains had left Savannah.

The six Chinook helicopters from Hunter Army Airfield now were re-grouped to re-fuel the three that discovered their target trains south and west of Savannah. They were then targeted to alternate routes generated from the three trains headed north. Richard was soon on the phone once more.

"Lieutenant Samson here, Big Bird 5. We are above a subject train heading northwest toward Ashville North Carolina, moving into mountainous terrain. We put the copter right in front of the engine with no effect except one person firing an automatic rifle from the engine cab. Please direct preferred actions."

"Thank you, Lieutenant," replied Owen. "We believe that your train is live. However, the bomb cannot be ignited prior to destination. We suggest that you de-rail by attacking the final rail car. Send troops to the engine to rescue the engineer—do not harm him—and then find the target container and capture the man inside. Return both prisoners, engineer and freight label to base. We will contact rail management to remove the damaged train."

"Roger that, sir. Operation underway. Will report results when complete."

Within minutes, Owen was back on the phone. "This is Lieutenant Brownlee, Big Bird 4, reporting from south of Charlotte, North Carolina, where we have stopped a train and we are pursuing an armed African American running from the scene. We have identified the subject carrier and we are extracting its occupant."

"Excellent work, Lieutenant. Please return to base with the engineer and two bad guys plus the shipping label. We will notify rail management to extract the subject carrier and re-route the other freight."

Owen then took a call from Big Bird 3. "Rick O'Shea checking in. We are hovering over 30th Street Station in central Philadelphia, one of the busiest passenger stations in America—over ten thousand passengers daily—and a station building listed on the National

Register of Historic Places. We have been following a suspect train which entered the tunnel system east of the Schuylkill River fifteen minutes ago and has not emerged in the freight yard adjacent to the 30th Street Station. This is primarily a multi-purpose passenger station on two levels serving both through trains and commuter trains. Freight traffic customarily is routed to the adjacent Penn Coach Yard and maintenance facility. We suspect that the target site for this container bomb is inside the station, so we need law officers to join us for a facility search. Also, there is no safe landing place for our copter. I suggest you brief local police to close the station and define a landing place for our troops."

"Okay, Rick, I am on it and will get back to you."

After a brief discussion with McBride, they decided to utilize the services of General Cassidy, and she placed the call.

"General Cassidy here!"

"General, this is Margaret McBride at the newspaper office in Savannah. We have a problem in Philadelphia and we need your personal assistance." She went on to describe the issue.

"I am on it as we speak, Ms. McBride. I will contact Bird 3 with the landing site and then report back to you. Are we in danger of the bomb exploding?"

"We do not believe so, General. The men riding with each bomb have the arming capability, but they did not enlist for a suicide mission. The plan is for them to arm it for ignition on Colombus Day, October 8, and then escape prior to the explosion. Please note, however, that we now believe that this train may be carrying two bombs, the second one destined for New York."

"Okay, we will approach with caution. I will get back to you shortly."

FIFTY-SIX

Philadelphia, Pennsylvania
September 27, 1977

As dawn was emerging over downtown Philadelphia, the Chinook Army helicopter landed in the blocked-off street adjacent to the 30th Street Railway Station. Police cars, with emergency lights flashing, were parked in the street one-hundred yards from the station in each direction to detour any traffic to streets to the north. No vehicles or pedestrians were permitted into or adjacent to the entrance of the station where members of the police bomb squad were suiting up for dealing with the potential bomb inside.

The officer in command of the soldiers emerging from the helicopter was briefing the city police captain about the bomb scare just as the Chief of Police arrived with his special assistant and driver in an unidentified black Yukon utility vehicle. He waived off the opportunity for a repeat briefing—General Cassidy had already provided that by phone—and asked everyone to gather round.

"Ladies and gentlemen. We are not certain of all the facts, but the President of the United States woke me up this morning to ask me to personally direct the search of this station for one or two ordinary-looking open freight cars with ordinary-looking containers on them. If we locate them, we are to stay our distance and report back to me for explicit directions from a knowledgeable source through the Army helicopter.

"Captain Murphy beside me has copies of the station plan with assigned search areas for the groups of six identified with each plan. A two-way radio is assigned to each group and one person per group named as communicator. Now, please assemble with your group identified with an alphabetical letter matching your own ID label and proceed into the station to your search area. Captain Murphy will contact each of the communicators to test the radios and confirm the search areas.

"One last note: there may be one or more armed men guarding these containers so exercise appropriate caution. Also, there is a reported kidnapped female reporter tied up in one of the containers who will need medical care, so report finding her immediately to Captain Murphy for emergency aid. That is the mission. Let us proceed at a steady pace and minimum noise. Return here upon completing your area search. The residents of Philadelphia thank you for your diligence on their behalf."

The combined police and army groups assembled and proceeded to their designated areas to begin the search. Although the internal lighting had been switched on, many members carried flashlights to better see darker parts of the station. Within thirty minutes, the Team H communicator reported the described vehicle on a little-used rail siding near the southern boundary wall of the historic building. The rail car with the container was unattached to an engine or other rail car. No other rail cars other than surplus commuter passenger cars were discovered, along with more than a dozen vagrants, who were assembled at the station entrance for transport to a holding center.

As instructed, Team H members spread out in a rough circle about ten yards from the freight car and waited for further orders. The Police Chief, accompanied by Captain Murphy and two or three aides, appeared within ten minutes. The Chief carried a battery-powered megaphone and began to speak into it.

"Attention, attention, inside the container. You are completely surrounded by armed military officers. There is no place for you to hide. Open the entry hatch and come out immediately and you will not be harmed. Do it now, or we will come inside and drag you out. I repeat, come out now."

Slowly, a panel at the end of the container opened and an average-size man of middle age crawled onto the open surface of the freight car. He continued to the edge of the car and was helped to the ground by three Team H members directed by Captain

Murphy. After they patted him down for potential weapons or electronic gadgets—they found nothing other than his crumpled attire—Murphy took out a battery-operated tape recorder to interrogate the man, who had not uttered a word.

Although he had the skin complexion of a Latin-American, the man from the container spoke English with no apparent accent. He admitted to being hired for this trip for five thousand dollars of which one thousand was paid in advance and the rest was due after the bomb was exploded as directed on instructions given him the evening prior to departure in Savannah. He was to escape by walking three blocks to an unlocked Toyota Corolla parked at the address shown, with keys under the floor mat and his remaining pay in an envelope in the glove compartment. A police car dispatched to that location a few blocks from the station found no car of any description. Either the terrorists had not yet parked the escape car, or there was no escape intended.

A search of the container by Team H members found that it contained a large welded vessel attached to a tiny metal cabin of six feet per length, width and height, with a marine toilet and wash basin, and single mattress for sleeping. Temperature could be controlled with a ceiling heating/cooling unit with fan. A single light bulb was mounted in the ceiling. The Police Bomb Squad examined the bomb ignition device and found no electronics for radio dispatch. It would explode the assumed fuel in the adjoining vessel immediately upon setting the mechanical switch wired to the adjacent vessel. Assuming that it was filled with volatile liquid gas, the captain of the bomb squad estimated that it would devastate most of downtown Philadelphia along with any humans in that area and possibly beyond.

As to how he arrived, the man from the train claimed to have left Savannah on a train with two diesel engines, one at front and the other at the rear. His car was next to the rear engine. The train stopped in a large rail yard during the night—he guessed Wilmington, Delaware—and his car and the rear engine were uncoupled and the front of the train departed behind the front engine. About thirty minutes later his car, pushed by the second engine, moved on at a seemingly high rate of speed and eventually slowed to a low speed before stopping at the current location, after which the engine was detached and disappeared, leaving him in the location indicated in his directions for ignition and escape. The police report that no escape car was parked at the designated location implied that no escape was planned for him.

The bomb squad quickly removed the igniter and assured the Chief that the remainder of the bomb could be moved to a safer inspection location determined by the appropriate federal agencies. The Chief instructed his aide to return to the office and send a secure note to President Carter—copy to Margaret McBride— that the Philadelphia bomb was disarmed.

During the Chief's instructions, Rick O'Shea questioned the prisoner in more detail about his experience of the prior night. But, he learned nothing new in addition to the man's story already stated to the Chief of Police and the search team. Rick then pressed the chief for more assistance on locating the front section of this train. The Chief responded by ordering his aide to contact the Amtrac manager and arrange a meeting for O'Shea that afternoon. He reported back in a few minutes that Philadelphia Manager Thomas Schultz would meet with him as soon as he could be in his office in the top floor of the 30th Street Station. Rick dashed back to the helicopter and asked the pilot to contact Ms. McBride at the Hunter Army base. He explained to her that he needed the helicopter for further tracing of the New York train. He was about to interview the Amtrac Regional Manager for assistance. She agreed immediately and put General Cassidy on the radio to confirm those orders.

As agreed in his telephone discussion with General Cassidy, the Chief of Police turned the prisoner over to the Army Lieutenant for delivery back to the Savannah army base. After O'Shea returned from his meeting with the Amtrac Regional Manager, the helicopter then loaded its soldiers and took off. The police vacated the area and the Thirtieth Station was opened for its daily travelers by eight o'clock that morning.

FIFTY-SEVEN

Savannah, Georgia
September 28, 1977

Detention facilities at the Hunter Army Airfield base on the edge of Savannah were taxed to the limit with four bomb monitors and three formerly armed guards. Margaret McBride had moved her temporary headquarters from the newspaper office to the base so that she could interview each of these men immediately. The first container monitor was already seated in the interview room when she arrived. He was in the same clothing he wore when captured.

"I see that you have written your name on the prisoner questionnaire as George Stinson. Is that correct?"

"Yes, ma'am."

"But you do not carry any identification with your name on it?"

"No, ma'am."

"Why not?"

"Because The Don took all of our identification before we left Fort Lauderdale."

"Who is The Don?"

"I dunno who he is, really. But he is the boss man who paid us each an initial thousand dollars to guide these bombs to their blast sites. We were supposed to receive an additional five thousand dollars in our escape cars after we set the timer on our bombs."

"How would you find your escape car with the final payment?"

"The final payment is supposed to be in the glove compartment of the escape car parked a short walk from the bomb site. I have directions to find it that the Don gave me. Each of us got a separate letter with directions. But, your army boys stopped the train before I could get to my site in Dallas."

"Yes they did. You should be thankful that they did, because your Don planned no escape car or five thousand dollars. You would have been blown away when you thought that you were arming the bomb for a delayed explosion. So, instead of talking to me about your jail term, you would be dead—blown into little pieces—all five of you. Probably, your armed guard riding with the engineer would have been blown up as well. Your Don would leave nobody behind to identify him. It appears that even your "Big Moe" was destined to be blown up in New York City. But we saved your useless hide. If you can't give me any useful information, you can return to your cell."

"But wait! Perhaps I can give you some good information. If I tell you where The Don lives, could you have my sentence reduced?"

McBride jerked her head up in surprise. "Well now, do you really know where he lives, or you just about to make up a location as a bargaining chip?"

"I swear to you that I have good information. I overheard The Don talkin' to Big Moe about his luxury apartment overlooking the ocean, that the Prince rented for him, and . . ."

"Whoa back, my man," interrupted McBride. "You may have something useful. Sit tight for a minute while I get a witness." With that, she left the room and returned with her stenographer, Janet Sproule.

"Janet, this man, whose name is on the form on the table, has some information that may be useful to locating the ringleader of this plot. As you are my witness, I promise to testify on his behalf for a reduced prison sentence when he goes to trial for attempted mass murder. Now, my man, go ahead and tell me about where the Don lives."

"First of all, Ms. McBride, The Don is always in disguise. He wears a white wig and face mask and beard to look older. I don't know his real name, but I heard him brag to Big Moe that his name is on the FBI's 'Most Wanted List.'"

"I heard him tell Big Moe that the 'Prince' rented him a luxury condominium apartment overlooking the beach at Amelia Island Plantation north of Jacksonville, so he could be close to the Prince's new home in this same community. He added that they both have fake American passports with new names. That's all I've got, Ms. McBride. Now, I'm counting on you to keep your end of the bargain."

"I am as good as my word," replied McBride. "If what you gave me is correct, it will impress any judge. Janet, please type it up and we will get someone working on it right away. Tell our Army liaison man that I will interview the other captured monitor prisoners one at a time, beginning now."

McBride sent her prisoner back to his confinement and spent the rest of the morning interviewing other prisoners, but could find little information to add to that of her first interviewee.

FIFTY-EIGHT

In Transit, New Jersey
September 27, 1977

The monitor for the New York bomb target turned out to be very uncomfortable sharing his tiny compartment in the bomb container with a bound-up prisoner, especially a young woman. He was not an aggressive personality, but he had jumped at the chance for this job because of his meager income that barely supported him and his aging mother in their small apartment in Fort Lauderdale. He was well aware that he was engaged in a criminal act, but he did not expect it to include close-quarters guard duty.

The train had stopped in the night and apparently released the second engine and a second bomb car for placement in a city between Savannah and New York. While the train was stopped, Big Moe came by to explain the stop to him and check on the condition of the prisoner. She had squirmed around in an apparent attempt to find comfort, but she clearly did not succeed. He did his best to ignore her. The big black man was too large to fit inside the container, but he suggested that the monitor remove the tape covering her mouth to give her some water. He wanted to make sure that she survived the trip to New York in case they might need her for an unexpected barter if their plans were exposed.

So, after they moved ahead, the now-frightened monitor moved the prisoner into a sitting position and carefully stripped the duct tape from her mouth. Then he held a cup of water for her to drink. When it was finished, she asked in a very faint voice if she could have more. He filled the cup once more and held it for her to finish. She smiled her thanks and closed her eyes.

About an hour later, he heard her moan, and he became disturbed that she might be ill. She told him that she had to pee. If he would release her, she promised not to cause trouble or try to escape. At first he refused, but then reconsidered as he recognized her obvious discomfort. So, he told her he would cut the bindings on her wrists if she could manage to drag herself to the small toilet. But her ankles would remain bound. She nodded her compliance, and he produced a pocket knife to cut her wrist bindings. He then shifted his body to the rear of the compartment to give her room to move her rear to the toilet while he stared at the wall. The operation was a struggle, but she eventually sighed in relief, and managed to tug her slacks back up to a covering position.

"Thank you, sir. You are most generous. May I call you by name?

"Tom."

"My name is Chandra."

"Very pretty name."

"Thank you. Do you do this sort of work often?"

"Never! But I need the money to care for my mother."

"Is she an invalid?"

"Arthritis! She can barely walk. Expensive medicine!"

"My sympathy to both of you! That is a difficult ordeal."

"Yes it is."

"What is your regular work, Tom?"

"I'm a dock worker in Port Everglades, but the hours are irregular. How about you?"

"I'm a television reporter in Jacksonville. My hours are irregular, too. But, luckily, they pay me a salary. As a matter of fact, they will offer a reward for my return."

"Really? How much do you reckon they will pay?"

"Well, I don't know. But the last time, they offered $10,000 for my safe return."

"This happened to you before?"

"Yes, I'm afraid so. What is even worse, it was the same man."

"You mean Big Moe?"

"That's the man."

"Wow! He is a dangerous fellow."

"He is indeed: robbery, blackmail, kidnapping, murder, the list goes on. What did he promise you after completion of this bombing?"

"Well, his boss, 'the Don,' promised four-thousand dollars in a rental escape car, but I must admit that I am beginning to wonder about it. Why wouldn't he deposit it into a bank account?"

"Why not indeed?!?! Is this 'Don' a short guy with white hair and a beard?"

"That's him, but the hair and beard, even the face, are false."

"Tom, that man's real name is Dimitri Chekov, and he is wanted in many countries for a wide range of criminal activities. He is employed by some wealthy Arabs to carry out these bombings. I think that your life is in real danger as well as mine."

"Do you think that your employer would pay me the reward if I help you to escape."

"I will make it happen."

"Okay, Miss Chandra. You've got a deal. This train is bound for New York City. There are no passenger train tracks at ground level, so they must be planning to park it underground. But, I imagine the tracks underground are difficult to negotiate. So, they must get rid of all the other cars before they cross into Manhattan. That's where we get off. But we must be super-careful, because Big Moe is fast on his feet and very strong, as well as armed with a gun."

"First of all, reach up and open that cupboard. Throw me an energy bar and pick out whatever you want. Here is my jackknife. Cut the duct tape from your ankles and massage them good to revive your circulation. Drink some more water. I have no idea how much time that we have before they stop, but we must be ready to move fast. Okay?"

"Okay, Tom. I'm with you."

FIFTY-NINE

Trenton, New Jersey
September 27, 1977

"Margaret, I'm glad I caught you before you left for lunch. I am on the ground just outside Trenton, New Jersey. The pilot and I were attracted by a group of railway workers huddled around a rail switch junction, so we came down to investigate. It turns out that the mechanism was damaged last night to shift main Amtrac traffic onto the New York bypass route through Newark, thus, clogging up rail traffic in the New York metro area, but leaving the center city open. When I interviewed the Amtrac Regional Manager yesterday, he told me that they would switch all northbound traffic through this bypass, thereby keeping all freight traffic from access into Manhattan. But, during the night, someone with knowledge of the system opened the switch for a train to go through, and then locked it back to the bypass route. Are you following me?"

"Yes Rick, and Janet is taking it down for the record. So, do I understand that our train is the only freight train into Manhattan since yesterday?"

"Exactly, Margaret. And there are many, many miles of rail lines both above and below ground in Manhattan. We need an army of searchers and a coordinator who is familiar with the routes in and around New York, and we need both yesterday."

"Alright, Rick, slow down to a walk. I will contact the President immediately to organize the search team. I will need you in New York to act as liaison with the new team. I am sending our

Amtrac VP, Richard, up to join you along with JD to double for your liaison. Please sit tight for twenty minutes and I will give you directions as to where the copter can drop you off prior to returning to base."

At virtually the same time as Margaret turned her attention to phoning President Carter, Big Moe was directing his engineer to find the designated site under Manhattan to park the New York bomb container. They had retained the diesel locomotive that originated in Savannah, despite the regulations permitting only electric-powered engines within Manhattan. However, the site chosen to place the bomb was not provided with electricity connection. It was an unused section of track three full rail levels below the intersection of 38th Street and Broadway. It had been selected because of its geographical position in the middle of the island, but also because the intensity of the anticipated blast at this point was estimated to topple the one-hundred and three floors of the nearby Empire State Building—a fitting symbol of destroyed capitalism in the world's business center. Prince Hassad El Saud and his cousins had side-stepped the more dramatic target of Washington because of its tighter security, and they selected the Manhattan site as their key blast for world attention. The pictures of the collapse of the Empire State Building would send a signal around the world that the presumed American economic might was not infallible.

The mid-Manhattan target site also had another strategic advantage. It was the terminus of a planned spur to a new rail line that had been halted for budget issues in 1932. No services had been extended up the spur, so no electricity was provided for lighting or engine power. It was a perfect spot to hide a rail car, after which the engine could be camouflaged along with many other inventory rail cars and engines in the Brooklyn Navy Yard. The Saud cousins thought it to be the perfect spot for their headline explosion and now Big Moe and his engineer were tasked with locating it in the maze of railway tracks under Manhattan streets and buildings.

Finally, at a few minutes past two o'clock that afternoon, the engine now pushing the single container car was aligned with the abandoned rail line leading into the designated target site. The engine pushed the car right to the end of the rusty track where Big Moe climbed down and set the brakes on the car and released the coupling to the engine. He then moved to the end of the container to open the access panel and ensure the monitor was in place and ready to play his role in arming the bomb. He also wanted to check on the prisoner, Chandra Jones, to confirm that she was still alive and fit for his sexual desires before her planned death on Columbus Day.

Big Moe's cry of despair was so loud and so anguished that it motivated the engineer to pause and investigate before he powered his engine out of the underground rail maze. But, when he shone his powerful flashlight on the end of the container, he saw only his big black companion furiously beating his fists against the steel wall of the container in uncontrolled anger. Upon closer inspection, the engineer discovered the cause of Big Moe's tantrum. He was alone. There was nobody else in the container. The monitor and the prisoner were gone. After his complete vocabulary of expletives was exhausted, Big Moe recovered his control and climbed slowly out of the container carrying the tote bag with provisions and the spare detonator. He closed the access panel and grabbed the engineer's arm followed by directing him back to the engine.

"Let's get out of here, Bill. Wherever they managed to escape, they don't know where we are. So, the first order of business is to get back into daylight and stash this engine. Then I can figure out how to find her. I should have known better than to trust that broad. She probably promised our man more money to free her and help her find the surface. So, now I've got another kidnap charge against me. I sure hope that the Prince has lots of money to pay for this caper."

224

During the same time that Big Moe and the engineer spent securing the bomb container, Margaret was making preparations for two search parties. Her call to the President resulted in the activation of a thousand-person search party under the command of an Army general, bolstered by senior railway personnel, to plan the complete inspection of the Manhattan underground rail system. They would stay at it until the freight car is found. No other option is tenable. Margaret sent Rick, JD and Richard, the Amtrac VP, to New York as liaison from her task force.

She then turned to the task of finding Chekov and Prince Hassad El Saud. She appointed Senior Agent Jordan Hale as director of a search team aided by Senior Agent Nigel Harris and a twenty-person contingent of soldiers requisitioned from General Cassidy's forces at Hunter Army Support Force outside Savannah. They were scheduled to occupy two Chinook helicopters for a flight to meet the Amelia Island Director of Security in the administration parking lot, which he would have cleared for the two copters. They would move out from there to probable destinations being researched by the resort rental staff.

From her second interview with the monitor informant, she added the two prisoners Walter and William, who had direct experience with Chekov out of disguise. They received the same promise that she gave the informant, that is, she would testify for clemency at their trial.

The two big Chinooks lifted off at two o'clock for the ninety-mile trip to Amelia Island Plantation to find and imprison the two leaders of this terrorist attack. They were met at the hotel parking lot by Director of Security Donald Stenback who handed out promotional maps of the property site plan. The rental staff had examined all furnished rentals for the prior three months and identified only twelve that had been paid for by resident owners that were in buildings overlooking the beach. They then reduced them further by owners who had purchased their own homes within the past three months and were somewhat surprised that they reduced the list to a probable three transactions, two of which involved condominium apartments in the same building.

Senior Agent Hale split his force into five sections: three to discretely surround the three homes of the resident owners and confine their actions to confining any persons coming or going to these residences. But, they were to desist from any invasive action. He named a communication leader for each section. The remaining two sections were to take invasive actions for the three rental apartments—two in one building—under the leadership of Nigel Harris and himself.

The results of the five-part action were good and bad. The three rental apartments were all vacant, but inspection by master key revealed only one was occupied by a single male of less than average size that matched Chekov's description. He was listed as Daniel Chester and confirmed as probable Chekov by receipts for helicopter rental from Charleston and commercial airline tickets to Fort Lauderdale and Charleston.

The entire five sections of troops then converged on the detached residence of the Stanton family of two adults, three children and two live-in attendants, reported to have moved from Montreal, Quebec in Canada. This house was vacant also, but contained un-washed breakfast dishes and signs of a hurried departure. Their reported two recent-vintage automobiles were both missing.

The troops were pulled back to the parking lot and the Security Director recovered vehicle registrations and Florida license plate numbers for all three vehicles in the names of Stanton and Chester. This information was phoned to the Florida State Police for an immediate "all-points-bulletin" including an alert for "armed and dangerous." The Security Director also promised to position a manned watch on both residences for any activity to be reported to

State Police for arrest on suspicion of murder. The force re-loaded and returned to base in Savannah.

SIXTY

New York City, New York
September 27, 1977

At three that afternoon, Mayor Abraham Beame of New York issued a special warning on all New York television channels and radio stations that a massive bomb threat created a full alert of all public and private security forces in the metropolitan area. September 28 and 29 were declared a public holiday for all government and schools in Manhattan. No public transportation facilities would operate on those days and all residents were advised to remain indoors. The underground transportation system would be subjected to a massive search by a team of Army militia coordinated by transportation experts and the city's own bomb squad on stand-by. The Mayor repeatedly pronounced that no terrorist organization would be allowed to operate in New York City.

Not to be outdone by local officials, President Jimmy Carter asked for and received national network time for his own message on the bomb plot. He announced that a crack task force under the direction of Deputy Security Advisor Margaret McBride had uncovered a terrorist attack financed by Prince Hassad El Saud and other members of the Saudi Arabian Royal Family. The threat had been targeted to five major American cities with non-nuclear bombs of extraordinary strength. Bombs for four of the five cities have been secured and de-activated. A massive search is organized in New York for the fifth bomb, known to be placed underground in midtown Manhattan. All exits from underground transportation are now being sealed to inspect anyone attempting to enter or exit that area. At midnight tonight, the combined Army and Police force of over one thousand men and women will begin a detailed search of underground transportation routes from end-to-end of Manhattan.

A spokesman for King Saud responded within an hour of President Carter's address to report that, "although Hassad El Saud is a member of the Royal Family, he has not lived in the Kingdom for many years and he takes no role in Saudi government. The King accepts no responsibility for his behavior. At last report he was domiciled in Monte Carlo."

"STOP RIGHT THERE! DO NOT MOVE!" Tom and Chandra stopped and looked across several tracks at a burly railway security officer with two other uniformed security men rushing toward them. Without discussion, the security men pulled out metal handcuffs and secured their wrists behind their backs.

"You are trespassing on government property and are under arrest. Do you understand English?

The two prisoners both nodded in the affirmative.

"Do you understand English?" They nodded again.

"Okay, men, take them straight to the Detention Center in the Brooklyn Navy Yard and have them locked up. We will question them later."

"With all due respect, sir, may I say a word?" asked Chandra in a quiet voice.

"Go ahead, but keep it short, I've got a busy schedule."

"My name is Chandra Jones. I am a television reporter from Jacksonville, Florida. This man and I just escaped from a railway flat car container carrying a very highly charged bomb. It was being pushed by a diesel engine to an ignition target under Manhattan. It

228

is important that I speak to the FBI immediately. They are searching for me."

"Lady, I have heard a lot of crazy stories, but that one tops them all. Take them away boys, and be sure and get fingerprints. They may be wanted."

The security men ushered them into an electric service conveyance for the underground trip to the Navy Yard where the detention center served all of the military and civilian security personnel.

About one hour after Chandra and Tom were arrested in Manhattan's underground railway yards, the Army Chinook helicopter landed Rick at the East River Public Helicopter Landing in Manhattan. As the helicopter took off to return to Savannah, Rick was met by an Army Captain standing by an official military car.

"Mr. O'Shea?"

"Yes, I'm your man, Captain." Rick turned and waved his goodbye to the helicopter pilot ascending into the sky.

"I'm Captain Tony LaRosa, sir, and I am instructed to take you to a priority meeting in the Federal Building." The two men entered the rear seat of the Army car and the driver drove off without delay.

Twenty minutes later, they arrived at the Federal Building in downtown Manhattan, and Captain LaRosa accompanied Rick to a large meeting room on the eighth floor. Two soldiers requested identification at the entrance after which LaRosa guided him inside through dozens of Army personnel and New York city police seated at tables displaying portions of the Manhattan underground. At a smaller table in the front of the room LaRosa stopped in front of a table, saluted a General and introduced Rick O'Shea.

General Martin Clark stood up, returned the captain's salute, and shook hands with O'Shea. He then dismissed the captain with thanks and turned to O'Shea.

"Mr. O'Shea, I have been hearing about your exploits on behalf of the American public all day. I am pleased to meet you and to thank you for your input. Margaret McBride told me that we cannot start without your briefing and description of our strategic plan. She will be here very shortly. In the interim, let me show you around our emergency 'War Room'."

At that same moment, an Army major stepped up to a microphone on a raised platform. "Ladies and gentlemen, I am pleased to introduce the President's appointed Chair of the Anti-terrorist Task Force, Margaret McBride. She strode to the microphone from the sideline and welcomed everyone to this vital project. She added a few words on the task force and the very successful efforts that they have achieved to date, with the cooperation of the Georgia State Police, the Army, FBI, CIA and Britain's Intelligence Services.

"Tonight's search of the vast transport network beneath the streets of Manhattan is being staffed and coordinated by the Army, with the cooperation of the New York City Police Department. Whatever role you are fulfilling in this search for a bomb more powerful than the bombs dropped on Hiroshima and Nagasaki to end World War II, it is a vital role and time is of the essence. Now, I would like to introduce Patrick M. O'Shea of Jacksonville, Florida, who has relentlessly tracked the origin of these bombs from the explosion in his city to their sources in Europe and Asia. He can explain the visual item that we are after. Rick!"

"Thank you, Margaret. First of all, I have taken the picture, now being displayed on the center screen, of a typical railway flat car with a metal container. These containers are designed to fit on flat cars, large truck trailers and ocean-going freighters. I am sure that you have all seen them in your travels. Our target looks virtually the same as the innocuous container in this picture, and we assume that it is still on the flat car that it rode here from Savannah, Georgia. The outside is typical, but the inside is custom-designed to kill Americans.

"The diagram now on the screen shows the floor plan of this weapon of mass destruction. The front two-thirds of the container is filled with a metal welded structure—a big tank full of liquid gas and a small ignition device controlled by a battery-powered timer independent of the tank. Behind the explosive tank is a two-meter square metal box over two meters high which contains the bare essentials for one man to sleep, eat, drink, wash and dispose for five to ten days. It has a small periscope fitted into the top so that he can see outside without opening the small sliding panel in the rear. He was hired and trained to ensure that the bomb arrives safely at the designated target without incident, and then he is to set a timer at noon on a Memorial Day—next Monday— designed to blow up the bomb five hours later, in concert with the other four bombs. The mission was projected to kill millions of people in these five American cities on this national holiday. Since capturing the other four bombs over the past 48 hours, we now realize that the escape time was a myth. The apparent timing switches on the timer are not connected. Therefore, unbeknownst to the watchman, he is destined to die in the explosion. Since he is unaware of his fate, he could panic when he sees a search party and set the timer in advance. So I caution you to stay out of sight and keep quiet when the target is located. The New York City Police bomb squad will take over at that point.

"Just one final point that I would like you to know. This container also includes a prisoner who is bound and gagged inside the living quarters. At least, she was so garbed according to a witness to her abduction. She is a television reporter from Jacksonville who became part of our team through her relentless pursuit of these terrorists. In addition to being an integral member of the search team, she is my partner. So, I have a very personal interest in finding this container. If any of you encounter her down below, I would be grateful if you would handle with care.

"Thank you for your attention and for being part of this team. If you have any specific questions, please step up to one of the three standing microphones in the aisles."

Rick then answered questions for another fifteen minutes before the Major released him and introduced Major General Clark to describe the strategic plan for the search planned to begin as soon as he finished and the busses loaded to transport the search team sections to their assigned start points. He did not take long, with the aid of a map projected on the large screen, to explain the strategy of leaving no stone unturned in the Manhattan underground. He also emphasized the danger of frightening the bomb's watchman into early ignition, and the need for absolute silence. Each section leader has received map orientation."You must follow his direction."

Big Moe and his engineer had been wandering around in the underground for several hours without finding any exit to the streets above, or even a stairway to the subway system which he had been told was the first level below the street. His usual calm demeanor was wearing thin by the lack of stairways, but even more by the absence of the sound of subway trains. Having traveled in the New York subway many years ago, he was well acquainted with the noise caused by the rapid acceleration and braking of the subway trains. The absence of that noise meant that, either the engineer and he had wandered beyond the perimeter of the subway system, or the entire system had shut down. "Why would they do that?" he mused to himself. "Only one reason;" he concluded, "those bastards have closed down the system because they know about the bomb. The next thing they will do is search the underground."

Luckily, he had the good sense to bring the auxiliary ignition package in its carrying case, so that he could set off the bomb from a remote location. He was determined to collect his promised bonus for the completed explosion.

However, he regretted his earlier decision to abandon the engine a couple of miles south of the blast site. He assumed that it was too big and noisy for their escape, especially if security people were searching the underground on foot. But now, it appeared that speed might be more important than noise.

"What's that, Big Moe? What did you say?" mumbled the engineer now feeling very tired from the seemingly endless distance they had traveled on foot.

"I said," repeated the irritated black man, "that the subway is not running, so they have shut it down figuring a bomb is down here. Now they are going to launch a search to find it, and us. We must find a hiding place, and quick."

Big Moe's lifelong optimism served him well once more as his flashlight beam illuminated an "Exit" sign less than fifty feet to their right. He grabbed the engineer by the arm and pulled him toward the welcome sign. The sign was mounted on a circular stairway which the two men mounted immediately to a doorway at the top. Moe pushed the smaller man aside and unholstered his weapon before slowly pushing the door open. But no light or sound was discovered at what appeared to be the subway track with emergency lighting a short distance ahead at a station stop. He immediately extinguished his flashlight and proceeded very slowly toward the station, followed by his tired engineer.

SIXTY-ONE

Manhattan Underground
September 29, 1977

It was long after midnight by the time all of the military searchers were stationed in their appointed locations and given the signal to initiate the search. Each searcher was equipped with a miner's helmet with battery-powered light and earphone connected to central command as well as a microphone allowing them to communicate at very low volume.

At precisely 2:33 that morning, the point man for Group Six reported to everyone that he had a visual on the flat car and container in an abandoned track and he turned off his light awaiting further instructions. The Search Director immediately replied, ordering every member of Group Six to stand down and extinguish lights and speech communication. The New York Police Bomb Squad had been mobilized and was en route to their location. They were to maintain complete silence. However, other groups should continue their search patterns in case the railway engineer and terrorist monitor were attempting to escape on their engine.

During the wait for the bomb squad to reach Search Group Six, radio silence was broken with a report from the Group Twelve point man that he had located an abandoned diesel engine at a location over two miles south of the container sighting. There was no sign of humans in or near the engine.

The Search Director once again replied without delay, and repeated his direction that all groups, except Group Six, should continue their detailed search, now on the lookout for one or two men anxious to escape the underground.

The New York City Police Bomb Squad arrived at the Group Six location just before three o'clock that morning. After conferring with the Group Six leader and the Search Director by wireless, the Bomb Squad Captain sent two of his most experienced troops, equipped with night vision goggles and side arms, to inspect the container. They approached entirely on their stomachs, using their elbows for propelling their bodies across the gravel soil and steel tracks over wood ties. After twenty minutes, the two scouts reported that no humans were aboard the container, although the interior cabin showed signs of recent occupancy by two persons. The ignition device for the liquid gas vessel was firmly in place, but the timer attached to it had no connection to the ignition. In short, the ignition would be instantaneous.

After reporting to the Search Director, the Bomb Squad Captain ordered the container fully illuminated, and he and his team began a detailed inspection of the rail car and the container. Thirty minutes later, the team inspection being complete, the Bomb Squad Captain reported to the Search Director that his team had disconnected the ignition, but it still retained the possibility of being fired by a remote device. He requested that a tank car be routed into an adjoining track and the liquid gas be removed from the container for shipment to a disposal site. Furthermore, he requested that this be done immediately. His Squad had the tools and expertise to carry out the transfer if the Search Director could supply the transportation.

The Search Director agreed with the recommendation and was communicating with the Amtrak officials on rapid delivery of a tank car. Current estimates were an hour best time. He requested the Bomb Squad Captain to remain on-site for further orders. In the interim, he advised all search groups to continue their search for the two missing men who abandoned the engine. It is possible that one of them is carrying a remote ignition. He also reported that the news reporter and the container monitor were still missing somewhere in the rail yard.

Just as the Search Director delivered the last message, an emergency call was sounded from a subway station police unit on lower Broadway. Shots were being fired by a tall African American man who had emerged from the tracks. Two policeman were wounded and in need of immediate medical care, and the other four officers in the guard squad were closeted in the ticket office trading shots with the shooter who was moving about in the track canal.

The Search Director ordered the closest Search Group 15 to move up to the subway level immediately and lend support, while a police patrol and ambulances were dispatched by road. Within twenty minutes, the subway station was invaded from below and above. Automatic weapons were pouring bullets into the subway canal to cover police recovering their wounded fellow officers. Wireless contact with Group 15 members revealed that their flashlights could not expose any shooters in or near the track, so the police unit from the street descended to the track platform without further firing to join the Group 15 members in searching all parts of the lower platform.

They finally found a dead body lying between the tracks about one hundred feet from the station. Examination of the pockets in his clothes determined that this was the body of the bomb train engineer. Bullet wounds from police weapons were assumed to have caused his death, after he managed to limp from the station this far down the track. There was no sign of the tall African-American who had fired a hand gun at the police unit guarding the entrance. They reported to the Search Director that he had left the scene, unable to escape to the street. They surmised that he could have continued down the subway track or escaped back down to the train level through a door that they discovered opened onto a spiral staircase. They assumed that this was the exit from the train level by which the two men had arrived at this station.

The Search Director ordered remaining healthy members of the police troop to barricade the track and he would send Group 10 from the next station to search the subway route back to them. In the interim, he ordered Group 15 to return to the railway level via the circular stairway and begin a detailed search to the west. He cautioned them that this man was armed and dangerous. Further he may be carrying a wireless bomb ignition which he could set off at any time. "Approach with extreme caution."

Big Moe had indeed returned to the train level via the circular stairway and headed due west toward what he now assumed would take him toward the terminus of the subway at the end of Manhattan. After thirty minutes of hiking in that direction, he encountered a six-passenger security vehicle approaching from what he believed was the tunnel to Brooklyn. He stepped into the glare of the headlight and waved the vehicle to a stop.

Two armed security officers stepped out of the vehicle, but stopped when they realized that the tall man held a pistol pointed at them. The newcomer ordered the two men to stand with their hands on the front of the vehicle while he removed their weapons, portable radios and hand-cuffs. Next, he ordered the smaller of the two officers to cuff his larger companion with hands behind his back. Finally, he removed the cuffed officer's peaked hat and put it on his own head and ordered the man to return to his seat. Realizing that the vehicle could operate in either direction, he motioned the smaller officer into the reverse driver position prior to delivering a massive blow with his pistol to the head of the cuffed officer, who then slumped forward unconscious to the floor of the vehicle.

Moe then jumped into the bench seat behind the driver and ordered him to reverse direction and return to Brooklyn. The smaller officer obeyed without a sound, and they moved forward at a brisk pace.

Dawn was breaking as the electric-powered vehicle moved out of the tunnel on the other side of the East River. Moe told the driver to stop at the first major street bridge over the tracks. He instructed him to move back to the second bench seat where he cuffed his hands behind his back and around the seat frame. He then applied the same massive blow to the officer's head causing immediate unconsciousness. The American terrorist then picked up the case with the ignition and quickly climbed the embankment to the major street.

The retail stores and offices were still closed, but he lost no time in finding a taxi with a sleeping driver. He pulled a roll of bills from his pocket and allowed the African-American driver to glimpse them before asking the driver for the fare to the Newark airport terminal. The driver named a reasonable fare and Big Moe climbed into the back seat. Newark was beyond the blast impact range and within visual distance. He had decided that he would not wait for the blast target date, but arm the ignition after arrival at the airport; perhaps not as devastating as during a national holiday, but still strong enough to kill a great many Americans for publicity around the world.

Rick O'Shea was dejected about the lack of any word about Chandra. The Search Director had reported by radio that all search groups had completed their assigned tours successfully, and the rail car containing the massive bomb was in the process of being disarmed by the New York City bomb squad. Nothing else of interest had occurred except for a shoot-out at a lower Manhattan subway station at which two officers had been wounded and the dead body of the bomb train engineer discovered. A tall black man had apparently escaped through an exit stairway to the lower train track level and disappeared. All search team members were on the lookout for him and the Search Director refused to let any team member end the search until these men were discovered. In the meantime, no rail traffic moved in Manhattan.

SIXTY-TWO

Manhattan, New York
September 29, 1977

Daylight over New York City revealed a clear blue sky and mild temperatures. Mayor Abraham Beame, resplendent in a black suit over a white shirt with red tie and matching pocket handkerchief, was right on time for the eight o'clock news announcement. The Mayor's Press Secretary had been at her post before six that morning faxing the meeting announcement to all media outlets in the city, as requested by her boss by phone in the middle of the night. The Mayor decided to hold forth on the front steps of City Hall, so the press corps was assembled down the steps as well as television cameras perched on the top of specially equipped vans parked in the street, although the traffic ban was still in force.

Mayor Beame stepped forward to the podium, where he was immediately joined by officers of the army as well as the Chief of the New York City Police Department.

"Ladies and gentlemen of the news media and millions of viewers watching on television. This is a wonderful day for New York. Thanks to the bravery of over 2,000 army and police who searched the Manhattan underground through the night, we have located and disarmed the enormous bomb hidden below our midtown streets. Members of our City Bomb Squad finished neutralizing it just three hours ago. They estimated that it contained enough explosive to flatten midtown New York, including the Empire State Building and the Chrysler Building. Clearly our precautions in closing down Manhattan were not excessive. We did the wise thing! Now, we must rely upon our federal forces to track down the terrorist instigators of this unimaginable act and bring them to justice. We have captured some of the messengers guiding this bomb, and four other bombs headed for other large cities; they are in custody. But, the people who financed and planned this operation are still at large. The Federal Bureau of Investigation, aided by the United States Army, the Central Intelligence Agency and local and state police, are hot on their trail. Our nation will not stand for terrorists to damage our cities and kill our citizens." Applause then broke out from the hundreds of news people and early workers at City Hall, causing the Mayor to pause for several minutes in his remarks, before continuing.

"Ladies and gentlemen, the success of our troops and police officers over the past twenty-four hours cannot be minimized. They saved your life and mine. Standing on either side of me are Army Major General Martin Clark and our New York City Chief of Police Patrick Murphy, representing all of the brave men and women who performed this outstanding service. Please show them your appreciation as we all return to our safe jobs. I hereby declare New York City open for business." And the Mayor then disappeared back into City Hall as the thundering applause and cheering continued outside the entrance.

Captain Murial Wilson had been a uniformed lawyer in the Judge Advocate General Corps for over twenty years, but the behavior of security personnel still tried her patience. The personnel at Brooklyn Navy Yard seemed especially dense, and at nine o'clock in the morning, Officer McGinty was particularly annoying.

"Let me get this straight, Officer McGinty. You found a man and a woman walking in the railway yard. You assumed that they were criminals because they were not supposed to be there. So you instructed your two men to handcuff them and lock them up in the brig. Is that correct?"

240

"Yes Captain, except for one more thing: she insisted on telling me a cock-and-bull story about being a television reporter from someplace in Florida and that her companion was an important witness in a terrorist plot to bomb Manhattan."

"I see. Do you watch television much McGinty?"

"I sure do, every day when I get off work."

"Did you watch it yesterday?"

"Absolutely!"

"What did you see?"

"Well, the Jew Mayor was spouting off about closing the subway."

"And why would Mayor Beame do that?

"Well, he said something about finding a bomb in . . . oh damn! Well, I'm sorry, Captain. I guess that I just didn't think. You know, we get pretty tired after walking around these yards all day and . . ."

"Forget it, McGinty. I should have expected no better. Please bring the man and woman out to this office immediately.

"Yes sir . . . I mean yes, Captain."

"Right, just do it, please."

Within a few minutes, Chandra Jones and her new friend, Tom, appeared in front of the gunmetal desk occupied by Captain Wilson.

"Please sit down. I understand that you may have been imprisoned by mistake. I will correct that error immediately. But, before I do, please show me your identification."

Chandra Jones quickly opened her purse and produced a Florida driver license and a certified press pass. Unfortunately, Tom had nothing to present because he and his companions had been required to leave all their possessions with Big Moe in Savannah.

But Chandra launched into her depiction of the search for the five bombs and reported that she had committed Tom to her care until he could be secured along with his collaborators at the Army base in Savannah.

"Okay, Miss Jones, I understand. Officer McGinty, please bring a release paper for Ms. Jones and her prisoner and order me a car to deliver them to the bomb search headquarters in Manhattan. And McGinty, I believe you owe her a major apology for false imprisonment. However, I will try to treat her kindly from here on out, and perhaps, just perhaps, she may not press charges and get you discharged from the Navy."

Captain Wilson returned Chandra's identification cards to her and the two women walked to the car, whose driver was standing at attention with the car doors open. Tom and McGinty followed with the latter man still muttering apologies and begging Chandra's forgiveness. She had decided to ignore him completely, and they drove off without another word.

Chandra, in the back seat with Tom, leaned forward to speak to Captain Wilson."Captain, I am most indebted to you for coming to our rescue. If you ever come through Jacksonville, please contact me for the best dinner our city has to offer."

"Thank you, Chandra; I might just take you up on that offer."

They arrived at the bomb search headquarters soon after and, Captain Wilson escorted her two companions through security and up to Major General Martin's desk.

"Good afternoon, sir. I have brought you a present from the Brooklyn Navy Yard, where I discovered Ms. Chandra Jones and her former captor in detention. I understand that you have been looking for her."

"Indeed we have, Captain, especially our star civilian, Rick O'Shea. In fact, Ms. Jones, I believe that you will find him standing right behind you."

Chandra immediately turned, and happily fell into the arms of Rick, who had almost given up hope of finding her in this huge city. No words were spoken, and the rest of the group resumed their discussion on accepting Tom as a prisoner to be shipped back to Savannah.

SIXTY-THREE

Destin, Florida
October 2, 1977

The summer season was drawing to a close on Florida's Emerald Coast, the Chamber of Commerce name given to beachfront development fronting the Gulf of Mexico from Panama Beach to Mobile Bay. Occupancy of multi-level hotels and condominiums was declining rapidly along with daily temperatures, as the first cool nights of the fall season discouraged sun bathers and swimmers from entering the crystal-clear Gulf waters. Sport fishing and golf remained popular throughout the winter for the smaller numbers of residents and visitors from northern climes.

The St. Pierre family, reportedly from Montreal, Canada, occupied a double penthouse suite on the top floor of the Hilton beachfront hotel within the sprawling Sandestin Resort. At over 1,750 acres stretching from the Gulf Coast to the panoramic views of Choctawhatchee Bay, this magnificent resort was filled with amenities for residents and guests of all ages and interests.

Henri St. Pierre and his beautiful wife, Claudette, maintained a personal live-in staff of two security men as well as a full-time female housekeeper for attention to their three children. Monsieur St. Pierre booked the top floor double penthouse for twelve months until he and his wife could locate a suitable residence to purchase. In the interim, they accepted no visitors, except by specific invitation, and the family members were always escorted by one or both of their security staff. A limousine with driver was kept available for their exclusive use twenty-four hours each day.

St. Pierre also kept a one-bedroom suite on a lower floor for his "business manager" who was registered as David Carson, and had credentials being prepared to match. It was here that he was meeting on the terrace with Henri St. Pierre on this lovely early October morning.

"David, you must get accustomed to your new name. It will suit you with your new glasses. Please remember that the security agencies of this country have extraordinary capabilities to uncover identities. Do not make it easy for them to do so. Put all of your former identity documents away in a safe place and do not use them. You will have new ones within a day or so."

"Right, sir. I have already put them away safely."

"Good! Now, completely erase Dimitri Chekov and Daniel Chester from your memory as well as Prince Hassad El Saud and Henry Stanton. Do not be guilty of any slip-ups. We are talking about the difference between life and death. Do you understand?"

"Yessir, please have no fear on my account."

"Good! Now, even though we had some bad luck on this venture. We will perform much better on our next one. Here is what you must do immediately. First, we must find Big Moe and put him in a safe place. I thought of eliminating him, but he has skills that we can use in our next venture. Do you have any idea where to locate him?"

244

"Yessir, he will almost certainly contact his cousin Alfred for assistance, and I will bribe Alfred for his new location. Where should I put him?"

"Re-locate him where he will not be noticeable; that is, in the midst of other black-skin people. I think Jamaica would work well. Provide him an existence income on a monthly basis and warn him to stay out of trouble if he wants further income."

"Right. I will get on it today."

"Good! Now, of greater importance, I want to establish a residence off-shore, preferably where French is the primary language and where they have an international school for my children. I am thinking the Caribbean islands of St. Barts and Martinique, or, perhaps, the French portion of the larger St. Martin. You know my needs: a large comfortable house with room for my family along with staff and security personnel. It probably should have a wall or suitable security fence, and a secure entry gate. Please fly down there and see what you can find. Perhaps, you can organize some contacts by telephone before you travel. Keep me advised."

"Right, sir. I will begin tomorrow, after I locate Big Moe."

"Excellent. In the interim, we will keep a low profile here in Florida. I believe that I will try my hand at some deep-sea fishing in the Gulf of Mexico. I have heard stories of some record catches off this coast." With that, the new Monsieur St. Pierre, rose from his chair and left his aide to begin addressing his new assignments.

On that same day, almost three hundred miles due east of Destin, Rick and Chandra had returned to Jacksonville, with both of them immediately reporting to their separate jobs. Needless to say, each of their colleagues was delighted to have them return. Chandra wasted no time in beginning to seek clearances for a special television feature on tracking down the terrorists, while Rick contacted his friend JD to schedule their promised follow-up meeting with Edward Ball and his attorney.

After repeated phone calls from the local news media to interview the happy couple, Rick's father and law partner, Michael O'Shea, had scheduled a press conference in his office conference room at four that afternoon, to be followed by a family dinner at the exclusive University Club on the top floor of the Gulf Life Tower. The Club manager had posted a "private party" sign in front of the ground floor elevator. Unbeknownst to any family members, Mike had asked his secretary and office manager, Maryanne, to deliver personal invitations to Bessie Solomon at the Times Union newspaper and to Mr. and Mrs. William Jones, Chandra's parents, to join the O'Shea family at this dinner. He arranged for a chauffeured car to pick them up at seven, a full hour after invitations to family members, so that they could be properly welcomed as honored guests by his father, the family patriarch, and by the entire assembled family which, at last count numbered almost seventy persons.

It was standing-room-only for late arrivals at the four o'clock press conference. Television cameramen lined the entrance wall of the conference room and reporters filled the extra folding chairs that Maryanne had wisely rented for the occasion. Michael O'Shea had barely completed the introduction of his father and the now heroic couple, when the news people relegated to hallway standing positions, moved aside to allow the entrance of Jacksonville's Mayor Hans Tanzler, along with several security men, The cameras recorded a short, but powerful speech honoring both Rick and Chandra along with his presentation of framed "Citizen of Honor" citations to each of them.

Not to be outdone, Michael Patrick O'Shea Junior delivered a brief speech of his own with his personal compliments to the research skills of Chandra Jones and his grandson in uncovering this terrorist plot against America.

After the Mayor's departure, Mike insisted upon silence so that Rick and Chandra could summarize their adventures prior to a limited question session. Chandra demurely requested that Rick speak for both of them. Rick led off with a concise account of their research in Jacksonville and court denial in Richmond, followed by his grandfather's suggestion of discovering their prey in Marseille, France, and the subsequent bombing of their hotel in Paris, followed by a charter flight to Washington and meeting with the Director of the CIA, prior to Chandra's kidnapping and the climactic train chases in Savannah and New York City.

However, he quickly realized that the real news sought by the media reporters was Chandra's two kidnappings and daring escapes, so he relinquished the stage to her and her genuinely exciting story of her near-fatal experiences with the dangerous "Big Moe" who was still being hunted by federal, state and local authorities. With more than her share of lucky escapes, she expressed great delight in returning safely home to Jacksonville and re-joining her news colleagues once again. Everyone crowded into the O'Shea office burst into lengthy applause, followed by questions from all sides.

Although it took several minutes of using his loudest courtroom voice, Michael O'Shea finally restored order and directed a half hour question and answer session. Of course, as he expected, almost all of the questions were directed to Chandra who responded to each one with the confidence that she had learned as a television reporter.

When Mike finally brought the session to a close, her fellow reporters were far from finished with their quest to learn more details about her adventure. The following days and weeks were filled with requests from both local and national reporters for additional details. The onslaught of invitations to television talk shows caused her editor to insist that they be scheduled on weekends or in the station's Jacksonville studios. Chandra was becoming a national, and even international, celebrity. Far from being envious, Rick virtually beamed with pride at her popularity.

The O'Shea family turned out in force for the Rick and Chandra celebration dinner. From the oldest, ninety-eight-year-old Grandmother Molly O'Shea, to the youngest, eight-month-old Great-grand-daughter Lucy Sobocheski, it appeared that every member of every O'Shea family was present and accounted for by the time Mike called for order immediately after the manager advised him that his special guests were in the building lobby and about to enter the elevator, wenty-one floors below.

"Please take your seats everyone. Since you all showed up for a free meal, you must abide by my rules in order to get served." He then paused briefly until he had their full attention before continuing.

"As you all know, we are gathered here to celebrate the safe homecoming of our internationally acclaimed Rick O'Shea and his accomplice Chandra Jones. For tonight, at least, she is an honorary member of our family." He was forced to pause again by the applause for their newfound heroes.

"What you don't know is that I have invited three other honorary guests who were instrumental in assisting to make this celebration possible. And they are just stepping off the elevator now. Please join me in welcoming to our honorary guest table, Mrs. Bessie Solomon, director of historical records for the Times Union newspaper, and, behind her, the parents of Chandra Jones, Mr. and Mrs. William Jones who live right here in Jacksonville."

Mike then stepped out and ushered his guests to the spotlight table where they were greeted by the obviously surprised and overjoyed Chandra, followed by Rick and his mother. The older Molly and Patrick O'Shea waited for the welcome from the others before approaching the new arrivals with their own sincere greetings on behalf of their entire family.

Mike stepped to the fore once more and advised his enthusiastic family members to be seated and enjoy the meal. "Before we resume our program, you may note that our honorary table is set for ten, but only nine of us are here. I will ask for your attention again in a few minutes to greet our final guest, who just landed a few minutes ago. He will be rushed directly here by our limo driver, at which time I will ask you to welcome him to our party."

Another twenty minutes elapsed before Rick's college best friend, JD, rushed out of the elevator and headed straight over to embrace Rick and Chandra before Mike could get to his feet for a suitable introduction. "Ladies and gentlemen, we are thrilled to welcome CIA Agent Joshua Dempsey from Washington. He is not only Rick O'Shea's former college room-mate at Harvard, but a key hero in the capture of the train terrorists. JD, we are honored to have you with us at this celebration." Another round of applause greeted the new guest.

As dessert was being served, Mike called upon his son to describe the surprising pathway that led from searching for a means of restoring the Flagler legacy to discovering the terrorist plot to bomb five major American cities, using the Florida East Coast Railroad cars to transport the bombs north into the target cities. He praised the research skills of Chandra Jones whom he met at Grandfather O'Shea's eightieth birthday party where she had come to film a special feature on the O'Shea family. "It was a stroke of good fortune," he admitted, "that her editor was the nephew of Bessie Solomon, whose vast knowledge of Jacksonville and its leaders made it possible for us to discover the link between the terrorists and the railroad. Another stroke of luck appeared in the person of his former college room-mate at the front door one evening with valuable information about the murders of the arsonists. These four demolition experts, subsequently murdered in the explosion of a chartered fishing boat in the Caribbean Sea, had killed two of our family members and set the bomb in the Broward Yard that snuffed out the lives of so many innocent Jacksonville residents. And as a bonus, JD turned out to be a talented attorney who is helping us to regain our family legacy.

"In a team meeting around my Dad's conference table, our grandfather came up with the brilliant plan for Chandra and me to fly to Marseille and eke out the name of the billionaire who was financing the entire venture, beginning with purchase of the Florida East Coast Railway. We discovered his identity, but he is still at large along with his two key aides, one of whom kidnapped Chandra in Washington and held her hostage in a Georgia farmhouse that had bars on the windows. Her escape from that near-death experience was a miracle in itself. She hiked six miles in the dead of night to a motel in Darien, Georgia to seek assistance." He was interrupted at this point by a burst of applause from the audience.

"But, the very next day, she received a tip from her cousin in Savannah that a freighter had arrived unexpectedly and was unloading suspicious cargo throughout the night. It appeared to be the very ship that the combined FBI/CIA team was expecting in Port Everglades south of Fort Lauderdale. She notified our team director, Margaret McBride, then picked up her cameraman in Jacksonville and raced to Savannah. Without due concern for their own lives, the two of them filmed the bomb containers being unloaded and her cameraman managed to get the videos to our team director. But Chandra was spotted by her former kidnapper, who was determined to kill her by wrapping her up with duct tape and stuffing her in the container bound for New York City. He then personally accompanied the engineer of that train to New York. They managed to escape army helicopters searching the tracks out of Savannah.

"Our assigned army helicopter unit out of Savannah captured four of the five bomb carriers by identification labels filmed by

Chandra's brave cameraman, Jimmy Brosovitch. I regret that a family emergency prevented Jimmy from joining us this evening. Chandra and I are most grateful for his participation in this dangerous venture.

"To continue, the missing fifth train somehow made it all the way to New York, where it reached its target below central Manhattan with a bomb carrying enough explosive to destroy all of the central city, including the 103-story Empire State Building. It also carried the bound –up body of Chandra Jones and the monitor rider paid by the terrorists to ignite the Manhattan bomb. One such monitor was assigned to each bomb carrier.

"Somehow, through another miracle and an extremely clever lady, Chandra managed to convince her monitor to remove her bindings and the two of them escaped into the labyrinth of train tracks under the city and under the East River to the Brooklyn Navy Yard, where they were arrested as trespassers by Navy police and put in detention.

"The security officer refused to listen to Chandra's admittedly strange story. At this time, I was with the search teams hunting the bomb as well as Chandra. The bomb was found and defused, but no sign of Chandra or her companion until the following afternoon, when an astute female captain in the Navy's Judge Advocate Guard discovered Chandra's detention in the Navy Yard and personally delivered her to search headquarters where we were re-united and returned to Jacksonville.

"I thank my Dad for inviting Chandra's parents here tonight so I can thank them personally for raising such a courageous and clever daughter." Rick paused and went to the Jones couple and hugged each of them. The audience broke into applause once again.

"I also am grateful to Dad for inviting Bessie Solomon, who provided us the information leading to the revelation that our search for railroad information was connected with the planned terrorist attack." He paused for another hug and another burst of applause.

"And of course, I also thank him for arranging the presence of my buddy, JD Dempsey, who managed to convince his CIA superiors to give him time off to help us settle our suit with FECR and hopefully restore the Flagler Legacy. Every member of this family owes him a great debt of gratitude." He paused for yet another hug and round of applause.

"Finally, my family members, I would like to give thanks to our honored matriarch, Molly O'Shea, who gave birth to our grandfather and thereby made possible to each of us in this family. I am privileged to be part of it and related to each of you." This time, everyone in the room rose to their feet and applauded their matriarch as well as the new leader-apparent of the O'Shea family. Chandra rose from her chair to join Rick in cheerfully waving to the joyful O'Shea family members.

SIXTY-FOUR

Jacksonville, Florida
October 3, 1977

Although both JD and Rick slept later than usual, after a late night of recounting memories, aided by a full refrigerator of beer in Rick's apartment, they still managed to arrive at the office by ten o'clock. Maryanne greeted them both cheerfully, and motioned to a pitcher of water, beside two glasses and a bottle of headache pills.

They both took her advice and then disappeared into the conference room to begin preparations for their scheduled afternoon meeting with Edward Ball and his attorney. After the excitement of the past week, they were ill-prepared to discuss the complex details involved in the history of the Florida East Coast Railway and its relationship to the Flagler Legacy gifted to the O'Shea family. There was little time to prepare and many documents to retrieve and digest.

Anticipating their task, Maryanne had set the office files on this topic in chronological order down the middle of the conference table. There were few historical files prior to 1940, the beginning of the modern era for FECR when government freight and soldiers became the priority cargo for the railroad after the December 1941 declaration of war by President Franklin D. Roosevelt. All of this government railroad cargo boosted FECR profits during the war years and made the company a much more valuable asset by the 1945 peace in Japan. They soon had sufficient annual financial statements summarized to support a substantial financial settlement for the O'Shea family for the twenty-five non-payment years following the judicial decision supporting cessation of the annual payment in 1952.

"Okay, my friend," smiled JD, "the FECR reserves are sufficient to pay the twenty-five million to the family if we can achieve a favorable judgment from an honest court. Now, let's turn our attention to the argument revealing a dishonest court. Although John Mason, the former Chief Justice of the Florida Supreme Court is deceased, we still have significant evidence that he was corrupted by FECR officials. More importantly, Senator Ebeneezer McCloud was clearly the bagman for the company and his testimony will directly threaten the credibility of FECR Managing Director Edward Ball. The clincher will be the testimony of our former news reporter, Florida Assemblyman Edward Cosgrove, who actually procured sworn affidavits from witnesses to money exchanges between McCloud and principal legislators. In short, old buddy, all we need to do over the next couple of hours is organize this story into a summary of wrongdoing to convince Ball and his attorney George Atkins that they are in a pile of deep cow dung.

"There is no question in my mind that we have a solid case against Ball and FECR, JD. Let's hustle and get it in presentable order so we'll have time for a relaxing lunch prior to ascending the lion's den." The two young attorneys immediately set to work.

SIXTY-FIVE

Destin, Florida
October 4, 1977

It was three o'clock on a beautiful sunshine day on the "Emerald Coast" when a tall African-American man rang the doorbell of an apartment labeled to belong to David Carson on the fifth floor of the waterfront condominium in the Sandestin resort. Carson, formerly Dimitri Chekov, answered the door and welcomed his longtime associate into his new home. He showed him to an upholstered chair and then went to a nearby desk and dialed a phone.

"Good afternoon," Carson spoke into the receiver. "Carson here, let me speak to Mr. St. Pierre, si'l vous plait. . . Merci . . . Monsieur St. Pierre. Carson here, our guest has arrived. Would you like to meet with him now? Very well, sir. We will await your arrival." He hung up the phone and offered Big Moe a beer before informing him that Monsieur St. Pierre would be with them in a few minutes.

"So, who the hell is Mon-soor Saint Perre?" asked his guest.

"You may remember him by another name. But be sure not to mention it in his presence. He is now Monsieur St. Pierre from Montreal." At that moment, the doorbell rang and Carson admitted the former Prince Hassad El Saud dressed in typical American beach clothes. He nodded to Big Moe and took a seat beside Carson across from Big Moe.

"Big Moe, I am delighted to see you have eluded the authorities once again. I am truly happy that you managed to escape from New York without incident, although I must admit that I am disappointed that you did not terminate the news reporter."

"If I had seen her, I would have killed her. But she must have soft-talked that dumbass traitor we assigned to that bomb, and they both escaped under Manhattan. Since then, she has been on television every day posing as the big hero of our failure to ignite a single bomb."

"Yes, that is unfortunate, but she will be repaid at some future time. In the interim, we must go undercover until we can mount another attack on these stupid Americans. And I need you as part of our team. I would like you to stay here for a few days in a room I have reserved for you. Mr. Carson will be arranging for a new identity for you, after which he will purchase you a one-way airline ticket to Jamaica where we have rented you a pleasant cottage by the sea. You will enjoy it there blending in with people of your own color and speech. Mr. Carson will send you monthly checks for rent and food until we need you for a new assignment. Then we can discuss a larger compensation package. Do you have any questions?"

"Yes I do, Mr San Pere. I have several questions." The big man sat up straighter in his chair and looked directly at the man he knew as the Prince.

"First and foremost, an article by the *Associated Press* claims that the FBI examined the ignition boxes for each bomb and discovered no connection to the timer displayed next to the trigger switch. In other words, the bombs would ignite immediately rather than the delay that you promised the monitor volunteers. Please explain."

The Prince appeared astounded, and he turned to his colleague now known as Carson. "David, what do you make of this finding? Were we sabotaged or did the FBI make up this news release to stimulate information from their captives?"

"Well, sir, I cannot believe that anyone could have sabotaged all five bombs. I personally observed the packaging on both freighters and again the re-loading in Savannah. I believe that your second reaction is more likely. The FBI informed their captives of this action to coerce then into cooperating in the investigation. Yes, that must be the answer, Moe. They create animosity toward us to gain cooperation from our employees."

"I see," responded Big Moe, quietly, as he sat up even higher in his chair. "Then that brings up my second question. When I escaped from the train with the engineer, I took the spare igniter with me to set it off at another location. I tripped the switch the next morning in a remote corner of the Newark Airport and learned personally that the timer did not activate. Of course, the bomb did not explode either, but I learned in the same article that the New York Police Bomb Squad had spent the entire night draining the liquid gas out of the bomb to render it harmless. Now my second question to you, Your Highness, is why did you insist at the last minute that I accompany the New York bomb personally? My conclusion is that you planned to kill all of your staff, thereby eliminating any connections to you and saving twenty-five thousand dollars in promised payments."

"Now see here," interjected the Prince angrily as he jumped up from his chair. "You cannot accuse me of such underhanded tactics after the money I have paid you over the past few months. You were never paid so well in your entire life." He stepped forward and confronted Big Moe still in his sitting position. Furthermore, I just promised you another ten thousand dollars and a beach house to live like an African king in Jamaica. Your lack of loyalty moves me to withdraw my offer."

"Go ahead and withdraw it," replied Moe quietly, "but I plan to take the money anyway."

As he spoke these words, the big man withdrew an Army-issue forty-five caliber handgun, fitted with a noise repressor, from his raincoat pocket. He quietly shot the wealthy Saudi-Arabian between the eyes causing the contents of his skull to spray over the opposite wall. Before the new David Carson could react to retrieve his pistol from a desk drawer, his head also was blown away by his former colleague.

"Live by the sword, gentlemen," muttered Big Moe as he stood and picked up the envelope full of one-hundred dollar bills. "You won't need to worry about my loyalty any longer."

Moe then pocketed his handgun and the envelope full of money as he quietly slipped out of the room and returned to his car in the parking lot below.

SIXTY-SIX

Jacksonville, Florida
October 4, 1977

As Big Moe drove west out of Sandestin, Rick and JD were entering the luxury condominium building where Ed Ball, and his attorney, George Atkins, awaited them in the penthouse suite. The meeting had been scheduled for five o'clock and Rick noted that they were ten minutes early. But JD did not hesitate in ringing the doorbell with confidence that their case against Mr. Ball was well prepared.

Ball's manservant answered the door and ushered the two younger men into the main lounge where Ed Ball and his attorney, George Atkins, rose from their chairs to greet the two visitors. They were offered the two remaining chairs in the group of four separated by side tables that contained fresh glasses of ice water. Ample illumination came from recessed ceiling lights.

Upon being seated, JD opened his briefcase and withdrew a brief over one inch in thickness and set it on his side table, indicating his readiness to begin. Ed Ball moved forward in his chair to open the conversation.

"Before we begin, gentlemen, I would like to extend my congratulations to both of you in playing key roles to defeat the terrorist threat launched by use of the railroads. Although the planned bombings did not take place, it was, nevertheless, a clever scheme and I applaud your separate roles in bringing it to a peaceful conclusion. Well done!"

"Thank you, sir," both men replied simultaneously.

Then, Rick continued: "We learned a great deal about the railroad business, as well as the military business, in a very short time. Some of our new knowledge is reflected in the brief that we have prepared for you. We have copies for each of you. If you would like to review it prior to discussion, we can re-schedule this meeting."

"No, I don't think that an extension is necessary," spoke George Atkins for the first time. "Mr. Ball and I have reviewed the potential directions that this case can take, and we would prefer to begin with our conclusions and reference back to your findings as necessary."

"By all means, sir, please take the lead and we will intercede as we feel necessary," replied Rick.

"Excellent," replied Atkins. "If you have no objection, I would like to summarize our findings for your response. Of course, Mr. Ball may interrupt as he feels necessary." Ball nodded his agreement, followed by smiles and nods by Rick and JD.

"We reviewed this case back to the beginning in 1897 when Henry Flagler registered the Patrick Michael O'Shea Trust to be funded annually by the Florida East Coast Railway, which then was entirely in his personal ownership. He did so in perpetuity, which I am sure you know is defined in American law as twenty-one years after the death of the last principal to the signing of the trust. That person is your grandfather, Patrick Michael O'Shea Junior. While we wish him a long and healthy life, he is now eighty years of age and our best estimate is that the Trust will expire within thirty to thirty-five years. Whereas that may seem like a very long time, both Mr. Ball and I can attest that these years can go by very quickly.

Nonetheless, under the original terms of the Trust, if we, in fact, agreed to continue it from its halt in 1972, the total payout could exceed fifty million dollars. I cite these facts just to ensure that the four of us understand the monetary value involved." Both Rick and JD nodded their understanding of the arithmetic.

Atkins continued: "When the 1931 FECR bankruptcy was enacted, Mr. Ball asked his staff to analyze the company as a potential investment. At that time, please remember, Mr. Ball was the confidant and investment manager for Alfred DuPont, a position he earned by several years of service to Mr. DuPont, who, as you know, was his brother-in-law. He and DuPont agreed that FECR was worth DuPont's investment and Mr. Ball began purchasing discounted mortgage bonds through the 1930s until they had acquired a primary ownership position.

"Unfortunately, DuPont died in 1935. His estate was left to his wife, Jessie Ball DuPont, and she retained Edward Ball as manager of the Alfred I. DuPont Testamentary Trust. In 1941, after considerable debate between suitors of the FECR, the federal court awarded management to the DuPont Trust, as primary owner, with Edward Ball as chief executive. Are you with me so far?" Rick and JD nodded their agreement.

After a sip of water, Atkins continued, "In examining his new management role, Mr. Ball ascertained that it was his responsibility to reduce costs and increase revenues, a normal description of the role of management. I won't bore you with his various cost-cutting strategies, including the court decision to uphold his non-union workers, but suffice it to say that the exclusion of the PMO Trust was part of this policy. Furthermore, under his management, FECR is now a profitable enterprise. Do you wish to add anything, Ed?"

"No, George. You have given an admirable summary. Please go on."

"Very well. We have established the fact that FECR is now a positive asset, compared to its operations thirty years ago. Any judge would need to take this economic recovery into account for settlement of a legal case affecting the FECR." JD moved to the front of his seat with intention to speak. "One moment, please, Mr. Dempsey. I just have a few more points to make."

"Yes, sir. I will exercise patience until you have finished."

"Good, patience is a wonderful trait, unfortunately not practiced by many in our profession. As you know, Ed Ball is entering the final years of his life. He has an envious financial management reputation that he would like to live after him. We understand that you gentlemen have built an impressive case that has potential to damage the reputation of at least three Florida jurists in addition to Mr. Ball. So, Ed and I have defined a concept that we believe can satisfy your family's concerns as well as bury the past deeds of our jurists." Here Atkins paused to pass copies of a single sheet of paper to Rick and JD.

"This paper summarizes our proposal to you and the O'Shea family. It sells all of the ownership notes held by the Alfred I. Dupont Trust to the Patrick Michael O'Shea Trust for the sum of one dollar and, in turn, you and your family formally agree to halt and terminate ad- infinitum any legal actions against anyone involved in this relationship. If you agree, I am prepared to draft a formal agreement between us immediately. Oh, by the way, we also intend to purchase all of the notes authored by Assemblyman Edward Cosgrove and held in the Times Union historic records. Do you have any questions?"

The two younger men exchanged looks, not quite believing what Attorney Atkins had told them. Finally, JD spoke up.

"Mr. Atkins, I'm afraid that my friend Rick and I are a little puzzled. We came here this afternoon to discuss a potential legal suit to restore the Flagler Legacy, or PMO Trust, and you have presented an opportunity for the family to take over primary ownership of the Florida East Coast Railway as a tradeoff . May I assume that you are concerned that restoration of the PMO Trust might place too great a financial burden on the FECR, so you have come to the conclusion that our potential lawsuit may have merit to bankrupt FECR? I find that hard to believe, unless there are other hidden liabilities of which we are unaware. Is that the case?"

"George." interrupted Ball. "Let me address Mr. Dempsey's question in less legal terms."

"Absolutely, sir. Please continue."

"Gentlemen, I have been fighting lawyers for the length of my pretty long career. And, I must admit that I have been damn good at it. But, you two, or perhaps three if you count your apparent girl friend, have dug up some pretty strong ammunition on me. I don't like it. But I do admire you for your success. Frankly, although George will not like my admission or my language, you have me by the balls. If we take this issue to court, we might be able to keep you at bay for several years just by throwing a bunch of legal bullshit at you and causing you to spend a great deal of time and energy reacting. But, in the interim, my name will be publicized throughout Florida as the crafty bastard that I really am.

"So, I told George and his associates that I do not want to end my days in defense of my life's work. I know that I have made many enemies and I do not believe that I will change their minds about me. But I would prefer to live the rest of my days more peacefully. So, in answer to your question: no, there are no major liabilities threatening FECR; and paying off the PMO Trust will not bankrupt FECR. However, I believe that putting your family back on the dole, so to speak, would neither benefit your relatives nor me. Easy money never really helped anyone in my view. And I do not want to be on the public witness stand for the rest of my few years. Furthermore, I have all the money any man could want, so I do not need to acquire any more. My solution is to literally give you the damn railroad, if you will promise not to bother me anymore. It's as simple as that."

"Wow!" exclaimed Rick. "This is amazing, and completely unexpected. I imagine that my friend Dempsey is disappointed that he cannot go to war. But, I am elated on behalf of my family. This is a far better solution than a victorious legal suit. Frankly, Mr. Ball, I do not believe that any of my relatives know diddley about running a railroad, but the prospect of turning the Flagler legacy into a continuation of his dream fills me with excitement."

Ed Ball rose from his chair and began to pace around the room. "George, this young man is absolutely right. His folks know zip about this business. So, I will agree to help them on a limited basis, as an assistant to the chairman. My initial recommendation is to have the new chairman establish a bonus plan for all executives based on a share of net profits. That will keep all your management skills in place. Make your father or grandfather the chairman, and I will serve as his advisor on a limited basis. He can hand over the job to your father after he spends a couple of years as general counsel. Your time will come later. There is no reason that we cannot be friends, despite our fights in past years. You can be assistant general counsel, but you would need to undertake a two year training program in all facets of the operation, even riding a train. If you like, your friend JD can quit the CIA and become your deputy with an opportunity for advancement as soon as you recognize the best spot for him. At least, if I were you, I wouldn't let him go back to the government without a fight. George is past retirement age, but you need him as special counsel for a couple of years."

"Oh, I forgot. Before, we seal this deal, you will need the best independent auditors in the country to examine the FECR books to ensure to all your family members that there are no secrets. After all, they have good reason to not trust me. I just don't want you to tell them."

JD suddenly jumped to his feet. "Mr. Ball, I would like to shake your hand. I just found out why you have been so successful all these years. Your enthusiasm for an idea sprouts creativity like the Fourth of July fireworks. I am humbled to be in your presence."

Ball stopped pacing and held up his hand. "Stop that kind of talk, Dempsey, or I might withdraw the whole idea. I am not used to people speaking nice to me. You do better as an active adversary. Keep it up. You could be really good in court. Now, gentlemen, do we have an oral agreement?" Both men nodded yes without hesitation. "Alright, go back and discuss it with your father and grandfather. They will be skeptical at first, so invite George over to explain the deal. But, I caution you to keep this confidential until we have a written agreement. Your girl-friend will want to put it on television. So promise her an exclusive if she will keep her mouth shut until we are ready. What do you think, George, about three months minimum?" Atkins nodded yes in reply.

"Excellent, let's get started." Ball then went to a cabinet and pulled out a bottle of very expensive bourbon. He poured a couple of ounces in each of four glasses and handed one to each of his guests. "Gentlemen, here's to the success of the FECR under new management."

SIXTY-SEVEN

Jacksonville, Florida
October 12, 1977

The meeting convened in the O'Shea Law Firm conference room at ten o'clock on Monday morning. All those invited were seated at the table with Mike O'Shea at the head of the table, and his father and grandmother at the opposite end. The other participants were Chandra Jones and her mother, Matilda Jones, Bessie Solomon, and Rick O'Shea.

"Ladies and gentlemen, began Mike O'Shea, thank you all for joining me this morning. The excitement and terrorist killings of the last few weeks have convinced me that the O'Shea family needs to invest some of the unearned money entrusted to us by Henry Flagler toward positive actions to achieve inter-racial harmony in our city. It is a terrible lesson for us to have foreigners from another land hate us just because of our religion and economic success, but it seems to me far worse to hate each other for the same unwarranted reason. So, I have asked each of you here today to volunteer to help my family and I decide upon the best means of financing activities to bring racial harmony to our city. If this is a cause which you feel that you cannot support, I thank you for coming and wish you well. But, if you will join us in this endeavor, please remain seated." Nobody moved.

Then, Matilda Jones held up her hand and looked at Mike O'Shea. He nodded back as a sign that she had the floor. "Mr. O'Shea, I am eager to help anyone who plans to promote racial harmony, or, for that matter, any kind of harmony. But can you tell us what you have in mind?"

"No, I cannot. That's why I invited you here today. I have discussed this general goal with my father and my son, but we have no plan except to enlist your help. We have been gifted with more money than we need, so we can donate to a good cause, but I have no idea what that cause, or causes, may be."

"Well, I can give you one idea," spoke Patrick Michael O'Shea Junior in his strong voice. "We don't need to spend time addressing each other by last names. So, Matilda, unless you object, I plan to call you by your first name, and you can call me Patrick. My mother beside me is Molly and my son is Mike. To avoid confusion, my grandson, Patrick Michael O'Shea the fourth is called Rick. That leaves Chandra and Bessie. Any objections? Hearing none, Mike, I suggest that we proceed by hearing ideas on how to promote our goal. And, frankly, I believe that Bessie knows more about our town than anyone else I know. So please speak up, Bessie."

"That's very kind of you . . . Patrick," responded Bessie Solomon. "And it is true that my forty-four years at the newspaper have provided me with a great deal of knowledge about Jacksonville and its people. But I certainly did not come this morning with a priority list of positive actions. However, I do have a suggestion if I may."

"Absolutely," responded Mike. "Please proceed."

"Well, despite evidence to the contrary, we have a number of organizations in this city that have activities complementary to Mike's initial statement of purpose. One suggestion might be to hire someone to identify them all and catalogue their programs and successes. Perhaps we need to examine them as a learning exercise. It may be that we could support the most promising activities anonymously like the United Way, rather than start our own programs."

"Super suggestion, Bessie," chimed in Chandra. "Mike, you might consider providing a name for our endeavor and making us the directors or steering committee. With the information in front of us that Bessie suggests, we could discuss each as a group and decide how best to lend our support."

"Well," began Molly in her soft voice. "If we do not need to solicit money, there is no need to publicize ourselves. As a start, why not just call our group 'Harmony' and proceed with Bessie's educational program. If it is appropriate, Michael, I would like to ask Chandra to identify a person or group to research all of the groups in the city contributing to racial harmony and catalog their activities for each of us to examine. Can you do this, my dear?"

"I can, and, subject to Mike's approval, I will," replied Chandra.

"Wow! This is going better than I anticipated," said Mike. "I propose that we meet here again one month from today. I nominate Rick as secretary to summarize this session and send it along with Chandra's proposal for a survey to each of you prior to our next meeting. Any other comments? Hearing none, I thank you all for coming, and I look forward to seeing you at the second meeting of 'Harmony' next month."

EPILOGUE

Saturday, June 18, 1978, was a beautiful, cloudless day for a wedding and the bride was gorgeous in her white gown with a classic veil and train, on the arm of her beaming father, William Jones. The happy couple descended on the walkway from the former DuPont mansion to the sounds of the "Wedding March" played on a portable organ by the venerable Molly O'Shea.

The setting was the riverfront garden of Epping Forest, the Florida homestead of Alfred and Jessie DuPont on a fifty-two-acre estate bordering the east bank of the St. Johns River in Jacksonville. The magnificent garden was filled (perhaps for the first time) with prominent citizens from both African American, Asian, Arab and White cultures in Jacksonville. They focused on the white latticework backdrop to the Roman Catholic Bishop of St. Augustine and the Senior Minister of the AME Church in Jacksonville who had agreed to collaborate (also for the first time) on an ecumenical wedding of Chandra Matilda Jones to Patrick Michael O'Shea IV.

Rick's youngest sister was Maid of Honor in a light brown, full-length gown and JD Dempsey was Best Man in a tuxedo of matching color to the Maid of Honor gown.

The Directors of 'Harmony' were all in attendance, along with many directors of charitable organizations throughout the city.

Over sixty members of the O'Shea family were gathered in the white pews along with friends and relatives, as well as many prominent political and legal figures, including Edward Ball (who had arranged the use of Epping Forest for the wedding). Clearly it was a major social event for a city that only deleted the law against racial intermarriage two decades earlier.

Almost one year later, Chandra gave birth to Margaret Matilda O'Shea, the first of five O'Shea children to expand the already large family. She would be known as "Molly" in honor of her great, great grandmother who died earlier that year at age ninety-nine. Her son Patrick Michael O'Shea Junior survived in robust health to age ninety-six. He controlled the Patrick Michael O'Shea Trust to his final year, and he was pleased to announce the Trust's college sponsorship of ninety percent of the family's high school graduates. Of even greater joy to him was the number of prominent citizens who donated funds to "Harmony" without public disclosure. The number of annual Harmony grants became so numerous that a small staff had to be organized under the direction of Chandra O'Shea when she retired as senior anchor of her station's evening news.

Patrick's son Mike reached his final year at age 94, after passing the family patriarch responsibility to his son Rick, a respected attorney in Jacksonville with both a daughter and son joining the O'Shea Law Firm and later becoming directors of 'Harmony'. Rick and Chandra became prominent supporters of many charitable organizations in addition to the confidential work of "Harmony." Chandra became an active spokesperson for resolution of interracial issues.

Edward Ball died in 1983 at the age of eighty-one. His obituary made no mention of the transfer of the Florida East Coast Railway or his anonymous gift to "Harmony" in 1980 of one million dollars to support racial harmony programs. The railroad was sold two years later to a major investment company and continues to operate successfully serving Florida's east coast. Henry Morrison

Flagler would be pleased to learn that the Patrick Michael O'Shea Trust became one of his finest investments in the growth of Florida.

www.ingramcontent.com/pod-product-compliance
Lightning Source LLC
Chambersburg PA
CBHW031104260626
47172CB00001B/210